D0194309

KILLER CONTENT

KILLER CONTENT

KILEY ROACHE

WITHDRAWN

UNDERLINED

This is a work of fiction. All incidents and dialogue, and all characters with the exception of some well-known historical and public figures, are products of the author's imagination and are not to be construed as real. Where real-life historical or public figures appear, the situations, incidents, and dialogues concerning those persons are fictional and are not intended to depict actual events or to change the fictional nature of the work. In all other respects, any resemblance to persons living or dead is entirely coincidental.

Text copyright © 2021 by Kiley Roache
Cover photo © 2021 by Robin Macmillan/Trevillion Images

All rights reserved. Published in the United States by Underlined,
an imprint of Random House Children's Books,
a division of Penguin Random House LLC, New York.

Underlined is a registered trademark and the colophon is a trademark
of Penguin Random House LLC.

GetUnderlined.com

Educators and librarians, for a variety of teaching tools,
visit us at RHTeachersLibrarians.com

Library of Congress Cataloging-in-Publication Data
Names: Roache, Kiley, author.
Title: Killer content / Kiley Roache.
Description: First edition. | New York : Underlined, 2021. | Audience: Ages 14 and up. |
Summary: Six teen influencers begin turning on each other when one member of
their group is found dead in the infinity pool of the Malibu beachfront mansion
where they all live.
Identifiers: LCCN 2021020527 (print) | LCCN 2021020528 (ebook) |
ISBN 978-0-593-42749-1 (trade paperback) | ISBN 978-0-593-42750-7 (ebook)
Subjects: CYAC: Internet personalities—Fiction. | Social media—Fiction. |
Murder—Fiction. | Criminal investigation—Fiction. | Mystery and detective stories. |
LCGFT: Novels. | Thrillers (Fiction) | Detective and mystery fiction.
Classification: LCC PZ7.1.R5775 Ki 2021 (print) | LCC PZ7.1.R5775 (ebook) |
DDC [Fic]—dc23

The text of this book is set in 11-point Janson MT Pro.

Interior design by Jen Valero

Printed in the United States of America
10 9 8 7 6 5 4 3 2 1
First Edition

Random House Children's Books supports the First Amendment
and celebrates the right to read.

Penguin Random House LLC supports copyright. Copyright fuels creativity,
encourages diverse voices, promotes free speech, and creates a vibrant culture.
Thank you for buying an authorized edition of this book and for complying
with copyright laws by not reproducing, scanning, or distributing any part in any
form without permission. You are supporting writers and allowing
Penguin Random House to publish books for every reader.

FOR ALL THOSE WITH CALIFORNIA DREAMS

KILLER CONTENT

PROLOGUE

11 DAYS AFTER

LA COUNTY JAIL INMATE #1438

The flash from the camera lights up my face. The officer tells me to turn. To hold the sign a little higher.

There used to be so much to prepare before I stepped in front of a camera. The right outfit, flattering and fashionable—but without appearing as if I cared about those sorts of things—and no visible logos, unless they've been paid for in advance. The right angle—determined through a series of test shots beforehand. The right lighting—I'd position myself 45 degrees from a window for natural light without the risk of being backlit, then prop up reflective boards to make sure both sides of my face were evenly bright, and of course, no shoot was ready without setting up my two-hundred-dollar ring light.

It was all about curating the right image: desirable, inimitable, unattainable, yet somehow still approachable. It was a balancing act so complicated that of course it required extensive preparation.

But I don't get to do any of these things before my mug shot.

So naturally, I look like absolute crap. And yet the picture performs better online than anything I posted in the two years I carefully cultivated my personal brand. In fact, this grainy image—shot on an ancient digital camera, against a flat gray background, under *fluorescent lighting*—beats my unique impression record in less than a day. Go figure.

I

17 HOURS BEFORE

GWEN

"I swear to God, if we don't get it this time, I'm going to kill you both." Cami's face is red with exertion. She grabs my arm, her grip a bit too firm, and guides me through the moves again. "It's right, left, turn, and pose, okay?"

"So basically, how we've been doing it?" I mumble.

"How *I've* been doing it. You're still off," Cami snaps.

Cami's full name is Dolores Camila Villalobos de Ávila, but almost everyone calls her Cami, since, in her words, *Dolores is a name for a grandmother, not a TikTok star.*

She thinks she's in charge because she's the only one with "real" dance experience. She went to the School of American Ballet for two years, until she hit puberty and her curves became too pronounced for the world of classical dance. Cami's always patronizing me for not being formally trained or knowing all the proper dance terms—*A frappé is not just something you get at Starbucks, Gwen.* If I wanted to, I could be just as condescending back. It would be easy to knock her down a peg—remind her that I'm the one with eighty million TikTok followers, while she lags behind by more than half. That although she may know the "correct" way to count music, there's only one queen bee in this house: me.

But instead, I keep my professionally plumped lips sealed and nod along as she walks me through the forty-five-second dance for the tenth time. If I say anything now, things will just devolve into another fight, and she's right, we don't have much time left to get this right.

I honestly can't tell the difference between what I was doing before and what she wants me to do now. But she seems pleased with my improvement.

"All right, let's run it again." She turns to Tucker, who had been filming us but is now lying across the foot of Cami's bed, scrolling through Instagram. He's gone ahead and made himself comfortable, with his long limbs sprawled out. Tucker is six foot two, and from what I can tell, there's not been a moment in his seventeen years of life during which he's worried about the space he takes up.

"Huh?" He looks up from the phone. His eyes go wide as he registers Cami's expression: so grumpy she looks kind of constipated. "Oh, ready." He stands up and adjusts the backward baseball cap on his head. He raises the phone and taps the screen to record. "Action!"

The music plays from TikTok, and we writhe and gyrate to the immortal sounds of the Pussycat Dolls.

"When I grow up / I wanna be famous / I wanna be a star."

Forty-five seconds later, Cami yells, "Cut." She snatches the phone from Tucker. "I think this is the one." She turns the phone so I can take a look. I watch us dance on the small screen. "See, I knew it wouldn't look off balance with just two of us."

"Yes, why apologize to your friend when you can just ignore the rule of thirds?" Tucker says.

"Exactly," Cami says, brushing off his sarcasm. She swipes through potential filters for our video. "And might I remind you that I'm not the only one Sydney's mad at."

Tucker bristles.

We haven't been able to dance in our usual formation—Sydney to my right, Cami to my left—since the big fight two days ago. Sydney stormed off that night, headed for her parents' house in the hills. She hasn't sent anyone here so much as a Snap or a text—let alone indicated she's ready to shoot TikToks with us again.

"Are you sure about the song?" Tucker changes the subject from his girlfriend's disappearing act. "You don't think it's a bit too on the nose?"

Cami shakes her head. "It's tongue-in-cheek, Tucker."

"What do you mean?" I say. Confused, I touch my own cheekbones, then the tip of my nose. Contour comes off on my fingers. "Does my nose look big in the video? Let me see it again."

Cami rolls her eyes.

Tucker laughs at me. "Not literally noses and cheeks, Gwen," he says. "They're expressions."

"Duh, I knew that." I straighten my shoulders. "I was just trying to be funny."

"Sure, honey," Cami says with a look of pity.

Embarrassment burns hot in my chest. I hate when people think I'm dumb. People assume that since I'm seventeen, platinum blond, and basically as close to looking like Barbie as La Mer skin care, the Tracy Anderson Method, and Dr. Malibu

(Plastic Surgeon to the Stars) can get me, I must also be shallow. But I'm not. I'm actually quite smart, in my own way.

I may not know much about the sorts of things they teach in school, or what "on the nose" means, which everyone else does, apparently. But I know the right time of day to post an Instagram, which is different from the right time to post a TikTok. I know which camera angles work best for me, and I know to match an ironic sound with a thirst trap, so you don't seem too into your own looks. I know how to put out enough content to stay relevant without becoming overexposed.

And I thought up this plan. Everyone forgets that, because it was Sydney's parents who signed for the mortgage. But it was actually my idea to form the Lit Lair—to gather a bunch of teenage TikTok stars and move into a Malibu mansion to create content together. I thought that if we appeared in each other's videos, our accounts would all grow much faster than they would apart. And I was right. I recently learned it's called synergy—when two plus two makes five instead of four. But even before I knew the term, I knew it was a good idea.

When it comes to turning myself into a brand, I have a gift. As Paris Hilton once said, "Some girls are just born with glitter in their veins." That's me. I always knew I was meant for this life. Even when my mom and I were living in a cramped studio apartment and my bed was a pullout couch, I'd look at my secondhand Barbie Dreamhouse and just know I was meant to live in a place like that.

It may look like fun and games, us all living in this house together—swimming in the infinity pool, making up dances, playing pool in the dining room—but really, it's serious business. We have thirty million followers on the @LitLair_LA account.

Plus, we all have our personal profiles, with at least ten million followers each (I'm the one with the most followers, and Sydney and Cami are always fighting for a distant second).

All these followers mean sponsorship deals, and not just with any random company—after all, we have our brand to protect. We work mostly with Fortune 500 companies. And my rate per post is at least $30,000. Since we moved into the house at the beginning of the summer, I've made more money starring in a series of sixty-second videos than most Hollywood starlets make for an entire film.

Not bad for a girl with no talent, as Kim Kardashian would say. And that's the blueprint, really. If you're going to monetize your personal brand, there's no better example than the patron saint of influencers out in Calabasas.

That's why lately I've been trying to diversify my portfolio. Things may appear perfect from the outside, but I'm terrified that one day I'll just be someone who used to be famous on an app most people have forgotten about.

Because, sure, TikTok is, like, the biggest thing in the world right now. But what if it goes the way of Vine or Myspace? So even though I currently have the most followers of any individual on the app, I don't want to just be a TikTok star. I want to be an It Girl. I want a makeup line, a lifestyle website, maybe a shoe collab. I want to publish a book made up mostly of my Instagram photos and have it hit the *New York Times* bestseller list. I want it all.

Some old dude once said, "The unexamined life is not worth living." This is how I know my life is worth a lot: it is examined by eighty million people every day. That's like, more people than the population of France. Having all these people caring about me and the way I dance and the clothes I wear, it makes me feel like my life matters. I don't ever want to lose that. I don't know who I would be without it.

But my mom, bless her heart, is no Kris Jenner. Since I got famous, she's spent her days playing tennis and drinking mimosas, not strategizing for my career. So I have to figure this out on my own. And with every comment below one of my videos from some troll saying I'm overrated, that I'm gaining weight, that no, I'm losing weight and must be anorexic, that my dance moves are too basic, that I am actually a conspiracy created by the Chinese government, or—most commonly—that I'm dumb, I can feel my fifteen minutes ticking by. And I worry they'll be gone before I can build something that will last.

Comments questioning my intelligence coming from strangers stress me out enough. I don't appreciate them from people who are supposed to be my friends, and especially not from Tucker.

"I guess you're lucky that you know everything about everything, Tuck," I say. I glare at him, thinking all the things I can't say with Cami here as a witness.

He flushes under my glare. "If you have the shot, then I'm gonna go get ready for tonight." He walks out of Cami's room and away from my rage.

Cami captions the post *Dynamic Duo* and adds the two-dancing-girls emoji. Then she presses a button and the video posts to @LitLair_LA and its thirty million loyal followers.

Within seconds, I watch on my own phone as the video begins to gather likes and adoring comments. But even so, watching the TikTok back, I must agree with Tucker. It just feels like something's missing without our other best friend dancing beside us.

"Syd will be back tonight, though, right?" I ask Cami.

"Of course," she reassures me. "She might be mad, but she's not stupid. She wouldn't miss Drake for the world."

I nod, but I'm not totally convinced. All I can think about is Sydney as she stormed out of the house, her Louis Keepall on her shoulder and her Away suitcase clunking on the stairs behind her. Her cheeks were stained with mascara, but what I remember most is her eyes. Because even though she was crying, she didn't look sad. She looked pissed.

I leave Cami's room and head down those same marble stairs, which are now soaked in Malibu sunlight. My perfectly manicured hand slides down the railing, and as I make my way downstairs, I hum quietly to myself, Nicole Scherzinger's voice still stuck in my head.

"Be careful what you wish for | 'cause you just might get it."

➦

16 HOURS BEFORE

KAT

My father's side of the family has been in California since the gold rush. My great-great-great-great-grandfather raced across the country in a covered wagon and ended up somewhere near Fresno.

His first week in the state, he found a small nugget of gold. He grabbed the gold, left his sifting pan in the river, and went promptly to the town's only two permanent businesses: a saloon and a brothel. Within the month, the money was gone and he was back to searching for a glimmer in the California dust. He looked his whole life but never found more gold. He died completely broke; there wasn't even any money left for a proper headstone. His descendants have lived in central California ever since.

My mom tells this story like a warning. Her family has a very different history. Her parents immigrated from Jamaica. Her mom became a nurse, her father worked in construction. My mom grew up and became a middle school teacher. Theirs is a story of hard work, staying in school, working solid union jobs. An American dream, not of ephemeral gold dust and that intoxicating promise of quick riches, but of daily bread carved from steady work.

So you can imagine how it went when I told her about coming here. To this get-rich-quick-influencer-palooza mansion.

My TikTok started as something to do for fun. Everyone at school had an account, and my parents didn't care if I made silly short videos with my friends as long as I kept up my schoolwork. But for some reason, my follower numbers didn't plateau around two hundred, like most of my friends' accounts. My videos kept making it onto the For You pages of people I didn't know all around the world. I had a few videos go really viral—like I'm talking my phone crashed during AP History because a video got a million views in three hours. And then, all of a sudden, I had 150,000 followers, then 400,000 a few days later, and then . . . well, you know how exponents work.

I'd been making a bit of money—a few hundred dollars here and there to promote small businesses—when I got the DM from Gwen. She told me she was making upward of twenty thousand for one sponsored post, and that she would love to teach me how, and would I like to come live with her and her friend Sydney in SoCal?

At first my parents gave me one month—June. This could be my summer job, my mom said. But I needed to make at least $480 a week—the equivalent of what I would make if I worked my old jobs scooping ice cream and babysitting in Fresno. In the first month, I made $40,000. It went right into the college fund, of course, except for what I spent on rent and an allowance for food and new clothes. But I still shopped at American Eagle and Target. I certainly wasn't buying the latest Gucci with my income, like some of the other TikTok kids. And that was fine with me. The money just meant I could show my parents that what I was doing here was work and help me negotiate for more time. They agreed to let me stay the rest of the summer.

One summer making videos full-time. One summer in the now-famous Malibu mansion. And then I was supposed to go back, finish high school, take the SATs, and generally get on the path to a real, steady job that is definitely not being a comedian and relying on the whims of the internet to determine whether I boom or bust. As of today, I have three weeks left of living my dream.

My heart beats hard in my chest, my blood racing through my veins. The pool water slides off my arms with every slicing movement.

My Apple watch alerts me that I have reached my daily activity goal. But I want to do a lap or two more. The sun is bright, and I can feel it on my back as I swim. It's a beautiful day in Malibu.

I get to the end of the pool and flip, propelling myself back in the other direction, gliding through the water. I spot two wavy feet that have now appeared at the other end. Even though I am underwater, my cheeks twitch up in a smile. My limbs are tired, but I find a bit of energy I didn't know I had left and speed up to get to Beau faster.

"Hi," I gasp as soon as I pop up out of the water. I lift my goggles. Beau smiles down at me. He is shirtless and sweaty from his run along the beach. His wavy surfer-dude hair still somehow looks perfect.

"How was your swim?" he asks me.

"Good. I'm close to beating my record," I say. I pull my cap off and rub my temples where I know the cap and goggles have left weird, angry marks on my face.

"You didn't want to be part of Cami's video?" he asks.

"Believe it or not, I'm not a huge Pussycat Dolls fan."

"Ah, really?" he teases.

Beau knows I hate to do dance videos, and that it's mutually understood with that crew to just stay out of each other's way. Like me, he specializes in comedy TikToks. I'm the only girl in the house who doesn't focus on dance videos—I mean, except when I Renegaded to Bill Clinton's "I did not have sexual relations with that woman" speech and captioned it *When everyone asked Joseph how Mary got knocked up.* I don't mean to sound all I'm-not-like-other-girls about it, because there are plenty of other girls whose TikTok accounts are about being funny, not just being cute and dancing. I'm just the only one like that who lives in this house.

Beau extends his hand and helps me out of the pool. I wrap a towel around my body. The sun is sinking toward the horizon, but the late-summer heat still hangs in the air, and the breeze feels good on my skin.

"I stopped in town on my run and saw this." Beau reaches into his shorts pocket and pulls out a bracelet made of black string and white seashells.

He holds it out to me carefully. "I thought you might like it."

I turn it over in my hand. "I love it."

"I know it's not *Cartier*," he says with an affected tone. "But it reminded me of your style."

I laugh at his joke. For the first few weeks after we moved in, Sydney would not shut up about this Cartier Love Bracelet her parents got her. She bugged me for weeks to make a video with her to the "I can't take it off" sound, and I eventually had to pull her aside and let her know that a video about a six-thousand-dollar bracelet wasn't exactly relatable to a teenage audience. That was the last time someone from the dance posse tried to make a comedy video.

I tug the seashell bracelet onto my wet wrist and smile up at Beau. "It's perfect," I say.

"Cool." He blushes. "I'm glad you like it."

For a moment, we just stand there at the edge of the pool, squinting in the sunlight, smiling like idiots. I'm still breathing hard from my swim, and I feel like my heart is beating in my ears.

"*What* are you two doing?" We are jolted from the moment by Cami, who's racing down the pool stairs in a dress and neon block heels. "Do you not understand that *Aubrey Graham* is coming here in one hour? How are you not even showered yet?"

"I was about to go up," I say.

"Golden hour is seven. Be in the *foyer* by six-forty-five." She says "foyer" the French way.

"Of course!" I say as I pass her. Beau and I giggle like little kids and race up the wet stone stairs to the house.

Upstairs in the girls' bathroom, I peel off my one-piece and step into the shower. This is my favorite part of the house. The whole back wall of the shower is glass—a giant window looking out to the ocean. The house is on a cliff and was designed with as many rooms as possible facing the ocean so you can enjoy the view from everywhere, even from the crapper, as my dad would call it.

I rinse off the salty water from the pool and breathe in the scent of my grapefruit body wash. I watch the waves crash onto the shore, and for the umpteenth time this summer, I think: *How is this my life?*

For as long as I can remember, there have been two Californias in my mind: The real place where I grew up, where I went to school and scooped ice cream and did homework, and the mythical California of Jack Kerouac's writing and Lana Del Rey's songs. It's the place where people chase glory: Hollywood dreams, Silicon Valley riches, and, yes, if you are like my distant relatives, literal gold in the ground. California is where you go so that something happens to you. Something big.

But I never felt like that was going to happen in Fresno. And now here I am. Where my idea of California and my reality finally collide. Watching the sun set over the Pacific as I shave my legs.

I towel off and head to my room to get dressed. There was a big fight over who got the best room when we moved in, but I just picked the one with the lowest rent, which means I have a view of the pool rather than the ocean. I pull the curtains closed so I can change.

I have no idea what to wear to meet Drake, so I decide just to put on what I would if someone's parents were visiting. My usual look but dressed up a bit more, to show respect. I pick out a yellow floral sundress and dab on a bit of minimalist makeup in front of my seashell-framed mirror.

On the vanity, my phone vibrates. *Call from Mom*, the screen says. We usually talk about once a day. But over the last few days, I've been dodging her. I know she wants to talk about plans for moving me back to Fresno, but I'm not ready to think about that yet. I'm still working up the courage to tell her and my dad that I'd like to take a year off school and stay here longer. I already know how they're going to react. I click the lock button to silence the call.

I grab a scrunchy to wear around my wrist as usual. But this time, I put it on my right wrist rather than my left, so as to not cover up my new bracelet. I spin one of the shells between my fingers. *It reminded me of your style*, Beau said.

I sigh. I've been crushing on Beau since we moved into the house. Before I met him, I'd seen some of his videos, so I knew he was funny and quite cute. But to know him in person was a whole different level. He's one of those people who can make the vibe of a room better just by walking in. His laugh is infectious, and his smile makes you feel like smiling, too. When someone is sad, he says exactly the right thing to comfort them. He's the kind of person who'll notice whoever at the party doesn't know anyone and is lingering at the edge of the room and go talk to them. He always knows how to break awkward silences and what songs to add to a playlist to revive a waning mood. He just makes everything warmer, happier. He's like sunshine.

During the first week here, when everyone was nervous and competitive and constantly comparing sponsorship deals and video views, Beau just . . . didn't engage with that drama. He made his videos, and then he went surfing. He asked everyone if they wanted to go with, but I was the only taker. He patiently taught me how, even though it took most of the morning for me to stand up on the board. I was smitten by the end of the day, both with the sport and with the boy.

Sometimes I even think he might feel the same way. Like, we'll be in a group and I'll catch him looking at me even when it's someone else talking. Or he'll save the last piece of pizza for me. Small things like that. Then again, he's pretty much nice to everyone in the house and, really, everyone he encounters, so it's hard to tell if it means anything.

I know some of the people who watch our videos ship us. But others ship me with Spider-Man—not Tom Holland but the literal fictional character, Peter Parker—so, you know, it's hard to put too much stock in that.

I look down at the bracelet. That must mean something, right? I mean, you don't just get a bracelet for all your friends, right? Bracelets are for crushes, girlfriends, not just friends—

I'm barreling down this train of thought when I remember the concept of friendship bracelets. *Well, crap. Never mind.*

I take a deep breath and check my hair one last time before heading downstairs and into the fray.

2

15 HOURS BEFORE

KAT

Drake is here. Sydney still isn't.

I watch as two black SUVs pull into our driveway. The head-lights shine through the windows.

"What are you doing?" Cami swats at my hand and pulls the curtains closed. "They're going to think you're creepy if you're watching from the window." She spins on her chunky neon heels. "Everybody act natural."

"Oh, because it's natural for us all to be assembled by the front door?" I gesture to Beau and Gwen, standing at attention. "We're not the von Trapps."

Beau laughs at my joke.

"Squid, I'm starting to get worried." Tucker's voice floats in from the living room. Through the doorway he spots the rest of us watching him. Cami waves him over frantically. "Just—call me when you get this." He hangs up and joins us.

"I cannot believe Sydney," says Cami. She types rapidly on her phone. "This is so unprofessional. I mean, I know she was upset, but *come on*, it's been two days."

"I don't know," Beau says. "I've been reading up on twin

psychology, and it's some pretty intense stuff. If Brooklyn is hurting, Sydney is probably hurting, too."

"Okay, Dr. Phil," Cami scoffs. "It's still no excuse to blow off something this big."

Gwen ignores the scene. Instead, she examines her reflection in the large gold-framed mirror. Her blond hair has been slicked straight, and small gold hoops sparkle in her ears. She's wearing a long black dress with a slit high up one side.

She's still staring at her reflection when she says, "We can do this without Sydney." Her voice is a little shaky. "We have to. It's our only option."

Just then, the doorbell rings.

It turns out, Drake in person is pretty much the same as Drake on TV. Except maybe a bit shyer. He says hello to all of us but mostly lets his team do the talking.

A woman in a magenta silk pantsuit introduces herself as Bianca and presents her team. "And which of you is Sydney?" she asks. "I spoke to your mother about the location rights for the house."

Silence. I turn to Beau; he's looking at me. Cami looks at Tucker. Tucker looks at Gwen.

"She's not here," Tucker finally says. "She, um, wasn't feeling well."

"Well, all right," Bianca says. "Then who's in charge?"

We are all quiet again until Cami steps forward, her head held high. "That would be me." She extends her hand. "I'm Cami. I choreographed the dance."

Drake's new single came out last week, and this visit is part of his press tour. We're going to record a one-minute dance sequence to the song—with the hopes that it will become the next viral dance and promote the single organically.

"I know Sydney wanted to film in the *foyer*, but the lighting is better down by the pool," Cami says.

We all head down the narrow, foliage-lined path to the pool. Cami and Bianca lead the way, chatting about engagement rates per post and Google Analytics.

Then Bianca holds up her cell phone, stretching it toward the trees above us. "For some reason, I can't get a signal," she says.

"Oh yeah, I meant to tell you, this close to the ocean, no one does," Cami says. "I'll help you get on the Wi-Fi."

"You're a content house that doesn't get cell service?" Bianca smiles wryly but hands over her phone.

"Trust me, I had the same reaction when I moved in. Sydney had neglected to tell us that," Cami says, laughing as she types in the password. She jokes about it now, but it was a big fight at the time. "Don't worry," Cami reassures Bianca. "We have like industrial-strength Wi-Fi that covers the entire grounds. You can even pick it up when you're a few feet into the ocean."

"We tested it when I did my 'Lay All Your Love on Me' video," Gwen interjects.

Cami turns around and glares at her.

"Have you guys gotten a chance to hear the new song?" Drake asks the rest of us. He says this as if it isn't the number one song in America.

"Yes!" I say. I told myself I wouldn't fangirl, but it's hard to keep it together with the guy who rapped "Nonstop" and "God's Plan" here. "I'm a *huge* fan," I gush. "*Take Care* was the first album I ever bought. Like the whole thing. On iTunes."

"Really?" says Drake. "That's cool." And then, "How old are you guys again?"

"Seventeen."

"But *Degrassi* is my favorite show," Tucker blurts out. "I've seen the reruns."

Drake chuckles at this. "I'm glad."

"*Degrassi?*" Gwen hisses at Tucker under her breath. "That's what you bring up?"

"I panicked," he whispers back.

Cami turns around, eyebrows raised, and glares at us as if to say *Pull it together.*

Drake politely pretends he's unaware of our nervousness.

His team decides Cami is right about the pool. But it's a bit too dark, so they set up freestanding lights while Cami walks us through the dance. She's already taught it to the house members and often reminded the nondancers, Beau and me, that we would never live down messing up in front of Drake.

Drake gets it right away. "That's a cool dance," he says.

And tough-as-nails Dolores Camila Villalobos de Ávila absolutely *melts*. "Thank you so much. That means so much coming from you." She giggles, which is not something I've ever seen her do.

"All right, let's get filming. I want a few options," Bianca says, waving her iPhone. The deal is, they'll pick their favorite take to post to Drake's account, which we'll repost. And then we can post any outtakes to our personal accounts.

As Cami tells everyone where to stand, I run through the dance in my head: *right, left, turn, hip sway, arm, arm* . . . But then I notice something out of the corner of my eye.

"Hey, guys, hold on." I scoop up the tiny salamander that's

chilling right next to Tucker's sneaker. "Don't want to step on this lil guy while we're dancing."

I walk over to the bushes at the edge of the pool and hold out my hand. The salamander blinks at me. "Go on," I whisper. He tentatively reaches one of his slimy hands toward the leaf. He must decide it's all right, because he hops onto the branch and scurries deeper into the bush.

I turn around to see Cami, arms folded across her chest, staring at me. "Really?" she scoffs. "She's not from here," she says to Drake. Then to me, "They're not, like, rare or anything. It's like a squirrel or a . . . pigeon."

I just shrug. Because I didn't think it was rare. I just thought it deserved to live.

"I think it's nice," Drake says. "No animals should be squished in the making of this video." And then he leans down to me and says, "And don't worry about not being from here. I'm not either."

"You're from Canada," Gwen says. As if Drake may have forgotten this.

"Yeah." Drake nods.

"Seriously?" Cami glares at Gwen. But then she reassumes her ever-professional smile and addresses Bianca: "How about we get rolling?"

After a few takes, I think we've got it. And two more after that, Cami concludes we have the shot, so we actually get to be done.

"That was wonderful," Bianca says. "And hey, while we're here, maybe let's get one with just Gwen?" Her words suggest that this is an idea that just occurred to her, but her delivery could use some work.

"Sure," Gwen says, and moves closer to Drake, a saccharine smile on her lips.

The rest of us clear out of the way. Cami lingers the longest before stepping out of the spotlight. Her eyes stay on Gwen like lasers. We film a few more takes with just the two of them, and everyone else's eyes are on the two true stars in the room—TikTok's most followed person and, well, Drake. But I'm watching Cami. Because as Drake and Gwen dance and laugh through Cami's choreography, Cami looks like she's trying not to wrap her perfectly manicured hands around Gwen's throat.

"Okay, I'm sure you've got it by now," Cami says after the third take. She's straining to keep her voice cheerful.

Bianca watches the video on her phone to make sure. "Yes, that's good." She looks up. "Thanks again for having us to your beautiful house. Give Sydney my thanks as well."

"We sure will," Cami says.

In all, Drake was here for about fifteen minutes. Still, I know it will be the thing my cousins ask me about every Thanksgiving for the next twenty or so years. Once the adults are gone, the night devolves into a classic Lit Lair party. Tucker pops champagne, spraying it toward us girls before passing the bottle around. And I'm too happy to even be annoyed with him. We drink straight out of the bottle and blast Drake songs.

When "Started from the Bottom" comes on, I realize I still know every word. As I mouth the lyrics I used to listen to jogging around Fresno, I look out across our pool and beyond to the ocean, and I think about how lucky I am. To be in this place. In this time. And to have the opportunity to meet one of my heroes and make silly videos with my friends, and with them make more money than I'd ever imagined.

I watch Beau dance poorly, his drink sloshing in his hand, and

I can't help but giggle. I'm giddy from champagne bubbles and the sweetness of success.

Cami climbs onto the diving board, a bottle of champagne in hand, and dances, her moves casual and carefree but her form and rhythm still excellent.

"Yes, Dolores!" I shout.

She flips me off—she hates her full name. But she's smiling. I blow her a kiss, and she pretends to almost fall off the diving board to catch it.

As the song winds down, Tucker looks up from his phone. "Hey!" He turns down the music. "Drake posted!"

We all scramble together to look at his phone. But on the screen, there are only two figures. They used the take with only Drake and Gwen. My heart sinks.

"Oh, cute," says Gwen. She barely glances at the screen before walking to the table to top off her champagne. A post with Drake is just another day in the glamorous life of Gwen Riley.

Cami, who had to make her way from the diving board, is the last to see what's happened. Pain flickers across her face before she corrects herself to look impassive.

She charges over to the table and grabs a bottle of Patrón. She takes a long swig, then turns her focus on us. "Enough champagne! Let's do shots."

She starts to splash heavy pours into Solo cups and hand them around.

"Oh, I'm good with champagne," I say when she tries to hand one to me.

"Don't be soft, *Kitty-Kat*," she says. It's a nickname Beau uses often and others sometimes adopt as well. But I don't like it coming from her. Particularly in this mood. She glares at me, and I decide not to cross her.

Cami raises the bottle and spins around to take us all in. "Lit Lair forever!" she toasts before downing another long pull of tequila.

I grimace at my shot.

"Here, to chase." Beau hands me a cup of strange brownish liquid.

I take a sip. It's so sweet it hurts my teeth. "Thanks!" I manage to smile despite the taste.

"It's peach vodka, AriZona iced tea, and Diet Coke. Here, I'll make you one."

I'm not sure if I like it, but I really like him, so I smile and nod. "That'd be great, thank you."

Beau mixes me his weird drink, talking me through the details with the pride of a cooking-show host. "The trick is not too much Diet Coke," he says.

"Interesting."

Before moving to SoCal, I'd drunk alcohol only once, besides wine at church. It was last Fourth of July, and one of my older cousins had brought a bottle of blue Gatorade spiked with Taaka vodka (a concoction she called Fader-ade) to the picnic. We kept walking around the fairgrounds away from our parents to sneak sips. The whole thing was so clandestine, and by the time the sun had set and the fireworks were going off, we were giggling and hiccupping, and I was seriously scared one of our parents was going to figure out what we'd done. It was fun that day, but I was on edge for like a week after, hoping my mom wouldn't bring it up and ground me. But here, in the little bubble of the house, we're totally unsupervised. Tucker has a fake ID, and even though we make sure to hide any trace of alcohol when we film, most weekends everyone drinks like we're grown-ups or, I mean, at least college students. At this point, I've gotten kind of used to being able to drink with my friends. I've almost forgotten how rebellious I felt last summer just because I had a few sips.

In the background, "God's Plan" fades out and the opening bars of "Say So" play from the outdoor speakers.

"Hey, that's not Drake," I say teasingly. But I know why someone queued it. Our first-ever house video—the one that proved that this experiment would work, that put us on the map, not as individuals with solid followings but as a house of superstars— was a dance choreographed to this Doja Cat song. It's always a hit at our parties.

"It's not the same without Sydney here," Gwen says from her spot by the edge of the pool. She dangles one leg in the water, making slow, melancholy circles with her foot.

"Whatever," Cami harrumphs. She steps around Gwen, walking along the edge of the pool like it's a balance beam, swinging the tequila bottle in her hand. The liquor has set in: her eyes are bright with fire; her typically perfect makeup is smudged around the edges. "You know what, I'll say it." Her platform heels totter on the edge of the pool, and I worry she's about to fall in. "I'm glad she's gone. We're all thinking it, I'm just not sorry to say it: Sydney's a bitch, and I don't miss her!"

"All right, that's enough." Tucker crosses over and rips the bottle from her hand. "Can you be a bit nicer when talking about my girlfriend?"

"Is she even your girlfriend anymore?" Cami shoots back. "Have you even heard from her since she left?"

Tucker's broad shoulders fall. His voice is quiet when he says,

"I think she just needed space from the group, after everything that happened." They share a tense look. He takes a swig of her tequila, then shoves it back toward her.

And then a new song comes on and Beau does a cannonball into the pool. Cami lets out a yelp as droplets splash her legs, and she becomes preoccupied with whether any got on her dress. And as many drunk arguments go, the participants get distracted and pretty much forget about it. At least for now.

A few hours later, when the full moon is hanging low on the horizon and the night is winding down, Beau and I sit at our favorite spot: the flat part of the roof we climb onto from the window by the staircase.

Clouds blot out most of the stars, but through the darkness you can just see the ocean. "Steal Tomorrow" by The Tallest Man on Earth plays softly from Beau's cracked iPhone.

The wind has picked up a bit, blowing my hair back. Below, the rhythm of the waves crashing picks up slightly.

"Surf tomorrow?" Beau asks. "Looks like the weather will be good."

"Sure." I nod sleepily.

Beau's phone pings, interrupting the song. He checks it, and even in the darkness, I can see his cheeks turn rosy.

"What is it?" I lean forward, but he pulls his phone into his chest so I can't see.

I flinch. Is it a girl texting him?

"It's nothing," he says. "Just a comment on my TikTok that's blowing up."

I narrow my eyes. Would that really make him react that way?

"It's . . . well, here." He hands me his phone. It's open to the video he posted from Drake's visit: a blooper in which he trips over his own feet and almost tumbles, then I grab his arm and steady him. He captioned the video: *Trying to be a dance TikToker today. Not sure how well it went . . .*

I slide up the comment section, and my eyes widen at the 40K likes the first comment has garnered. It reads: *Omg love that these two are next to each other in the video! And when Kat touches his arm!!* 😱 *I ship #Keau or is it #Bat? lol which one do you guys think?*

My cheeks grow hot. I understand now why he was being so awkward. Beau and I have never talked about the internet's opinions of us before.

I look up to find Beau's steady gaze on me. "So what do you think?" he says.

"Do you mean, do I think we should call ourselves *Bat?*"

He smiles, but his eyes convey nervousness, not joy. "No, I mean . . . Okay, how do I ask you this?" He looks away and twists one of the rubber wristbands on his arm. "It's so weird, because I usually feel like I can talk to you about anything. And I've never felt that before." He looks into my eyes. "I've only known you for a few months, but you're the only person in the world I feel like I can completely trust." This warms my heart in a bittersweet way. Beau avoids talking about his family, but I know things are strained. I'm glad I can be a person he trusts, but I'm sad that I'm the only one. Beau deserves to feel as good as he makes so many strangers feel.

"But in this particular case, it's strange," he continues. "I find myself in this situation where there's something on my mind, and it feels like the whole internet is asking me about it, but the only person I want to talk to about it, my best friend, is the one person who I can't, well, talk to about it," he rambles, avoiding eye contact again.

My heart sinks into my stomach. I'm not sure what he's trying to say, but I think he might be trying to let me down easy. That he might be about to tell me that he's noticed my feelings and he doesn't share them.

"Because," he continues, "well, like, how do you get advice on asking a girl out from the girl you want to ask out?" He looks at the ocean and runs his hands through his floppy hair. "Because really, if you think about it—"

I put my hand on his cheek, bringing his face toward mine, and kiss him.

His breath catches in surprise. But then his lips soften, and he kisses me back. His hand grazes my waist, the warmth of his skin seeping through the thin fabric of my sundress.

My heart pounds against my chest. And it's like the world has slowed down around us.

Beau pulls back and smiles, his forehead pressed against mine in the dark. "I've been wanting to do that since the day I met you."

I smile back at him. "If I'd left it up to you, it would've taken three more months."

He laughs and gently plays with the end of one of my braids. I look into his sea-green eyes and shiver.

"It's getting cold up here." He runs his hand down my bare arm. "We should get inside."

I nod, although I wasn't shivering because of the weather.

Beau climbs down first, easing himself from the edge of the roof into the window below. I follow. It's a move I've done dozens of times since Beau and I discovered this spot the first week in the house, and I'm pretty much sober at this point, so it'll be no trouble. I scooch to the edge of the roof, then dangle down toward the windowsill. My right shoe makes contact with the sill. I swing down for my left to meet it and—

Thunder cracks and a bolt of lightning strikes the water behind me.

I scream and my left sneaker slips on a small pebble on the windowsill. My foot catches nothing but air. Beau lunges for me, wrapping his arms around my hips. I grab the side of the window and hold on for dear life.

Beau pulls me through the window into the house. "Are you okay?" He holds me tightly.

"Yes, yes, I'm fine," I say into his soft T-shirt. Adrenaline pulses through my veins. My hands are a bit scraped, minor cuts I didn't even feel happen, thanks to the shock. But besides that, I am okay. I tell myself that I'm fine, I'm safe, I'm here in Beau's arms.

"These old Vans just have no traction anymore," I say breathlessly. "I need to get new ones."

Beau lets out a relieved laugh and runs a hand down my back softly.

We're so caught up in the moment that we almost don't notice the shadowy figure emerging from Sydney's room.

"Hey, you're back," I say.

She startles at my voice. Then lightning strikes again, and the light from the window illuminates the girl's *blond* hair. But Sydney's hair is black.

"Gwen?" I ask.

Gwen's usually rosy cheeks are pale. I haven't seen her like this since the day Kylie Jenner unfollowed her on Instagram.

"What are you doing?" I ask. My eyes dart to the closed door behind her.

29

"I was just, um, borrowing something," she says. She looks down at her empty hands, then tucks them behind her back.

I tilt my head, incredulous.

"At two a.m.?" Beau asks.

"What exactly were you borrowing?" I add.

"Ugh, okay." She lets out an over-the-top sigh, and her empty hands fall to her side. "I needed a maxi pad, okay? Sydney had a stash." Then she looks at Beau when she explains, "I put it on in her bathroom."

"Right, okay." Beau's face goes crimson. "Well, night, Gwen."

"'Night! Sleep well." She sashays off toward her room.

"Yeah, good night," I say. Beau takes my hand, and we head down the hall. I glance back over my shoulder at Gwen. Beau seemed to believe her explanation just fine. But a thought nags at me: Wasn't Gwen's period two weeks ago? I'm pretty sure she borrowed a tampon from me when we were stuck at a three-hour meet-and-greet.

At my door, Beau pauses, twisting the end of my new bracelet in his fingers. In the dim light, his eyelashes cast long shadows on his cheekbones. "See you tomorrow," he whispers.

He kisses me again.

I float into my bedroom in a dreamy haze. Beau *likes* me. Beau *kissed* me. I grab my headphones off my dresser and turn on the sappiest, most over-the-top romantic songs I can think of. Because right now, they don't seem like an exaggeration. They seem just right.

I flop down on my bed, still in my clothes. I listen to Death Cab for Cutie and replay the night in my mind again and again. I'm smiling so much my face hurts. I stare at the ceiling, my room dark except for the bluish light coming in the window from the pool below. And there's one thing I know for sure: there's no way I'm going back to Fresno in a few weeks. Not when my life is happening here.

Before I go to sleep, I close my curtains so the pool light won't wake me later. I notice that the rain has settled and the stars have started to peek out through the clouds.

I sleep soundly in the afterglow of the night. Except for around three, when I hear a cracking sound like thunder.

It must be storming again, I think, half-asleep. I have the vague worry that we've left the cushions on the patio furniture. But I'm too sleepy to get up to check, and it's too late now.

I roll over and fall into a deep, luxurious sleep until long after the sun is high in the sky and shining through the cracks in the curtains, when I'm awakened by a bloodcurdling scream.

3

1 HOUR BEFORE

CAMI

Where's Sydney?

It's the first thing I see when I open my eyes. Well, I mean, the first thing I see is my lock screen: a photo of me and Gwen at Coachella, the day we met. But as soon as I pull up TikTok, I see the comment. It has nine thousand likes, and it's stuck at the top of the comment section on my Drake video.

Ugh. I fight the urge to throw my phone at the wall. Instead, I send it into the plush pillow beside me and hop out of my California King bed.

I can't believe I'm in a video dancing with Drake, *Drake,* and everyone just wants to talk about stupid Sydney.

That girl has never been more relevant now that she's disappeared.

I was finally making progress toward Gwen's most-followed crown, and now I have to deal with Sydney's surge in status. I can't wait till she's done licking her wounds at her parents' house. I want her down here by the beach and at her fighting weight. That way, I can beat her and reestablish myself as the one for Gwen to watch. It's hard to compete with a ghost.

I pull off my silk pajamas and throw them into the hamper. For a second, I examine my naked body in the mirror. My olive skin glows in the Southern California sun.

When I was in New York, I was always trying to make myself smaller. I'd do cardio constantly—running on a treadmill even after hours of dance, dieting obsessively—trying to whittle myself down to that lithe ballerina shape. But it still wasn't enough. I was fighting my body type for a figure that isn't even possible for most adult women to achieve, at least not in a way that isn't wildly unhealthy.

Now I love my curves. They're my signature. I work hard in the gym multiple times a week—but now it's to highlight my hourglass shape, not fight it. I lift weights and do squats. I want to emphasize the curve of my hips and the strength of my legs. I no longer want to make myself smaller.

But as much as I love my body, it seems much of the internet still prefers stick-thin girls like Sydney. She doesn't have to work hard in the gym. She doesn't work for anything.

I'm going with athleisure vibes today, so I pull a pair of black Gymshark leggings out of one drawer and a Puma crop top from another. I have to have a dresser because Sydney took the room with the biggest closet—something about how she should have the main suite because her family put up the down payment. Gwen took the next-biggest room, so she has space for all the clothes her sponsors send her. You can barely even walk into my closet; it's ridiculous.

I sit at my vanity and straighten my hair before pinning a few clips above my ears. I lace up my chunky Filas and grab my phone.

At least a hundred TikTok notifications have gathered while I was getting ready, but I swipe up to ignore them.

I take the stairs two at a time. "Everyone be quiet! I'm about to go live!" I yell over the railing.

I start by the front door. I hold my phone out like I'm taking a selfie and start my livestream.

"Hello, TikTok! Welcome to our crib!" I say into the live video. I've never seen *MTV Cribs*—after all, I was a baby when it was a hit show—but I know that was, like, a catchphrase. "Thanks for tuning in to part three of my house tour!"

I walk backward through the foyer, keeping my face in the shot while making sure to pan to the boxes piled in the entryway.

"Here you see just some of the mail we get every day." I make sure to get the box of shoes from Nike, the clothes haul from Revolve, and the package from Kylie Cosmetics in the shot. I try to avoid showing shipping labels so stalkers don't see our address, and so no one sees how many are addressed to Gwen or Sydney rather than to all of us. I keep my face neutral and move my tour along.

"Over there's the formal living room—no one really goes in there—and the dining room, which has a pool table and old arcade games in it. And here is the TV room, where we can see a Gwen Riley in her natural habitat."

Gwen lies across the couch, a cool eye mask on her face, scrolling through TikTok. Her eyes are kind of glossed over, and she's going quickly, just allowing the beginnings of a sound to play before flicking past. "Don't get me on camera," she says without looking up. "I look so gross."

Which is of course a ridiculous thing to say. Gwen is the most beautiful person I've ever seen. Not that I'd say that to her, or to the thousands of people on this live. Sure, people know I like girls; I've been out for almost three years now. But the internet knowing you're gay is super different from it knowing that you're crushing on your housemate and best friend, who is almost definitely straight. If people knew I liked Gwen, they'd pity me. If Gwen knew, she'd probably pity me, too, and make some big deal about letting me down easy and making sure I know how much she values our friendship and all that. I'm mortified just thinking about it. I could never let that happen. I'm Cami de Ávila, and I'm clever and mean and unapologetically strong. An unrequited crush does not fit with that image. There is no state more vulnerable than being in love.

So instead of telling her how great she looks right now, I deflect. I turn to the camera and say, "As we can see, Gwen is hungover."

"Cami!" She chucks a throw pillow at me.

I yelp and step out of the way. "Teen drinking is very bad," I say into the camera.

"Yo, I got a fake ID, though!" someone yells from the kitchen, completing the reference.

"Beau's awake!" I take my broadcast to a more willing cohost.

In the kitchen, Beau is constructing an elaborate breakfast sandwich with eggs, bacon, and pickles, it appears. He's got cameras on tripods so he can film each step.

"Say hi to the people, Beau."

"Hi to the people," he says with a big smile.

I roll my eyes exaggeratedly. "Beau thinks dad jokes are funny."

"They are!"

I pan to show his elaborate cooking setup. I notice he's put out two plates and two sets of bagels for his sandwiches.

"Oooh, is that one for me?" I ask, fluttering my eyelids.

"Oh, um, it wasn't." He gets flustered. "But I can make you one, too."

"Relax, I'm just joking. We all know who it's for." I wink conspiratorially toward the camera. Everyone knows Beau and Kat are obsessed with each other, except for maybe Beau and Kat.

Beau blushes at the suggestion. I cackle and head to the door. It's 80 degrees but it's not humid, and there's a nice breeze off the ocean. I leave the door open.

"And of course, for many of us, our favorite part of the Lit Lair isn't inside the house at all." I head down the greenery-lined path to the pool, walking backward down the steps.

"The weather is beautiful here in Malibu, so we try to use the pool as much as possible." This is a bit of a white lie. The boys use the pool, and so does Kat. But the rest of us girls barely use it—it's too much work to have to start hair and makeup again. Mostly we just pose beside it in swimsuits.

The stones on the path are a bit slick. My sneaker catches and I almost wipe out. A small yelp escapes my lips.

"Be careful!" Beau yells down from the house.

My ankle hurts and I want to swear, but instead I giggle, aware of the camera. "Walking backward is harder than it looks." I readjust the camera and regain my composure.

On the phone, the pool comes into view over my shoulder. For some reason, the water looks a sort of bronzy-red color.

What is that? I wonder if there's a flare on the lens or something.

I turn around to look at the pool directly, my phone—still broadcasting live—in my hand.

I gasp and my phone clatters to the ground. It lands in a puddle of murky pool water, traced with red tendrils. Under

36

the water, the freshly cracked screen lights up with thousands of alerts before the device fries out.

In a matter of minutes, more people will see my "House Tour: Part 3" video than watched last year's NBA Finals. I won't just beat Gwen's single-video record; I'll blow it out of the water. But none of that registers until much later.

Because in this moment, all I can see is my friend facedown in the pool, her beautiful, shiny black hair tangled in the bloody water.

A scream rips through my body.

4

23 MINUTES AFTER

TUCKER

I wake up to Gwen standing above my bed, crying. "It's Sydney," she gasps.

I look up at her from my mattress on the floor, and it feels like I'm drowning. All I can think is *She knows.*

This can't be happening. My heart pounds in my chest as I struggle to sit up.

"What about Sydney?" I try to keep my voice as normal as possible.

She tumbles from tears into full sobs. "You—need—to—come—downstairs," she manages to say between gasps for air.

"Okay, okay." I search my room for a pair of basketball shorts. My head throbs. I try to remember last night, but it's all a blur of tequila and champagne. I must have blacked out. Jesus, why did I drink so freaking much?

I find a pair of shorts on a pile of video game disks and pull them on over my boxers. My room is a bit of a disaster on a good day. *Ugh, I guess teenage boys are teenage boys no matter how much money they have,* Sydney said when I told her I was done decorating my room. I'd mounted a flat-screen, taped up my Tarantino posters and SATURDAYS ARE FOR THE BOYS flag, and started an alcohol bottle graveyard on top of my dresser. That seemed like enough to me. She kept offering for her parents to pay for furniture, like they did for her bedroom and the rooms downstairs. But that made me feel like we were on a fast train toward marriage and a house down the cul-de-sac from the in-laws. Even more than usual.

"I didn't— This summer was just supposed to be fun—*for* fun," Gwen babbles through her tears. "No one was supposed to get hurt."

I grab my sunglasses from my Herschel backpack and pull a semiclean shirt off the top of my laundry basket. I lead an unsteady, sobbing Gwen out of my room. As we descend the stairs, I try to put on my best loyal-boyfriend face. I'm still figuring out what that might look like when we reach the entryway.

The front door is wide open, and police are everywhere: barking into radios, taking notes while listening to a tearful, pajama-clad Kat, and taking pictures—of the floor, of the photographs on the wall, of a Solo cup left in a puddle of beer from last night.

What the fuck?

A passing cop gives me a disgusted look; I glance down and realize I'm still shirtless. I pull my T-shirt on roughly, wishing I'd looked for a clean one. Gwen could've warned me that the damn police were here. Since she's taken up residency on the bottom step, digging her nails into the wooden banister like it's the door in *Titanic*, maybe that would've been asking a bit too much from her.

A flashbulb goes off near my face, and I flinch.

I think there's something wrong with my hearing. Everyone is talking at once, but I can't make out any words.

I stumble to the kitchen to see a very pale Cami. She opens

her mouth as if she's about to say something to me, but then she vomits all over her white Filas.

I sidestep her chunks and follow the flow of police out of the house. They seem to all be heading toward the pool. The more cops I see, the more I start to panic. I race down the steps, weaving around blue uniforms, my bare feet sliding on the stone steps. I stop short just before the edge of the pool.

And then I see her: my girlfriend, my gorgeous, vibrant, wickedly smart, and sometimes just wicked girlfriend. Floating facedown, unconscious, in the pool. I look around. But no one is doing anything to help her. But they must see her; they're all looking at her. Some are even taking pictures.

I turn to the nearest cop. "Why is no one helping her? Shouldn't we be doing CPR? Didn't someone call 911? Where is the ambulance?"

I start to charge forward, but a cop extends his arm to stop me. "Stay back, son," he barks.

A soft hand flutters on my shoulder, and I process what I'm seeing at the same time Kat whispers the words "She's already gone, Tucker."

The cops pull yellow police tape across the entrance to the pool deck and usher us back inside the house.

In the front room, the police are taking a statement from Beau. Cami sits on the stairs with Gwen, pulling sticky strands of blond hair from her wet cheeks and whispering soothing, indistinguishable words to her.

"I don't understand," a burly uniformed cop says to Beau.

"You've been up for two hours and you didn't notice that your friend was dead in the pool?"

Beau flinches at the word "dead." He opens his mouth to defend himself, but someone else speaks first.

"You can't see the pool from the house," Gwen says. Her voice is clear. It's the first coherent thought she's expressed this morning. She's presumably answering the cop, but she cuts her eyes at me.

3 MONTHS BEFORE
GWEN

"You can't see the pool from the house," Tucker whispers in my ear. "Don't worry."

His warm lips kiss down my neck, and I sigh, leaning back against the cool tile wall of the pool. Our limbs are tangled together under the water, skin touching everywhere, thanks to our swimsuits. I'm wearing the Oh Polly bikini they sent me to model—basically a thong. I wear stuff like this a lot, but right now I'm so much more aware of how barely covered up I am. How every lasered-hairless pore on my body has turned to goose bumps. Because right now, my scantily clad body is not being photographed but is pressed up against Tucker. *Tucker*—who's been my closest guy friend, my only guy friend, really. Tucker, who every straight teenage girl with a data plan is absolutely obsessed with. Tucker, who has a movie-star jawline and eyes that catch the stars, and whose face recently became the one I can't help but picture when I hear a love song. Tucker, who, despite all this, is still *Sydney's boyfriend.*

I press my palm against his chest and push him away. "Wait," I whisper. "What about that one girl—Kat? She can see the pool from her room, I think." I peer through the palm trees, trying to see if I can make out her window through the leaves.

"She's down on the beach with that stoner guy." He brushes off my concern and leans back in to kiss me.

I lean away. "But what if someone decides to come down here? I mean, if anyone finds out—like, Tuck, can you imagine if *TMZ* got this . . . it would be—"

"God, for once can you not worry about what *TMZ* thinks? Can't you do something you want to, without an Insta poll to see if your followers approve? Something just for you?" He looks down to my hand, still resting on his bare chest. His skin feels electric on mine. My heart begins to race. "Something just for us."

"But Sydney . . ."

"I know you care about her, and I do, too. But this thing between you and me, Gwen, I've never felt anything like it before. And we deserve to find out what it is, without the whole world watching or losing Syd and our place in the house. And I know you think that I'm just saying this because I'm drunk, or because it's Malibu or 'cause Sydney and I are fighting. But really, Gwen, it's not any of that." He lifts my hand away from his chest, wrapping it in his. "I've wanted this for so long, you don't even know."

But I do know. His words so closely mirror my own pining thoughts over the last few weeks that I'd think I was hallucinating if I couldn't feel his solid touch against my hand.

But I also don't need a poll to know what people would think if they found out: *Gwen can have any guy she wants, and she hooked up with her best friend's boyfriend, like, really?!?* But it's more complicated than that.

The truth is, it's hard to find love, even for me. Maybe even especially for me.

Sure, I mean, there are tons of people who *think* they'd love to date me. People like my looks, my clothes, my lifestyle. They want to be close to me, to kiss me, to sleep with me. But they don't know me. They just think they do.

Usually when guys get to know me outside of the Instagram and TikTok posts—when they see the hours it takes to look this way, or that, although I'm smiling in all my videos, believe it or not, I'm not always happy; that, like everyone else, I have bad days, foul moods, and family troubles (shout out to my parents and their *three* rounds in divorce court across marriages); or even when they find out that I watch cheesy reality TV like *The Bachelor* and don't, in fact, know everything about sports or comic books or whatever else they love and therefore have projected onto me—well, then, I'm no longer the girl in the Instagram thirst trap or crop-top dance video. I'm just a normal, real girl, asking them for normal, real things like good-morning texts or to hold my purse during a photo shoot or to hold me when I cry. And when they wake up from their dream of me, they leave.

I've only ever been loved like a Top 40 song—the latest hit, the hot new thing. Something fleeting, bubbly and fun; nothing serious. But just once, I'd like to be loved like a poignant, timeless ballad. With a melody that moves you and lyrics that burrow deep in your heart. Like Leonard Cohen's "Suzanne" or "Something" by the Beatles or—oooh, "Speak Now" by Taylor Swift. But that never seems to happen.

To be loved so broadly, and so shallowly, well, that's a thought that sticks. It's what keeps me up at night: *What does it say that strangers love me but those who've known me best have rejected me?*

But with Tucker it's different. He does know me. He's talked to me and listened to me plenty, even when there wasn't anything sexual between us. When it seemed that there couldn't be anything sexual between us—since, after all, he's been dating the girl whose been my best friend since eighth grade, when my mom got a job as Sydney's dad's assistant and we moved to Beverly Hills.

Throughout high school, Syd, Tucker, and I were all so close. Sitting at the same lunch table, hanging out in Sydney's basement, at her family's ski lodge over holidays. *The three musketeers*, Sydney's dad called us when he caught us sneaking vodka last New Year's.

Tucker's seen me without makeup. He drove me to McDonald's after my parents' custody hearing and brought over soup when I was recovering from my rhinoplasty—he saw my face all bruised and everything. He's not some follower or fan. He's my friend, truly.

So of course, when Sydney and I were putting together the Lit Lair and she asked if it'd be cool if her boyfriend joined, I said duh.

Which brings us to today, our first official day living in the house. Tucker helped me carry in my boxes, we met the other TikTokers, and when the sun went down, we popped champagne. We all drank for hours, enjoying the thrill of freedom, of no adult supervision or eight o'clock school alarm the next morning. The only sour point of the night was when Sydney went to bed early, claiming a headache, even though we all knew it was 'cause she had some big fight with Tucker about a bed frame.

A few tequila shots after she huffed off, Tucker and I stumbled down to check out the pool. Giggling and giddy. High on the weed that Beau shared and the excitement of our growing celebrity status. Just the two of us. Half naked and cross-faded.

And now, being here with him, the way he's looking at me, it does feel like I'm living that iconic-ballad sort of love.

"Here, I have an idea," Tucker says, breaking our embrace and swimming across the width of the pool in a few graceful strokes. He reaches over the edge and clicks a switch, extinguishing the pool lights.

He makes his way back over to me. Under the water, his hands find my waist, and I bring up my legs and wrap them around his hips.

He smiles at me in the darkness. "See, now it's like we're the only two people in the world."

And then I kiss him. And he tugs the string on my bikini. And that's how I start hooking up with my best friend's boyfriend. In the very same pool where she'll later be found dead.

5

1 HOUR AFTER

CAMI

Uniformed police officers are swarming about everywhere. Trekking in and out. Going to the driveway to report into their car radios, then back through the front door, through the house, to the pool, and then back. They leave the doors open, and I can hear the air-conditioning clicking on and off over and over, pumping cool air into the scorching August heat.

Their boots track in dirt. My mind is swimming, but my eyes focus on the muddy footprint in the middle of the white hallway runner. The one Sydney's mom picked out from West Elm. I think about telling them to take their shoes off. But then I realize the boots are also tracking blood across the carpet. So I keep my mouth shut.

And then, amid the boots, there's a pair of sensible black dress shoes, walking through our front door and down the hall. My eyes flicker up.

"Catch me up," the woman tells a cop. There's a badge hanging from a silver chain around her neck, but she's not in uniform. Instead, she's wearing a gray pantsuit, made of what I must say is a quite tacky polyester.

"Call came in at nine-fifty-two," says one of the officers. His name tag says MOORE. The same guy who was just asking Beau questions. "I was first to respond." Officer Moore flips through his notebook. "Arrived on scene less than six minutes after the initial call . . ."

The woman doesn't stop walking, and Officer Moore follows closely at her heels. As she passes the other cops, their eyes turn to her, and they stand a little straighter or nod. Right away, despite the fog in my brain, I recognize the dynamic: she's in charge. She's the queen bee. So I do what I always do: I make sure to stay close to her.

My brain clicks into focus. I turn to Gwen, who is still slumped on the bottom stair. "Come on," I say, pulling her up by the arm. "Let's get you some water." Gwen just nods and looks at me with her wide, glossy eyes as I drag her into the kitchen after the woman and her posse.

When we enter the kitchen, the woman has already gone to work. She examines the surface, wiping a gloved hand across the mustard Beau left spilled on the counter. The sandwiches are still half made, the cameras still on tripods. "What is this?" She looks through the camera at the bagels. She turns to a cop: "Are these ours?"

"Oh no, those are Beau's," I say.

The woman turns to us. "Why is your kitchen rigged up with lights and cameras?"

"We're the Lit Lair," Gwen replies, her voice proud, if strained.

"I'm sorry?"

"Like"—Gwen does a few of the arm movements from our most famous dance—"you know. The Lit Lair." She looks around expectantly, mascara tears still staining her face.

47

The woman in the suit looks at Gwen like she's crazy.

"We're six TikTok stars," I clarify. "Or I guess . . . five now." That's weird to think about. I shake it off, try to keep focused. "We live together and make videos about our lives."

"Oh!" Officer Moore's eyes go wide with recognition. "My niece loves you guys."

"Great," Pantsuit sighs. "So it's an investigation on the *Big Brother* set."

"What's *Big Brother*?" Gwen asks.

I step in front of her, because there are more important questions. "I'm sorry, but how much of an 'investigation' is there? Because to me it seems like she came back late and tried coming in through the pool deck. Then she hit her head and fell. It's very sad, of course, but really, how much is there to investigate?"

I'm hoping for some reassurance, but her face remains neutral and she replies, "What's your name again?"

"Cami," I say. "Dolores Camila." I hold out my hand, but she doesn't take it.

"Hmmm." She writes something in her notebook, her gaze still on me.

I squirm. I decide it's best I show her I had another reason to come to the kitchen. One that makes me a kind, thoughtful friend. I grab a cup and turn on the sink, since a cop is blocking the fridge with the La Croix. I hand Gwen the glass of lukewarm liquid, and she sips carefully.

A man comes through the screen door wearing a white plastic jumpsuit and safety glasses, like the kind I used to wear in AP Chem.

"Detective Johnson," he says.

I make a mental note of Pantsuit's real name.

"Reyes." She nods in his direction. "What do we have?"

"GSW to the right temple, exit wound out the left," he tells her, handing her a notebook. I don't know what any of it means, but I decide here's the place to be if I want to find out. I lean closer to hear better.

Detective Johnson reads from the notebook, then says, "So she didn't drown?"

"No," the cop replies. "She was dead before she hit the water. The gunshot killed her."

The glass slips out of Gwen's hand, shattering against the tile floor on impact.

"Sydney was shot?" I croak.

"No, no, that can't be," says Gwen. "I mean, she hit her head, like Cami said, and fell in the pool. This was an accident; she wasn't murdered. People don't just, like, get shot in Malibu."

The world is swirling colors again. I feel like I'm drowning inside myself. My mouth fills with a bitter taste.

The detective ignores Gwen. She turns to the guy in the jumpsuit. "Can you do a spatter analysis?"

"We can try, but it'll be hard, with the water. My team found blood and brain matter in the pool filter."

And at that, I throw up for the second time that morning.

The detective sighs and looks at me like somehow my bile is more disgusting than Sydney's *brain matter.*

"Can someone get these kids out of my way?" she says.

The police herd us into the formal living room at the front of the house, a room we almost never use. I have a feeling that after this day, we'll want to spend even less time in here.

Gwen paces, practically bouncing off the wall. Kat sits on the window seat in the sun, rubbing her red eyes. Tucker man-spreads across most of the couch. I sit on the edge of the piano bench and try to catch my breath.

Beau enters the room and drops an armload of Kind bars and bottled water on the coffee table.

"They said I couldn't touch my sandwiches, but I got these."

"Thank you," Kat says, looking at the Kind bars like they're magic. "That was smart of you."

I roll my eyes. "The police will *allow* us to eat some of our own food. How generous of them." My stomach is still rolling from vomiting, so I just take a water.

"So," Tucker says carefully, "they think someone just, what? Shot her, and she fell into the pool?" His face is pale; his eyes are glassy.

"No, no, no, no, no," Gwen mutters, but more to herself.

"I guess," I say. "They didn't really explain their thinking. But yes, they, um, they said she'd been shot in the head."

"Shit." Tucker rubs the back of his neck.

"Wouldn't we have heard that?" Beau asks. "If she was shot right outside the house?"

"I—I may have heard it," Kat says. Everyone turns to look at her. "My room is by the pool and . . . I heard a sound last night. I thought it was thunder. I guess it could've been a gunshot." She twists her scrunchy between her hands.

"You guess?" I say. "How can you not know?"

"I don't know. I've never heard one before."

"Ugh," I sigh. "You're useless."

"Jeez, Cami," Beau says. "Have *you* heard a gunshot before?"

"No, but I would know if I'd heard one or not, okay?" I snap at him. "Unlike your precious Kat, who can't tell the difference between thunder and Sydney being murdered."

Kat rolls her eyes. Beau crosses the room to sit next to her. He wraps an arm around her shoulders.

"I just don't understand who would want to hurt Sydney," Beau says. "She's such a sweet person."

Tucker and I share a look across the room. Only an oblivious, gullible stoner like Beau would think Sydney was sweet. That girl was a lot of things. Some admirable. But *sweet* wasn't one of them.

I flick my eyes away from Tucker's before anyone else notices the look we shared.

"Let's think about it," Tucker says. "Besides us, who else had access to the house in the last twenty-four hours?"

Gwen's eyes go wide. "Drake?"

"No, not Drake." He sighs. "Who was here early this morning? I mean, there are always people in and out, you know, cleaning or gardening, delivering things. . . ."

"What, are you saying that just because someone's working class, they are more likely to have killed Sydney?" Kat asks.

"That's not what I'm saying." Tucker holds up his arms in innocence. "But, I mean, do you really think someone in this room killed her?"

We stare at each other.

"What about a stalker?" I offer. "Sydney got weird messages from men all the time. All of us do."

"That's true," Kat says. "I've had some messed-up messages."

I think back to all the weird and inappropriate DM requests, emails, and comments I've received. Strangers proposing marriage or asking for a lock of my hair. And those are the ones who claim to like me. There's also the hate messages. Some of which have contained death threats. And just like that, this day gets even more frightening. Because if one of those people killed Sydney, they might be after the rest of us, too.

"Excuse me." Officer Moore pokes his head into the room. He flips through his notebook. "Beau, can I double-check a few things with you?"

"Oh, sure." Beau stands and follows him out of the room.

Left alone on the window seat, Kat starts to softly cry again. She rubs her face with her hands, probably getting snot in the scrunchy on her wrist. I wrinkle my nose. *Gross.* I want to judge her, but then I remember the vomit soaking into my socks.

I rise and walk toward the officer stationed at the doorway. "Are we being detained?" I ask.

"Uh . . ." He glances from side to side. "There are no suspects at this time," he says. "We are just gathering information."

"So . . . no?"

"No," he admits.

I reach into the small pocket at the waistband of my leggings and pull out a fifty-dollar bill. "Then you won't mind if I go up to my room." I press the bill into his hand.

Tucker scoffs: "Cami, he's a cop, not the hostess at Nobu."

But I just shrug and saunter up the stairs. I'm not sure if the cop pockets the fifty, but he doesn't stop me.

I round the corner at the top of the stairs, and there's Sydney's room, as always. But it's not as always. Because there are more people in white jumpsuits in there, rooting through her things. Her Away suitcase, the one she took with her when she left last week, lies open on the floor.

One of the moon-suit guys reaches down with tweezers to

pick something off the carpet. It's a long *blond* hair. There's only one person in the house with hair like that.

Another moon suit notices me and shuts the door between us.

I go straight to the bathroom. I try not to think about the hair and just focus on what I came up here to do. I turn both faucets of the clawfoot bathtub on full blast. I take off my shoes and peel off my damp socks, trying not to gag at the smell. I throw them right in the trash, not even bothering with the hamper or trying to wash them.

I slide my feet into the water and scrub them with Floris London soap. The smell usually calms me. It has ever since I was a little girl, when I would sniff all the samples while my mother got her hair done. But today there's no such luck.

I watch the water, laced with vomit and luxury soap, circling the drain. I calm down enough to process: *My friend is dead. My friend has been killed.*

I turn the thought over in my mind, but it really doesn't make sense. People die when they're old and sick. They die in hospitals, hooked up to machines, their loved ones gathered beside them, saying the rosary. They die having told their family how they want to be buried. With last will and testaments and life insurance plans.

People don't die at seventeen. Having just bought their first car. Having kissed only one person, that person being someone as annoying as *Tucker Campbell.* People don't die just a few months after finally getting decent SAT scores. People who still listen to One Direction every time they shower don't die. And they certainly don't die days after posting a thirst trap dance on TikTok. That can't be the last thing she ever says to the world, can it? Just at the top of her feed forever?

That's simply not how things work.

I'm jolted by a crash on the other side of the wall. I turn off the water and step out of the tub, my feet dripping.

Gwen's door is wide open. She's digging through her closet, throwing jackets, yoga pants, and makeup products toward the open suitcase on her bed.

"What are you doing?" I ask.

She chucks a Golden Goose over her shoulder, and it bounces off the wall. The crashing sound I heard, I guess.

"I'm getting out of here," she says. She pulls down a whole section of her closet, hangers and all, and crosses the room to plop it into her suitcase. I spot the Riverdale High cheerleader outfit she wore last Halloween in the stack, so clearly she's packing the essentials.

"You shouldn't leave," I say.

"Why not?"

"You're witness to a murder," I say. The words sound foreign.

"I didn't see anything," Gwen replies.

"But you were in the house, I mean."

She shrugs and pulls at the zipper of her suitcase.

"Where will you even go?" I ask.

"My dad is in Tahoe. I'll meet him there." Gwen sits on her suitcase, struggling to get the zipper closed. I cringe. Her relationship with her dad is . . . complicated. It seems like every time something goes wrong in her life, a sponsorship deal goes to a member of rival house Clout 9 instead of her, or a boy she's texting ghosts her, Gwen calls her dad, crying. And every time, without fail, he either doesn't answer or treats her distantly and coldly. And trying to get his support just makes her emotional state worse.

"The police will stop you at the airport," I tell Gwen.

"Then I'll drive."

"It'll look suspicious," I say. "If you run away."

"Well, then I guess it's good I didn't kill her," she says, venom in her voice. She gives up on her suitcase, leaving it half open as she pulls the handle and flees her room. I follow her.

"Don't you want to stay and help figure out what happened? Or just, you know, be there for each other—Gwen!" I grab the handle of her suitcase.

"I'm not staying in this murder house. I'm just not! There's someone dead in the pool, Cami." She tugs back her suitcase and starts down the stairs, her bag banging on each step and shedding articles of clothing and shoes. "When I said I wanted my life to be like *The Great Gatsby*, I meant the money and parties, not this!"

"Wow, you actually read a book I gave you," I mumble.

Gwen glares and continues to flee, dropping a lacy bra in her wake. But before she gets to the front door, two cops step in front of her. "Ma'am, where are you going?" one asks.

"Tahoe." She tries to sidestep him, but he extends his arm to block her.

"We're asking that you stay in the state for now," the other cop says. I give Gwen an I-told-you-so look.

"That's fine, I'll just stay on the California side." She tries to sidestep him again.

The other cop takes the suitcase handle out of Gwen's hand. "Actually, we're gonna have to ask that you don't leave the premises," he says.

That's a bit more than even I was expecting. "Why?" I step forward and ask. "I thought you said we weren't suspects."

BEAU

"In here, son." Officer Moore leads me into the dining room. Someone's put the cover on the PAC-MAN machine and pulled chairs up to the pool table. It looks so different, so adult. "The detective will just want to know the same types of things I asked about: What time did you go to bed, when did you wake up this morning . . . did you see anything from the kitchen."

"Okay." I push a hand through my hair. It's getting long. My dad would say I look like a punk.

"If you want a parent or lawyer let us know—but you're not a suspect, just a witness," he says.

"Nah, my parents are at work. And I'm almost eighteen anyway." They'd be pissed if I made them come all the way to Malibu just to hear me tell these people I got up and made a sandwich without noticing anything was wrong. My mom's gallery has a major opening this week. And my dad is never not busy with work.

Officer Moore leaves me alone, and in the quiet, I can just hear the sound of the TV from the other room.

". . . where seventeen-year-old Sydney Reynolds was found dead this morning," a voice says. I lean forward to see through a small crack in the slightly ajar doors.

On the news, the anchor talks about how Sydney was last seen alive last night at her parents' house, and they play our TikTok videos as B-roll.

Internet Star Slain, the caption reads.

"It's better to tune out the press," a voice behind me says. I turn to see the lady who's been ordering the cops around. "It can be difficult to be bombarded by strangers talking about you."

I'm confused. "They're not talking about me. They're talking about Sydney." Actually, this moment shouldn't be about me at all. It should be about mourning and honoring her.

"Right, of course," she says. "I just meant, they're talking about, well, your little group here."

The way she talks about us makes me defensive. "We've dealt with the media before." I clear my throat. "We can handle it."

"I'm sure you can." She smiles tightly. "Detective Elena Johnson," she says. "And that's my partner, Detective Jim Carney." She tips her head toward the burly middle-aged man coming through the door with a pile of blank legal pads.

I nod and smile, trying to remember all the things my dad is always yelling at me about eye contact and being polite and addressing adults properly. "Nice to meet you, um, ma'am and sir," I manage to say.

The male detective, Carney, cocks his head in confusion. "I wouldn't exactly say it was nice. Someone's died."

Johnson cuts her eyes at him. "I know what you meant, Beau." She gestures to the chair across the table from her. "Please, take a seat."

I bump on the fact that she knows my name even though I haven't said it yet. But I don't know, maybe she's a TikTok fan.

Carney closes the doors, and the sound from the TV becomes a faint mumble.

Johnson sits down at the table across from me and flips open a file. Carney takes the place next to her and clicks on a tape recorder.

"Has anyone in the house ever mentioned wanting to buy a gun?" She looks up from the paper. "Or perhaps receiving one as a gift? Or a family heirloom?"

"No." I shake my head. "We're from LA and New York. No one has a gun."

"Katherine Powell is from Fresno."

"I mean, we're all from, ya know, blue states."

"Yet you specifically said the kids 'from LA and New York' don't have guns. Does Ms. Powell have a gun?"

"What? No." It feels like my stomach has dropped out of my body. *How would they get that from what I said?* "Kat is a pacifist," I say firmly. "She did March for Our Lives. She would never own a gun."

The detective writes something down; her face is impassive.

"Why are you asking about that anyway? Officer Moore said you just wanted to know about things like if I heard anything last night. We're witnesses, not suspects, right?"

"There are no official suspects in this case," she says in response.

"Yeah, okay. So if you want a suspect, what you should be looking into are these cyberstalkers who message us constantly. I mean, I get weird DMs, too, but nothing like the girls—the messages Syd would get—all of them get. They're terrible. Any one of those creeps could have done this. Actually, one time I was at the Grove with Sydney and this guy asked us for a selfie, then followed us for an hour." I dig my phone out of my pocket. "I actually might still have the picture." I scroll back through my camera roll, through images of food we've cooked in the kitchen, candids from pool parties, different celebrity meet-and-greets. "I never posted the selfie, because, well, the guy was a creep. But I guess it's good I have the picture now."

I finally find the picture. The image of a smiling Sydney hits me like a punch in the gut.

I slide my phone across the table. "This is the guy."

"Thanks. That's, um, great." Detective Johnson barely glances at the image before setting my phone aside. "I'll have one of my associates look into that."

She turns back to her file. My phone screen times out and fades to black on the table, but the cops don't even seem to notice. I furrow my brow in confusion. This could be the guy. The guy who killed Syd. And they barely want to look at the picture.

"I'd like to hear about what happened two nights ago," Detective Johnson says.

I shrug. "There was a fight, an argument, I mean. About Syd's sister, Brooklyn. It wasn't a big deal." I'm itching for my vape right about now. I didn't want to use it with all the cops around, but now it's burning a hole in my pocket.

"But Ms. Reynolds left after that?" Carney asks.

"Yeah, but, I mean, Syd was always talking about leaving whenever there was drama. You know, her family lives nearby. So it was easy for her to go—get away for a while to blow off some steam."

"But she left in the middle of the night?" Johnson asks.

"She left at like eleven," I say. "For a bunch of teenagers, that's not really late."

"Hmmm." Johnson presses her lips into a hard line. "And no one had heard from Ms. Reynolds since the argument?"

"No. I mean, I hadn't, at least. But I'm not tight with her. You should ask Tucker; he's her boyfriend. Or, I mean, was." I turn over the words in my head. Trying to get used to talking about Sydney in the past tense.

"What stance did he take in the argument Thursday night?" Detective Carney asks.

"He—" I stop myself. I don't want to dig Tucker into a hole by talking more about this dumb argument than is necessary. "Why are you so obsessed with the fight? It wasn't a big deal—"

"Wasn't a big deal?" Carney says, incredulous. "Then why is Ms. Reynolds dead?"

"No one in this house killed her, if that's what you're suggesting." I try to keep my voice down, but my anger wins out. "We were her friends. Her *best* friends. You shouldn't be wasting your time asking me about some dumb Lit Lair drama when you should be out there trying to find some—some stalker with a shrine to Syd and Gwen in his basement." I stand, my chair scraping loudly on the floor.

"Hey, son, calm down." Carney grabs my shoulder from across the table. His grip is a little stronger than it needs to be.

"Just take a deep breath, Beau," Johnson says. "Sit down."

I follow her directions. I'm still fuming when there's a knock at the door.

Officer Moore enters, looking shaken. He avoids eye contact with me and heads right to Detective Johnson. He hands her an iPhone, leans in, and says something to her too quietly, holding a manila folder up to block his mouth from my view.

"Okay, thank you," Johnson replies.

Moore leaves, and she turns back to me. "Beau, I'd like to see what you make of this."

She hands me the iPhone. My hands shake, but I try to steady them so I can see what's on the screen.

The phone is open to TikTok. It's a slideshow-style post containing different shots of Sydney—selfies, thirst traps, and zoomed-in group pics. A creepy song plays in the background.

The caption reads: *Everyone wanted Sydney out of the house. I just made sure she was gone for good.*

A chill runs down my spine.

I'm caught up in the disturbing pairing of the images of Sydney—alive and smiley and vivacious—and the music and caption, so creepy and dark. I'm about to ask why they would show me someone's disgusting, ambulance-chasing clout video when I notice that the likes count is climbing exponentially. If the likes are going up by hundreds at a time, then this video is being viewed thousands of times per second, which can only mean . . . I glance down at the handle, but I already know what it will be before I see it. This video was posted by the @LitLair_LA account.

My head feels foggy, like a thick syrup is clouding my brain.

"Care to explain?" asks Carney.

"We got hacked?" I struggle to keep my voice steady. "I mean, everyone saw Cami's livestream, right? And I guess some sick prankster thought this was their opportunity. What else could explain that?"

Even as I say the words, I'm not sure if I believe them. We have over thirty million followers; it's not like our password is passWord123. We have strict settings so we can only log in with facial recognition. I'm good enough at coding to know that the average hacker wouldn't be able to break into our account.

Detective Johnson looks even less convinced by my hacking

suggestion than I am. She turns to her partner, and they share a look, something passing wordlessly between them.

"This video was queued early this morning," Detective Johnson finally says. "Hours before Ms. de Ávila's livestream and the nine-one-one call. And according to your statements, hours before anyone had seen the body. The brand-new phone that queued it was connected to the house's Wi-Fi network." She pauses, looking at me seriously. When I don't react with anything but confusion, she clarifies: "Whoever posted that video was in this house."

"Can you explain that?" Carney asks.

"No, I can't." I keep my eyes on the table. I watch the looping video on the phone in front of me, transitioning between photos of Sydney with a swirling, blurry effect. I feel like I'm going to throw up. The house is quieter than I've ever heard it. I can feel the detectives' eyes on me.

I finally look up. "I think I'd like my parents and a lawyer now."

6

2 HOURS AFTER

GWEN

I've never cried this much in my life. Not when my parents divorced, or when my dad missed my sixteenth birthday because he was hungover in Vegas, or even when they canceled *Keeping Up with the Kardashians.* I've cried so much I think I should be out of tears. At this point, you'd think there would be no moisture left in my body and my skin would shrivel up like the mean witch in *Snow White.* But I look in my compact mirror, and I look as dewy and youthful as ever. Which doesn't match how I feel at all. On the inside, I feel wretched and ugly. Because the truth is, I don't deserve to be the crying best friend, not after what I did to Sydney.

The police have brought me and Cami back to the living room. They said we all have to stay downstairs while they sweep upstairs for possible evidence. I try not to think about how many things Tucker and I touched last night when we snuck into Sydney's bathroom to use the Jacuzzi. About the traces we left behind. Fingerprints and, *oh God,* other kinds of DNA.

Beau's in with the detectives now. And I guess they'll be going through us one by one. Just thinking about being asked questions by the police makes the tears threaten to spill over my eyelids again.

So I do what I always do when I'm stressed and need to distract myself. I focus on the one thing that never lets me down, that always makes me feel better: fashion. I sort through the clothes I threw in my suitcase: bandeau tops, flirty skirts, high-waisted jeans, skintight glossy bodysuits, bikini tops of every color. I take out the items that were shoved in haphazardly and refold them carefully.

From the outside, I might look silly and frivolous doing this. But it calms me down. And no one seems to know what we should be doing. Cami sits at the piano, plucking out notes at random, not so much playing anything as touching the keys like it's a nervous tic. Kat stares at the window, seemingly very interested in the lemon tree that arches over the driveway. Tucker stares at me and the items that surround me. At the clothes, some of which he has taken off me in the past. Some of which I previously lent to his now-dead girlfriend. Which I bet he took off her. I avoid his eyes.

I pull out my phone and head to Fashion Nova. I want another color of this crop top. Or maybe ten more colors.

A uniformed cop enters the room, carrying a blue plastic bin. At first, I think it's for Cami—after all, she's vommed quite a bit. But then he shoves it under my nose.

"Your phone," he says.

"What?"

"Your cell phones. We're gonna need to take a look at them." He glances around the room. "That goes for all of you."

"You lot already took mine," Cami says with a shrug. "I mean, whatever's left of the waterlogged thing."

I push the lock button on my phone, and the screen goes black with the sound of a camera shutter closing. I watch as the rest of my housemates dig into their pockets for their phones. But I pull mine closer to my chest as I turn back to the cop, look into his eyes, and say, "No."

"What?" The cop raises his bushy, unmanaged eyebrows.

"There's no way in hell I'm giving this to you."

"Why?" he demands. "Because it incriminates you?"

"No!" I say. I might sound a bit too defensive. "Because . . . well, because I have a major sponcon to post later today, and I already spent the check on a new car." That's actually true. After I totaled my Ferrari, I thought it made sense for my next car to be a Jeep, since Cher Horowitz is my style icon. I drove it off the lot yesterday.

"Sponcon?" the cop asks. "*Miss*, you understand there's a murder investigation going on, right?"

Anger swells in my chest. I *hate* the patronizing tone in his voice on the word "miss."

"What I understand is that you're trying to bully me or to trick me or something. Maybe because I'm young or female or an internet celebrity, you think I'm gullible. But I know my rights, and you can't take my phone." I step back. "That's, like, against the rules of America!"

He laughs at me. My heart starts to race against my chest; I hope I appear more confident than I feel.

I force myself to take a deep breath. "I mean, it's against the *constitution*, okay? The Fourth Amendment, to be exact. If you wanted to forcibly seize our possessions, you would need probable cause. And I doubt you have that for all our phones. You just thought you could take advantage of our ignorance." I spin my phone between my fingers, tauntingly. "If you want it, get a warrant."

Cami raises her eyebrows.

"See, there are some things I do know," I tell the group. "After all, *Legally Blonde* is my favorite movie."

The cop shakes his head and looks around the room. Everyone follows my lead and puts their phones away.

"Fine." He lets out an exasperated breath.

"I really wish you'd stop wasting your time worrying about our phones and focus on finding the psycho who killed my friend," I say. "After all, if someone's out there killing influencers, I could be next." It makes me shiver just to think about it. I gather myself, tossing a wave of blond hair over my shoulder. "I mean, really, I'm surprised they didn't go for me in the first place. If this is a, like, kill-a-famous-person-to-become-famous kind of thing, I'd be the Holy Grail."

Kat's eyes go wide at my words.

"Gwen." Cami stares at me like she's trying to communicate something telepathically. "Maybe a bit more sensitivity, eh?"

"I'm just saying." I shrug. "I mean, like, that crazy dude shot John, right? Not Ringo."

Cami has just opened her mouth to reply when all our cell phones go off at once. We pull out our devices, and the same TikTok sound echoes around the room.

Cami leans over to watch the video on Kat's phone. Her face as white as a ghost, she looks up and says, "Well, I guess now they have their probable cause."

4 HOURS AFTER

KAT

Last year, we read *Lord of the Flies* in English class. My teacher made a big deal about how it was a story about human nature. That Golding put those kids on that island to prove that humans' natural state was one of evil. That children, left without rules or society, would resort to hedonism, selfishness, and eventually, murder.

But here's the thing about that theory. Golding didn't put everyone on that island. It wasn't a perfect cross section of humanity that crashed in that plane. It wasn't like *It's a Small World: Survivor Edition* or something.

The group representing human nature in *Lord of the Flies* is a bunch of British boys from a *boarding* school. In the 1950s.

Which makes me wonder: Is the descent into selfishness, hedonism, and violence really about human nature? Or is it about the nature of privilege, of entitlement? About how those told their entire lives that they should be entitled to take whatever they want from the world and not worry about the rest, not give anything back, would behave if they could literally, and not just figuratively, get away with murder?

This is what I'm thinking about when all the rich parents and the lawyers start to arrive. After we first hear the words "persons of interest," the parents descend on the house in what seems like record time, arriving by chauffeured cars or, in one case, by helicopter. They've been flapping around like birds in shiny designer labels, circling their children and squawking into their cell phones, talking to lawyers who've been ordered to drop what they're doing and get here. Tucker's mom, who's wearing head-to-toe Lululemon paired with a Birkin bag, keeps demanding things of the police, as if they're concierges at the Ritz-Carlton and not, you know, the murder crime scene investigators. *Are you almost done gathering fingerprints from upstairs? I'd really love to lie down,* I heard her say to a cop. It's really quite surreal to witness.

My train of thought is interrupted by my phone buzzing. It lights up with a picture of my mom, a candid I took while we were baking peanut butter cookies back in our kitchen in Fresno. Just seeing her face, in this familiar picture, I feel relief. Like a bit of the weight I've been carrying has lifted off my shoulders. Like I can breathe again.

"Mom," I gasp.

"Kat! Are you okay?"

"Yeah, I'm fine, I'm—" I don't know how to explain how I feel. "I'm not hurt," I settle on. After all, I'm not physically injured. I can at least give my mother that assurance.

Cami is staring at me from across the room, her eyes locked on me. It makes the hairs on the back of my neck stand on end. I realize that I can't speak freely in the house.

"Hold on a second, Mom...." I walk to the back and pull open the glass door. The stairs to the pool are taped off, and just looking at them makes me feel sick. It causes a sort of prickly feeling behind my eyes, like all of a sudden, the sun is too bright. I turn the other way instead and take the steps down toward the beach.

"All right, sorry," I say into the phone. "I'm here."

"I was just saying to your father, that poor girl's family. I can't even imagine."

"Yeah, I guess they're on the way here to, um, get the rest of her things." I haven't really thought about what I'll do when Sydney's parents and sister arrive. What I will say to them. After all, any words will fall so short of comfort. No words can make this better.

I watch my feet as I walk down the stairs. My sandals brush against the worn wood, sand embedded in every crack from countless trips to the beach. It's all I can do to just put one foot in front of the other. I reach the sand and look out at the ocean, the waves crashing on the shore. Just like they did yesterday, except not. Because nothing is the same.

"Mom, I know it's really busy right now with the school year about to start, and I was so weird about you guys coming down here before . . . but do you think you could maybe drive down—"

"We're in the car," she says. "Your dad started to fuel it up as soon as we heard. We'll be there in less than four hours."

I hear my dad say something indistinguishable over the line.

"Your father thinks I should let him speed. But the last thing we need is to get in a car wreck on our way to you. So we'll drive safely."

This makes me smile. My parents bickering about how my dad drives is so familiar, so normal. I let out a small laugh and wipe a tear from my cheek.

"Thank you, Mom," I say. "For coming, and for not being mad about the last few weeks."

"Kat," she says seriously. "Listen to me. You're becoming your own person, an adult with views that sometimes might be different from mine. And that'll mean we'll disagree more than when you were just the little girl in a princess dress. But no matter what we fight about, no matter what you do, you're my daughter and I love you. And I will always be there when you need me."

Tears start to roll down my cheeks. I'm almost ashamed about how relieved I am to know that in a few hours my mom will be here with me. It makes me feel like a baby. I thought I was so grown up, living down here all on my own, and now here I am, crying and asking my mom to come help me. My face burns with embarrassment as my tears tumble into sobs.

"Mom," I choke out, "I think I need a lawyer. I didn't do anything wrong, I promise. But they, um, they think the person who hurt Sydney is one of us in the house. So everyone else is getting a lawyer or, like, kind of already has one. And—"—my voice cracks—"I don't think it's a good idea for me to be the only one without one."

"Of course, right," my mom says. "We'll figure it out."

I hear my father talk again. "She needs a lawyer," my mom says to him. "Hold on, Kat, I'm putting you on the Bluetooth."

"Hi, kiddo," my dad says. The line is a little choppy. I realize I've wandered all the way down to the water.

I turn around so I don't lose the Wi-Fi signal. And that's when I see them. Two figures down the beach. Gwen leads, walking with an intense, angry purpose, her platinum hair blowing in the sea breeze. Following is a visibly upset Tucker. He grabs her arm roughly. She says something I can't hear. But it doesn't look nice.

I avert my eyes, feeling like I'm intruding on a private moment. And then I think: *Maybe I* should *watch. What if this is important? What if this is evidence? What if one of them killed Sydney? What if they both did? What if that's what they're fighting about? What if snooping on these people who I thought were my friends is necessary to ensure Sydney's killer is found?* The whole world feels so topsy-turvy.

On the phone, my parents are discussing how to go about getting me a lawyer and how long it might take. I move up toward the house to hear them better.

"Oh, you know what I can do?" my mom says. "Kat, I'll call Mr. Lambert right now. He was in my dorm back in college. Remember, we had lunch with him on the way to Disneyland? Or I guess maybe you don't remember; you were five. But he's a lawyer down in LA. Helped your dad's brother with that DUI back in the day. I'm sure he'll know what to do."

"Okay," I say. I don't know if DUI court dates are quite the same as murder investigations. But I don't know any other lawyers to suggest, so I keep the thought to myself. "Thanks. Let me know what he says," I say.

"Of course, honey. Love you."

"You too."

After the line goes quiet, I look back down the beach toward where Gwen and Tucker were. But there's nothing there but sand and footprints. They've disappeared.

7

4 HOURS AFTER

TUCKER

"Gwen, stop running away!" I shout after her. But she ignores me. She's already made me chase her all the way down to the beach. I'm getting sick of her drama. I grab her arm.

She whips her head around, like my touch burned her. "What do you want?"

"What do I want?" *What the fuck does that mean?* "You wake me up crying but don't manage to tell me that Sydney is dead, leaving me to find out in front of like ten cops. And you've been avoiding me since. What's your plan, Gwen, just to ignore me forever?"

Gwen pulls her arm back but stands still. At least she isn't running away from me now. "I just don't know what to think," she says. She folds her arms across her chest, like she is cold, even though the sun is strong today. She avoids my eyes, looking down at the sand.

"You don't know what to think about what?" I ask.

She doesn't reply. After a moment, her head still down, she starts to make this little high-pitched noise. It takes me a second to realize she is crying again.

"Hey, no, here." I pull her into a hug. She whimpers and falls against me. Her tears soak into my shirt. I run a hand over her head and make shushing sounds, like I do when I pet my brother's polo horse.

Over Gwen's shoulder, I spot Kat down by the water. Which means she could see us. Which would not be good.

"Here, c'mon." I take Gwen's hand and lead her up off the beach. We have to go over a few rocks, which she complains about, but then we're at the pool house.

I pull her inside and shut the door. The pool house is really just a shed. It's dark, there's no lightbulb, just sunlight filtering in from the places where the wooden slats meet. The air smells stale, like sawdust and industrial cleaner. Between the tall blue tanks and haphazard piles of inner tubes and pool noodles, there's barely room for the two of us to stand.

I put my hands on Gwen's shoulders and study her face in the dark. Her cheeks glisten with tears, and there's snot under her nose. Her makeup is still somehow intact, though.

"Just take a deep breath, okay?" I say. Her body is so small, so delicate, my hand takes up most of her shoulder, and I can feel her bones through the thin fabric of her shirt.

She tries to inhale deeply, but her breath is still shaky. "Just be honest with me," she says. "Did you hurt her? Did you . . . kill her?"

She stares at me, waiting for my answer. Her eyes are so wide, so big. Have they always been that big? She looks like a deer. It makes me think of hunting trips with my brothers. Of staring down a doe, of my brothers egging me on, telling me to pull the trigger, to not be a sissy, to be a man and kill it. And me yelling at them to shut up, loud enough that the deer ran away, escaping me.

With ice in my veins, I look Gwen directly in the eyes and say, "Of course not."

"Oh, thank God." She pulls me into an embrace. But unlike down on the beach, she no longer feels like a rag doll falling into my arms. She feels present.

A wave of relief washes over me. She believes me.

Gwen tilts her head up and kisses me. Her lips taste salty, probably because she was crying. But they feel soft. Her body presses against mine. I hope she isn't too sad to hook up later. I really need something to look forward to at the end of this hellish day.

For now, the kiss is brief. After she pulls back, she keeps her arms around me, nuzzling her head against my chest. This extended hug makes me realize how hot it is in this little shed. I feel claustrophobic. I wonder how long I have to hold her before I can step back without being rude.

"Tuck," Gwen says quietly into my T-shirt. "Do you think we should tell the police? You know, come clean about you and me?"

"What?" My chest tightens. Suddenly, it's hard to breathe. "No. Absolutely not."

She leans back to make eye contact. "But Carmen always says the first rule of crisis PR is to get ahead of the story—"

"This isn't like your nose job, Gwen. This is serious, don't you get it? You slept with your best friend's boyfriend, and now she's dead. We can't let anyone find out about this."

"Okay . . . I guess." She pouts. "But then what? We just keep our love secret forever?"

"No, we can eventually tell people about our . . . thing." I sidestep that word. "Like in the future, picture this: you and I were both grieving Sydney, and in that time of grief we became closer friends and that friendship turned to a"—I take a deep breath; I have to sell her on this, because if I don't, we're toast—"a *relationship* that grew like a flower out of a time of sadness." That's some cheesy phrasing Gwen will like.

She tilts her head, considering this.

"Now, you're smart about these kinds of things, Gwen," I say, knowing exactly which buttons to push. "You have to know that's a better headline than if people found out now."

A small smile forms. "I guess so. . . ."

"Great." I reach out my hand. "Now give me your phone."

"What?"

"You did a good Reese Witherspoon impression earlier, but after that post on the house account, they'll get a warrant soon enough. We've gotta get rid of our texts before then."

She reluctantly hands me her phone. "It's just sad to lose the memories, you know, all those sweet texts."

Yeah, well, it would be sadder to spend twenty-five years in jail. I swipe to delete our conversations from her phone and then from her iCloud. Just like I already did with my own. "There." I place the phone back in her palm and exhale.

I reach for her free hand. "Okay, so for now, if anyone asks?"

"There's nothing between us," she says with a smile. "You're, like, totally gross."

I kiss her on the forehead, inhaling her perfume. "You're the best, Gwen."

I reach for the door and drop her hand before I step out into the light.

Gwen trips over an empty bottle of pool chemicals and swears under her breath. "Why are there like ten empty bottles in here?" she demands as she follows me out.

"Do I look like I clean pools?" I say.

Right at that moment, a flashbulb goes off in my eyes. I turn to see a paparazzo, dressed in black, squatting in the foliage.

"Hey!" I shout after him. But he's already running away, camera in hand. He got the picture he came for.

I'm fucking furious. Of course, we've encountered paps before. I mean, hell, half the time we go out we call ahead so we can make *sure* they get a shot of us. And yeah, there have been a couple times they've gotten an unplanned shot, an unflattering angle. Gwen once cried about a shot they got of her at the gas station without makeup. But they've never come to the house before. And they've certainly never hidden in the bushes.

"Do you think he got me in the frame?" Gwen asks.

"God, I hope not."

8

4 HOURS AFTER

CAMI

Denial is the first of five stages of grief. But for some reason, when it comes to the deaths of celebrities, people seem to get stuck on it. Witnesses claim they've seen Tupac on a beach in Cuba, laughing and talking with Suge Knight; others say they saw Michael Jackson walk out of the coroner's van. There's a Facebook group for people who think Elvis is still alive, and a whole book about how Marilyn Monroe grew old in Canada.

Maybe it's something about the nature of celebrity that causes people to spin these fantastical stories. It's like they can't believe that these people, who seemed to be larger than life, are somehow just as mortal, just as fragile, as every other human being.

But I always thought the people who believe those kinds of things were just plain crazy.

Then again, right now, sitting in the house and watching the spitting image of Sydney crying in our hallway, it's easy to imagine that she hasn't died. Tempting to pretend that she's alive and well and here.

But I saw the bits of her brain floating in our pool. And I know that she's now lying on a slab in the county morgue. And that the girl in the hall is her twin sister, Brooklyn.

Sydney's family arrived a few minutes ago. Her mother walked straight over to Tucker and embraced him. It was quite strange. After all, she just lost her daughter, but she seemed more concerned about how he was doing. I think some people are just so used to taking care of others they don't know what else to do in situations like this. Her dad hasn't said anything. Not to us, to the cops, to the rest of his family. He just stares ahead blankly, sparing only a half nod when the cops tell him something. Brooklyn hasn't stopped crying since she walked in the door. In that way, she's not unlike Gwen—ironic, since those two have never gotten along. The best friend and the twin sister. They competed for Sydney's affection when she was alive. And now, apparently, they're competing to see who can sob a greater volume of tears upon her death.

Sydney's parents are in with the police now, but Brooklyn is sitting in the hallway, her tall, model-thin body slumped into a chair the police moved for her.

I think about going over to talk to her, but I'm not sure if it would be welcome. After everything that happened this week . . . I know that I'm probably the last person Brooklyn would want to talk to. But maybe it's all water under the bridge now. After all, Sydney and I were once close. And Brooklyn and I were friendly before . . . well, before fame and drama got in the way.

She wipes snot from her nose with her hand, and her gold bracelet shimmers in the light. She wipes the gunk on her Reformation dress.

Ugh, I can't watch this any longer. I pull a tissue from the container on the side table and then, after a pause to consider, just pick up the whole box and head toward Brooklyn. The cop guarding the dining room briefly looks up from his phone but does nothing to stop me.

"Here," I say, holding the tissue in front of her face.

She looks up at me. Mascara streaks mark her face. *"Cami,"* she says, her voice singsongy and strange. She shakes her head as she unfolds herself and stands up. "You are the *nicest* person."

"Oh." I stumble backward as she hugs me.

People have called me a lot of things in my life. Beautiful, smart, cunning, passionate, clever. But no one has ever called me nice. Certainly not the nicest. It's just not accurate.

But I'm grateful Brooklyn is not mad at me, so I'm certainly not going to argue with her.

She pulls away, dabbing her eyes with the tissue. The white paper is quickly stained by her makeup. "God, I am such a mess," she says. She peeks past me, toward the large windows across the front of the house. "You just know the paparazzi are gonna use the shot where my makeup looks the worst."

"There's press here?"

"Yeah, you guys don't know? The police are trying to keep them down past the driveway, but yeah, like, every freaking photographer in LA is on your street. Walking in here was probably the most I've ever been photographed, and naturally I've never looked worse."

"Yeah, that sucks," I say. Her face falls and I realize a second too late that the thing one is *supposed* to do in this social situation is to say that despite the snot on her face and her bloodshot eyes, she's actually looking quite fabulous. I always mess up stuff like that. Forget when I'm supposed to lie. I try to make up for it by saying "Here, take the rest of the tissues."

I hold out the box, and as she reaches for it, I see the bracelet on her wrist more clearly. A Cartier Love bracelet, with a large scratch across the face.

I flash back to the night of the Neon Pool Party. It was one of our first big events. An energy drink company was sponsoring.

They dyed the pool water this crazy neon green and set up colored lights everywhere. They had us doing all sorts of games, including this thing called gladiator joust, where we stood on rafts and hit each other with giant things that looked like Q-tips. (I won all my matches, naturally.)

I'd told Syd to dress down that day, that the party would be more sporty vibes, but she didn't listen and dressed up, as always. When it was her turn to battle Kat, she lasted all of two seconds before she was knocked over into the pool. But it was long enough for Kat's stick to scratch the freaking Cartier bracelet Syd never took off.

I remember it so clearly: Sydney rising out of the green pool, looking at her bracelet, and seeing that not only was there a large scratch but that the grooves of the scratch had turned *green*. She screamed at Kat, even called her a bitch, and Beau and Tucker almost got in a fistfight. We had to pay half the money back to the sponsor to get them to delete that part of the footage.

I spent hours sitting on Sydney's floor as she cried, and I tried every method Google could offer for cleaning jewelry. I rubbed a Q-tip on that bracelet for what felt like forever, staring at that ugly green scratch that wouldn't budge. The same scratch I'm looking at right now.

I grab Brooklyn's wrist. "When did you— Where did you get this?"

Her eyes flicker between me and the jewelry. "What do you mean? It's mine."

She tries to pull her hand back, but I tighten my grip. "No, it's *Sydney's*. And the last time I saw her, she was wearing it."

"Our parents got us *both* Cartier bracelets for our birthday," she says. "Not to mention that like half of Beverly Hills has them. Stop being so crazy, Cami." She shoves me hard, and I stumble backward, losing my grip on her hand.

I want to say that *half of Beverly Hills* does not have a giant scratch across their bracelet. And that I'd bet only one bracelet in the world has a *neon green* scratch. But I don't get the chance.

"Hey!" The cop from the other end of the hall heads toward us. "Why don't you leave this poor family alone? They're going through enough."

The way he looks at me when he says that, like he'd prefer to spit at me, tells me that he believes he knows exactly who's to blame for what this family is going through. And that he thinks that person is *me*.

4 HOURS AFTER

BEAU

When I come back from talking with my lawyer, no one is in the living room. I ask the people in the kitchen if anyone has seen Kat, and Tucker's mom says she thinks she saw her headed toward the beach. I slide open the door and step out onto the patio.

"Roberts, what'd you find on the family?" I hear Detective Johnson's voice coming up the stairs from the pool.

I dodge behind a palm tree.

"Parents are Lillian and Jeffrey Reynolds," another female voice answers. "Married twenty years, live in Beverly Hills. They have two kids, Sydney and a twin, Brooklyn. Both influencers, but Brooklyn lived at home. The Reynoldses hold the deed to this house, too, and charge the other kids rent. They're on time with the payments for both houses. Let's see . . . solid credit score, substantial 401(k)s, typical rich LA family."

I peek between the foliage to see a younger cop, Roberts evidently, handing a red file to Johnson. They've stopped halfway up the stairs.

"So no clear financial motives?" Johnson asks.

"No, no significant debt. Oh, but they did have a million-dollar life insurance policy on Sydney."

"On a kid?" Johnson asks. "That can't be right. Are you sure it wasn't the parents' policy, with the girls as beneficiaries?"

"No." The younger cop points to the file. "I actually don't think it's all that unusual. I mean, she's a TikTok star, and you see this with child actors and the like. And when you compare it to her annual earnings, it's not a completely inappropriate policy."

"Right . . ." Johnson shuffles through the papers. "What did they take out on the twin?"

"Huh?"

"You said they had two kids. But there's only one policy in here."

"Well, I mean, they didn't take out a policy on Brooklyn."

"But isn't she also an, um, you said she's one of these web celebrities, too?"

"An influencer," the younger cop says. "And yeah, she is. But she's not . . . I don't know how to say, she's not that good at it. Has a fraction of the following her sister did. Guess the Reynoldses weren't nearly as worried about losing Brooklyn."

"Hmm."

"Detective Johnson, can I ask, um, why'd you have me do this? I mean, they traced the phone that queued the video to here, right? I thought we narrowed it to the five kids."

"We did," she says without looking up from the papers. "But you can never be too careful."

The younger cop nods. "Well, the parents are in with Carney now. So whenever you're ready for them."

A cell phone trills. Johnson reaches into her pocket. "My daughter," she says.

Her phone makes the swooshing FaceTime noise, and a girl, probably thirteen or fourteen years old, with a sandy blond ponytail, appears on the screen.

"Mom, is it true you're at the Lit Lair? Jess said she saw you in the background of a video."

"Yeah, do you know about these Tic Tac kids?"

"Oh my God, Mom, Tik*Tok*. And everyone knows who they are. They are like internet royalty. OMG, have you met Kat? Have you met Beau? Who do you think did it? Tucker? Ellie G. says it's *always* the boyfriend."

"Hannah," Detective Johnson scolds. "Someone's child is dead. It's not entertainment."

"Ugh, like it can't be both."

A hand clamps down on my shoulder and yanks me backward. I stumble as I turn around.

"What are you doing?" Roberts demands.

"I was, um, just looking for my . . ." I guess I shouldn't refer to Kat as my girlfriend to a cop before I ask her to be that. "For Kat. For Katherine Powell."

Roberts looks confused. "You both should be inside. This is an active crime scene." She tugs my arm and herds me back inside.

I look over my shoulder to Detective Johnson and the red file under her arm. Wishing I could find out what other information it holds.

9

5 HOURS AFTER

TUCKER

"We're going to provide you with the best defense money can buy, Mr. Campbell," my lawyer says. "Don't you worry."

I nod, and then I wince. Even that bit of movement hurts my head. I think when I first woke up I was still a little drunk, which was blunting the full blow of my hangover. Which is now here. My head throbs and my skin feels like it's crawling with grime, like the champagne and tequila is trying to escape through my sweat. I've never been this hungover in my life.

Last night keeps coming back to me in flashes. The underwater lights in the pool, blurry and doubled. Gwen's hair tickling my face as she straddled me. A glass bottle shattering against the patio. Someone's cackling laughter. A flash of lightning. The splash of the pool water. A sudden scream.

I can't sort out what was where and when. What was real and what was a dream. What was at the party with everyone else around, and what seems like . . . it may have been after that.

"Tucker, are you listening to me?" my lawyer asks.

"Huh? Yeah, of course," I lie.

"Because this stuff about Miranda is no joke."

"Miranda. I got it." I nod. I wonder if that's the name of the lady detective Beau mentioned. 'Cause I gotta admit, the only Miranda I know is that chick who used to be on *iCarly*.

My lawyer rubs the shiny part of his head, where his hair would be if he had any left. His name is Tom Fleming. He's got a potbelly that stretches out his shirt, and he is always sweating a little, even though the air conditioner is pumping. Gwen texted me that he looks like a bad lawyer. *If he doesn't know that black shoes don't go with navy socks, how can he know anything?*

I told her to stop judging people based on how they look. Although I have to admit, the sweating thing is kind of gross. Still, my dad said he's the best criminal defense lawyer on the West Coast. And my dad always knows what's best—whether it's what wine to order, what colleges to apply to, what hotel to stay at in Aspen, or, it turns out, which murder lawyer should defend you.

Tom Fleming looks at me seriously. "All right, now, this is important, Tucker. Before we go in there, is there anything I need to know? Anything that might come up that would make it seem, well, like you did this?"

"No." I shake my head. "Nothing."

"Great." He chuckles and slaps me on the shoulder. He seems relieved. He seems to believe me.

He pushes open the door to the dining room, where the two detectives are waiting. I've seen them wandering about the house, but this is the first time I've talked to them. Up close, the girl cop is kind of a MILF, or at least she would be if she weren't scowling at me.

"Tucker Campbell?" she asks.

"In the flesh." I flash her the smile that usually does wonders with the "Stacy's Mom" demographic. The one that got me ten-dollar tips from the tennis moms when I used to hand out towels at the Bel-Air Country Club. The one that made the homely clerk at Malibu Liquors look the other way at my fake Nevada license.

But this time, the smile doesn't work.

"Sit." She points to the chair. "I'm Detective Johnson, that's Detective Carney. You will address us as such."

Okay, so charming my way out of this isn't an option. Noted. That's fine. I can figure out something else.

Detective Johnson turns a page in her notebook. It seems that pleasantries, if you can even call them that, are over. "Where were you at three this morning?"

"Asleep in bed," I answer. That's where I should've been. I'm 95 percent sure I was. Maybe 90 percent.

"Any witnesses who can confirm that?"

"That I was asleep in my own bed? No." I'm not sure I like what she's implying. *Do they know about Gwen? I mean, how could they? Unless, oh shit, did Gwen already fold?* She's so dumb sometimes, I can't believe she holds my fate in her stupid hands.

But the cop moves on, asking me other questions, about when I last saw each member of the house last night and if I heard anything unusual.

And then, "Have you ever seen a gun like this before?" Detective Johnson takes a photograph out of a red folder and slides it toward me. My knowledge of guns is basically just from video games, so I'm about to say no when I pick up the photograph. I freeze.

I recognize it immediately. It's not the exact gun I remember. This photo is the official kind, like from a magazine or website or something. But I'm sure it's the same kind.

My mind flashes back to dinner with Sydney's extended family for the twins' sixteenth birthday. Their grandparents were in from Nevada, and we were all gathered in the Reynoldses' living room, eating cake and watching the girls open their gifts. I was bored and trying to act enthusiastic about a bunch of girl clothes that looked the same as the shit Squid already owned. And then the girls unwrapped matching handguns, and the room fell silent.

"Of course, they'll be in your father's name," Grandpa Reynolds explained. "But now that you're sixteen, you can go to the range and learn how to shoot."

Brooklyn fumed, asking if the gift was a passive-aggressive response to the gun control op-ed she'd sent her grandfather earlier in the month. Grandpa Reynolds shot back that firearms were a family tradition passed down through generations and how could she not appreciate this gift and what exactly was she learning at her California school?

The argument carried on, but Sydney just set the box on the floor, said thank you with a tight smile, and went to get another piece of cake.

A few weeks later, Sydney's dad brought them to the gun range. Brooklyn refused to go inside and ended up waiting around in the parking lot while the rest of the group went in. When I asked how it went later that night, Sydney didn't want to talk about it much, only to joke that she was a better shot with the paper targets than I was in *Call of Duty* before changing the subject. She never again mentioned going back to the range, or the gun, really, at all. Back at school, when people asked what she got for her birthday, she just mentioned the Cartier bracelets their parents got them, never the guns.

"Yeah, uh, the Reynolds twins got those as a gift." I look up from the picture to the detectives. "What, do you think it was Sydney's gun that someone . . . used on her?"

"Preliminary ballistics suggest this is the type of gun," Johnson says. "And it's not uncommon for individuals who keep a gun for self-defense to have that very weapon used against them in the course of a struggle."

"What, you think someone like ripped it out of her hands? And then shot her with it?" I try to imagine someone wresting a gun from Sydney's hands. Beau could do it. Cami probably could. But Gwen? Kat? They're not that strong.

"It's quite possible," says Johnson.

"Of course, there's always the other option," Carney says, "that someone knew about the gun and took it from her room."

Oh, shit. Maybe I should've lied about recognizing it. "I didn't even know she'd brought the gun here," I say. "Last I heard, it was locked in a safe at her parents' house."

"The others mentioned that you helped Sydney unpack when you moved in," Johnson says. "You didn't see the gun then?"

"No way," I say. Before Sydney and I got in a fight that day, I helped unpack, like, a billion shoes and hair products. But definitely not a gun.

"Did she ever say anything about having cause for fear, living here in the house?"

I shake my head.

"We'll need a verbal response." She taps the tape recorder in the middle of the table with her pencil.

"No."

"She never mentioned wanting any sort of weapon for self-defense?"

"Listen, lady, she never talked to me about the gun, okay? I told you the first time. If she brought it here, she didn't tell me."

"All right, all right." She holds a hand up. "I hear you. She didn't tell you." She shrugs. "Hey, wouldn't be the first secret between couples, would it, Tucker?"

What the hell is that supposed to mean?

Detective Johnson is smiling, but I can't read her eyes. And I can't tell if the thing I'm trying the hardest to hide, she already knows.

10

7 HOURS AFTER

CAMI

"Is it true that a week ago, in front of multiple witnesses, you called Sydney Reynolds, quote, 'a tacky bitch with no ass who'"—Detective Carney flips the page of his notebook—"'looks like a puppet when she dances'?"

I clear my throat. "I actually said 'Muppet,' not 'puppet.'"

The crease in his forehead deepens. "What?"

"If she danced like a puppet, that could actually be cool, like in NSYNC's 'No Strings Attached' or something. When Sydney danced, she looked like a *Muppet*—you know, sort of overexcited and flailing about." I gesture with my hands to illustrate.

"Oh. Right," says Carney. He turns to Detective Johnson, who seems just as confused as he is.

Jeez, do these cops know anything?

My lawyer gives me a tired look. He told me not to be sassy, but I can't help it. Whatever. He's making five hundred dollars an hour; he can get over it.

"And last night, did you say you were 'glad she was gone'?"

"Yeah." I scrunch my nose. "But I meant not here, not, you know, dead."

91

Carney continues: "A few weeks ago, did you scream at her from across the pool that Ms. Reynolds was 'faker than a Depop bag'?"

"I honestly don't remember," I say. "But yeah, that sounds like me." I chuckle to myself. "That's pretty funny, actually. I'll happily take credit."

"Ms. de Ávila," Detective Johnson scolds. "Can you please take this seriously?"

"I take the murder of my best friend very seriously," I say. "But I'm not going to take these questions seriously. They're ridiculous."

"You don't think it's noteworthy that you said these things to Ms. Reynolds?"

"No, not really."

"You were quite mean to her," Detective Johnson observes.

"Yeah, but I'm mean to everyone." I pout my lips. "Never killed anyone, though."

My lawyer clears his throat. "What my client means is these insults, they are just overreactions to teenage drama. Which, I think we can all agree, hardly amount to motive for murder. These arguments you're bringing up, they are just silly disagreements."

"No," I correct him. "That's not at all what I mean."

My lawyer turns to me. "Excuse me?"

"It wasn't silly teen drama," I say, "and by the way, I resent the implication that something I care about should matter less just because of my age." I fold my arms over my chest. "But I didn't overreact. I said those things to her because what she did to me was really messed up."

"Cami," my lawyer scolds.

"What? I'm just saying I was rightfully pissed. First of all, *she* was always trying to edge *me* out. Acting like she and Gwen were better friends than *me* and Gwen, just because they knew each other longer. But that's dumb, because Gwen liked me better, she told me that all the time when Sydney wasn't around. Sydney was actually kind of a bitch to Gwen a lot of the time." I know you're not supposed to speak ill of the dead, but I always pride myself on being honest and blunt, and I don't think that should change now. "And if you think about it," I continue, "I'm a better fit to be Gwen's number two. Gwen's super popular on TikTok but doesn't have dance experience. I do. What did Sydney bring? Nothing. She was like a lame copy of Gwen, almost like her brand was 'Diet Gwen' or something. If you're gonna have a power-couple best-friend thing going, you need to be like Sprite and Coke, not Coke and Diet Coke. That's Branding 101."

This seems to have severely confused Detective Carney. But I don't know how I could've been clearer. Maybe he's not that bright.

But Detective Johnson seems to get what I'm saying; she nods along. "So now that Sydney's gone, it seems like everything can kind of fall into place. Just like you'd want it, right?" She counts out on her fingers. "You have Gwen as your best friend. You bump up to the second-most popular TikToker in the house instead of the third." And then, like she's just thinking of it, she says, "Huh, her death worked out pretty well for you, didn't it?"

"That's a cute little logic trick." I stare her down and tilt my head to the side. "But it's not going to work."

She just stares back.

"Yes," I admit, "I was competitive with Sydney when it came to Gwen's friendship and sure, sure, after what she pulled with Parker, would I have been happy if someone shaved Syd's eyebrows off while she was asleep? Yes. But am I happy she's dead? Of course not. I hated the bitch, but she was still my friend. You could list a hundred mean things, and yeah, I probably said them to her. But I didn't do this."

I check my watch. I'm wearing my Gucci timepiece, the one with a red-and-green-striped snake that curves across most of the face. A snake that my mom always says looks poisonous. "Are we done?" I ask with a fake smile. "I have things to do."

I start to stand, but my lawyer grabs my arm. "Not until they dismiss you," he whispers. I roll my eyes and collapse back into my chair.

"Who is Parker?" asks Detective Carney.

"Huh?"

"A second ago, you said that you were so mad at Sydney because of what happened with Parker. Who is he?"

"Parker is not a *he*. It's a what," I say. "Parker Records, the multimillion-dollar record company?" I spell it out in case Carney's really dumb.

"Oh yeah." His eyes light up with recognition. But then confusion clouds his face again. "But wait, what does that have to do with you and Ms. Reynolds?"

I brace myself; this interview might go on for a while.

CAMI

The deep red liquid glistens in the California sun.

I pour myself another cup of sangria, bopping my head along to the Tupac playing over the loudspeaker. The backyard is packed with partygoers.

Everywhere I turn, there are girls in Technicolor bikinis, most of them cut high up the butt like a thong, dancing on tables. Shirtless, six-packed guys in five-inch-inseam board shorts throw dice into cups of beer with athletic prowess. People drink saccharine, fruity mixed drinks from red Solo cups or shots of flavored liquor from neon plastic shot glasses. The sun is high in the sky and glistens off everything: the pool water, the highlighter on sharply contoured cheekbones, the tanning oil on bodies. A guy I recognize from his viral surfing videos throws a fitness influencer into the pool with a splash. At one end of the pool, a group passes around a piece of rolled paper, and a sickly sweet cloud floats up toward the palm leaves, the sunlight refracting through the smoke. A guy in a backward baseball hat, who I think recently starred in a rom-com, stands on the diving board and pops a bottle of champagne, spraying it onto the people in the pool, who whoop and shout back.

I soak it all in and take a long sip of my drink. California knows how to party, indeed.

Gwen and I are at the top of the pool deck, up on the DJ stand, surveying our kingdom, as it were. Every few minutes, Gwen will see someone she's actually met before in real life, or someone with enough followers and clout that we'd want to be photographed with them, and she'll pull them up onto the platform to join our little posse. Leaving the rest of the partygoers to watch from afar, seeing us but us not really seeing them, just like on the internet.

The song fades out, and the DJ plays a remix of old-school Katy Perry. Right below the DJ stand a gaggle of girls squeal at the opening notes. They proceed to shout-sing along enthusiastically about "greener grass" and "something in the water."

Gwen grabs my hand and twirls me around, singing along to every word. I giggle and spin. She's had more than a couple Black Cherry White Claws, and her eyes are wide and her movements a bit less controlled than usual. Her improvised dancing is a little awkward without the usual step-by-step choreography I provide for our videos. I can't help but smile. Usually I hate when people pantomime along with the lyrics the way she is, but for some reason when she does it, it's kind of cute.

"'California Gurls,' really?" I hear Tucker say to a group of guys on the far end of the DJ stand. "Nothing basic girls like more than songs they think are about them." He's far enough away that if I can hear him, so can the DJ and so can the girls below.

He's really been getting on my nerves today, taking up prime party real estate on the platform but barely making an effort to dance. Instead, he's been passing around a bottle of vodka with some dudes who, when he introduced us, looked at Gwen even when he said my name. One of the boys is his brother, and it appears that douchiness runs in the family. I wish Sydney was here to rein in her boyfriend. Last time I saw her was right before I came outside, when she was only just returning from her Pilates class to begin her two-hour getting-ready process.

The girls below us are unfazed by Tucker and keep singing in their off-tune way. But Gwen, I notice, stops dancing at the comment and goes over to Tucker to spike her White Claw further with his bottle of vodka.

When the song ends, the DJ fades right into another old-school Katy classic. Whoa, I haven't heard this song in a minute. It brings back memories of third grade, when I absolutely *insisted* on my mom buying me cherry lip balm at CVS without telling her why, of course.

One of Tucker's bro-y friends leans over the railing of the DJ stand and says something to the singing girls, gesturing between two of them. One shrugs, and then the other leans in and kisses her, just a little peck. The guys on the platform shout and cheer. The girls come away giggling. Then Tucker's friend leans down and pulls them up onto the platform. Something about the quasi-transactional nature of it all turns my stomach.

Someone touches my hand. I turn to see that Gwen has returned.

"Hey." She smiles. "Do you wanna?"

"What?" I ask.

She leans in and I smell a mix of sunscreen, perfume, and vodka. "Kiss," she whispers in my ear.

My heart leaps. But my body feels frozen in place. I can't believe she just said that. "What?" I ask again.

"Tucker dared me to," she says conspiratorially. "He said it would be *sooo* hot."

"Since when do you care what Tucker thinks?" I ask.

"Um . . ." She looks over her shoulder at Tucker, who is standing a few feet away, elbowing one of the guys to look toward us.

Another one of them is holding up a phone, to film. Gwen looks from him back to me, something strange in her eyes. She bites her bottom lip as if trying to decide whether or not to tell me something.

I flash back to last Friday, when we all played Truth or Dare. Gwen picked dare every single time. Even when she had to eat a bug and *even* when she had to post an unfiltered photo to her Instagram story. A few turns in, as we headed down to the pool so Tucker could do what Sydney dared him (a backflip into the pool—more a chance for him to show off than anything), I asked Gwen why she never picked truth. "I can't do truth because *I have a secret*," she singsonged as we made our way down the steps, just out of earshot of the others. "I like someone in the house. I mean, like, I *like-like* someone." I remember how my heart was pounding as she said that. Wondering what she was trying to tell me. Wondering if she felt the same way I did. But before I could ask her anything, Tucker pushed Sydney into the pool, and then everyone was pulling each other in and splashing and laughing and the moment was gone.

Now it's all so clear. She was talking about *Tucker*. I feel like such a fool that I ever took that comment as anything more than a friend half-confessing a secret. That I thought it could've been, well, her trying to say that she liked *me*.

"Oh," I say now, on the podium. "It's him. Isn't it?"

"Please, Cam," she says, tugging on my hand. "It would be such a favor. I'd owe you."

For half a second I consider it: closing my eyes and kissing her. Because it is something that I've thought about so many times before.

After I first met Gwen, it took me a few weeks to sort out how

I felt. I mean, I've known I liked girls since puberty, or really, even before that. I knew on some level when I heard that song and asked for that Chapstick. But sometimes it's hard to make sense of my emotions. Like with my very first crush, Johana Grant, in the seventh grade. I remember when I started to feel a sort of nervousness being around her, like she was going to read my mind, and know I thought she was pretty, not just in the way girls say to each other to be nice, but prettier than any boy I'd ever seen. Or I worried she would notice my face flush when she held my hand as we walked around the playground at recess.

I remember reading an article in *Seventeen* magazine titled "Do You Like Her or Do You Want to Be Her?" I remember studying the quiz until I had it memorized and trying to reassure myself that, really, I just admired Johana Grant. That I just admired Zendaya. That I just admired Rowan Blanchard. I even told the priest about it at confession and said a bunch of Hail Marys, hoping the feelings of intense "admiration" would go away. But eventually, around the same time I left ballet, I realized they weren't going to go away. Nor did I want them to. This was me. This was who I am. I'm not attracted to boys. I like girls.

Even so, I still sometimes think about that strange article in *Seventeen*. Not because I think it will turn out that I'm not really a lesbian but just really admire #girlbosses, but because on an individual basis, it's sometimes hard to untangle my feelings. I'm a fiercely competitive person, and I do get jealous of other people, and it's hard to know sometimes why someone else is causing such a strong reaction in me. *Do I like her or do I want to be her?*

With Gwen, I knew before I met her that I admired her. I knew about the following she'd built, that she was the most famous person on TikTok. That she had what I wanted. And that she was, in the eyes of most of the internet-connected world, incredibly, objectively beautiful.

Once I met her, I realized there was also something deeply intriguing about her in person, just as much as on the internet. Maybe even more so than on the internet. I found myself thinking about her when she wasn't around and wanting to hang out with her whenever I could. But still, I wondered: *Why am I so obsessed with her?* Did I want to be "The Next Gwen Riley," as a few blogs generously named me? Or did I *want* Gwen Riley?

But then, after just a week or so in the house, I knew. I realized it when we were all watching a movie in the TV room, some '80s rom-com Sydney was obsessed with. And there weren't enough spots on the couch. So Gwen and I were sitting quite close together. And then, as the movie wore on and she became tired, she leaned her head on my shoulder. And her hair smelled like pomegranate shampoo. And I found myself completely unable to follow the plot of the film. I hoped she couldn't hear how fast my heart was beating. And I knew I was toast.

I look at her now. Drunk, her eyes flickering between Tucker and me, waiting for my answer.

But no. I won't kiss her. Not like this. Not as a party trick. Not for the kicks of the guy she really wants to be kissing. Just no.

I refuse to have a fake version of something that I actually, truly want.

"No," I say, barely loud enough to be heard over the music. "No." I pull my hand from hers and turn around, tears burning in my eyes. I push through the crowd on the platform until I get to the edge. I start to lower myself down, and then the crowd shifts and I'm pushed off. I fall onto the ground, hard, my hands scraping on the concrete pool deck.

I stand and brush myself off. I'm right by one of the speakers, and the sound is so loud my ears throb. The song is still playing, but it no longer sounds bubbly and fun. Now it sounds like Katy Perry is taunting me.

Being in this crowd of beautiful, dancing people suddenly does not feel fun, exciting, or invigorating. Instead it feels claustrophobic and chaotic, the music too loud and the sights overwhelming. I head toward the house. I need to get a glass of water.

The same people who were just trying to catch my eye to get me to pull them onto the platform now act like they can't see me as I ask them to please let me through. "Excuse me, excuse me," I say again and again as I push through slack drunk and vaguely annoyed faces.

I couldn't see it before from the DJ stand, but the ground is covered with trash.

The pool deck is littered with toppled Solo cups and crushed beer cans. Someone's vomited behind the hot tub, and someone else has stepped in it, leaving a trail of disgusting footprints. On the grounds beyond the pool deck, the aftermath of a Slip 'N Slide has torn up the Bermuda grass, leaving long streaks of black mud. I spot multiple T-shirts and cover-ups soaked in puddles of muddy water, waiting to be found in a few hours when the sun sets and the now-sunny pool deck turns a bluish shadowy gray. When the party people realize that they're starting to get a splitting headache and maybe they're not so much drunk anymore as headed toward a hangover, and that actually it's quite cold to be in a wet swimsuit, and they will stumble around until they find their ruined clothes, or just leave them behind, piling into Ubers short a T-shirt or shoe but having gained the clout of an Instagram story from one of our parties.

I step around a cluster of broken green glass from a shattered champagne bottle, my stack-heeled sandals the only thing protecting my feet. Which is more than most of the dancers have, in their bare feet or flip-flops.

"Cami, omigod!" A group of girls stops me near the top of the stairs. I don't recognize any of them. But they all seem to know who I am.

"No way!" one of them says; she has thick Cara Delevingne–style, Glossier Boy Brow–perfected eyebrows. She unlocks her phone and starts to film me. "I can't believe it's you!"

"Well, yeah, I live here."

"I know! But even when we got the invite, I didn't think we'd actually get to meet you."

But none of them are meeting me, really. I can barely even see their faces behind the phones they hold up between us. They're more interested in making sure their followers know they "talked to me" than actually, well, talking to me.

"Hi, guys," another one of the girls addresses the people behind the likes on her phone. "I'm live from the Lit Lair with Cami de Ávila herself. Cami, do something!"

She pans. I plaster a bright smile on my face and do a few dance moves. The girls cheer. Then I wave sweetly and continue on my way, very aware of where each camera is, making sure to get out of all the shots before I let the smile fall off my face.

The house is mostly empty, since Sydney insisted party guests stay outside. I slide the glass door closed behind me, muffling the sound of the music.

The only people in the kitchen are Sydney and her twin sister, Brooklyn. Syd, hair and makeup perfect and looking very sober, is putting ice and margarita mix into a blender. Brooklyn is making guacamole.

"Hey, Camila," says Brooklyn.

I mumble in response as I grab a bottle of VOSS out of the fridge. I uncap the top and lean against the counter. I take a few slow sips, trying not to upset my nervous stomach any further. The sisters continue with their conversation, paying me no mind.

"Don't eat that until I get a picture," Sydney says, grabbing her phone off the charger.

"Of course." Brooklyn positions the bowl in good lighting and away from any alcohol so her sister can get a wholesome, postable party photo.

"I always say . . . if you don't post about it . . . it's like it never even happened," Sydney says between snaps. I resist the urge to roll my eyes at her favorite little catchphrase.

The two sisters take a series of selfies holding the guacamole they made. I decide this water isn't gonna do the trick, so I use their photo shoot as an opening to swipe the Patrón and pour myself a shot.

"This one is the cutest," Sydney says, showing off a shot of them. "Uh, I'm going to miss you so much next year." She side-hugs her sister.

"Actually . . . I've been thinking about taking a gap year," Brooklyn says as she returns to making the drinks.

"Since when?" asks Sydney. She notices I took the bottle and grabs it back. I step out of the way and take my shot.

"Since like before I even got in," she says. "I just don't feel ready for college yet. Like, what, I'm supposed to go and be a business major and study for a job I don't even want before I really even try for my dream?"

"Which is what?"

"Huh?" Brooklyn caps the blender.

"Your dream, what is it?"

"To be a TikTok star," Brooklyn says, like it's obvious. She clicks on the blender, the whirring sound pausing the conversation for a moment.

I raise my eyebrows. I've seen Brooklyn's videos, and they're not . . . well, not very good. She's so stiff and overrehearsed and self-conscious in them. You can tell this doesn't come naturally to her.

But I hold my tongue and avoid getting involved in this family matter. Instead, I just slowly reach across the island for the tequila.

"But I thought UCLA was your dream," Sydney says carefully. She takes the blender and pours two glasses.

"Yeah, when I was a little kid," says Brooklyn. "But now you don't even need to go to college to be successful. I mean, I think I could build a big enough following in a year that I might not even need to go to college at all. Like, you make way more now than I would in some office job. That's the way to build a career now, right? On the internet, not in some stuffy classroom."

Before Sydney can respond, her cell phone rings. "It's my manager," she tells her sister. "Hold that thought." She steps out into the hallway to take the call.

"Tell Carmen I say hello!" Brooklyn calls after her.

I toss back the tequila and bite a lime to chase. I reach for the bottle and pour another. "Shot?" I ask Brooklyn.

"Um, no," she says.

I shrug. "Suit yourself." I toss back another. My throat burns, but I kind of like the feeling.

"Oh my God, good news!" Sydney floats back into the room and sets her phone down. "Parker Records called Carmen. They want me to make TikToks for them!"

"Wait, what?" I set down the shot glass a bit too hard. "The whole house or just you?"

"Just me, I think," Sydney says. "Why?"

"Well, don't you think that I may be better suited for that . . . considering I'm a singer?" Sydney knows that I'm hoping to use my TikTok fame to launch a recording career. That this would be the ultimate sponcon deal for me if it got me in the door with Parker.

"You're not really a singer yet," Sydney says. "You have like three songs, and they're only on SoundCloud."

"I've written like a hundred songs; I've just only posted three. And if I knew the people at Parker, maybe I'd get further," I say. "Sydney, you know I've been trying to meet with them since I moved here. Did you even think to mention me?"

"No," Sydney says. "Because they called about *me*."

Just then, the glass door slides open and Tucker bounds in. "Squid, there you are!" he says. "You're missing your whole party." He kisses Sydney and then scoops her up, throwing her over his shoulder.

"Tucker!" she squeals. "I need to post a picture."

"Enough work. You should have some fun!" he says, carrying her off. She laughs and protests playfully.

Brooklyn grabs her margarita and follows them out to the party.

And I am left alone with my tequila.

My head is starting to spin, but my anger and pain about the Gwen situation hasn't numbed. If anything, it's only magnified. I look at the bottle, wondering if another shot would help.

And then a phone vibrates. I turn my head. It's Sydney's. She left it on the table. I look at the door, but no one is around. I pick up the phone carefully.

There's a text from Carmen Marrero, Gwen and Sydney's manager. The phone tries to recognize my face, and then prompts me for a password. She did use her birthday as the house security code . . .

I try it, and the phone unlocks. I click on the text.

Here's the info for Parker! the text says. There's a contact card below it.

My heart racing and my brain muddled with tequila, I click on the message and forward it quickly to myself. My phone vibrates in my pocket. I have it.

I delete the message from Sydney to me on her phone so she won't know what I did.

And then, without stopping to think too hard about it, I delete the text from Carmen to her, too. Sure, she'll probably call her manager and get the number eventually. But I might as well give myself a head start. I lock her phone and place it back where I found it.

CAMI

I tell the cops a version of the story about how the Parker thing went down. I don't exactly lie . . . I've watched enough TV to know what perjury is. But I spin. Like any good influencer would, I alter details and leave bits out that might make me look bad. I don't tell them about the Gwen thing or about how I was feeling rejected and brokenhearted. And I don't tell them that I "borrowed" Sydney's phone.

"The partnership rep texted both me and Sydney about the same opportunity," I say. No matter that I reached out to him first with the number I got from Syd's phone . . . he did eventually reply to me, so my words are accurate enough. "I was happy to compete fair and square, but when Sydney found out we were up for the same job, she got really mad. She told me to drop out of the running and threatened to kick me out of the house if I didn't. She was basically threatening to make me homeless if I didn't forfeit my dream, just so she could have what would be just another sponcon to her. We got in a big fight about it."

Carney raises his eyebrows.

"Don't start, okay? I don't mean a physical fight. I mean, like, we yelled and she called me a selfish bitch and I called her a spoiled brat, all right? But anyway . . . a house meeting was called to sort things out. Which we did, and I wasn't kicked out, obviously."

"And what did you do about Parker?" Carney asks.

"We explained the situation to them. But they only wanted one person for the campaign. So we both tried out. We each sent three sample videos, and they deliberated. The whole thing took, like, a month."

"So who got it in the end?" Johnson asks.

"Hmmm?" I blink. "Oh, um, she did. We found out on Wednesday."

"The day she left the house?" Johnson asks. "The last day you saw her alive?"

I bite my lip. Even I have to admit it doesn't look great.

11

8 HOURS AFTER

GWEN

I feel positively adrift without my phone. The police took it from me. They had a warrant and everything, so my lawyer, Sheila, instructed me to hand it over.

But now I keep thinking about all the people who might be trying to text me or call me or comment on my social media and don't know why I'm not answering them. I mean, it's already impossible to keep up with the utter avalanche of notifications I get every day, and this will set me even further behind. It's like the worst timing. Right now, my fans need me and I need them. Today has been so upsetting, and usually when I feel uneasy and anxious, scrolling on my phone is the best way to distract myself and get my heart rate to go back to normal.

"Gwen, are you okay?" Sheila asks. I like her a lot. She's one of the top criminal defense lawyers in California. She's also quite stylish, considering she's a lawyer. She has a perfectly tailored suit, blond hair, and no visible roots, and if she's had Botox, it's very tastefully done. "You look like you're going to be sick."

"I just feel like I'm missing a part of myself," I say with a sigh.

"Oh." Sheila places a hand over mine. "It can be so hard to lose a friend."

I realize that she thinks I was referring to Sydney. I don't know how to say I meant my phone, so I just nod solemnly.

"Can we get you anything?" she asks. "Water?"

"If you don't mind," I sniffle. "I'll take a sparkling water. Has to be La Croix. Unless there's only lime left. In that case, flat Voss, hold the ice, just a slice of lemon."

She turns to the paralegal on her right and raises an eyebrow. "You heard her."

He scoffs but goes to get it.

"Now, Gwen," Sheila says, "while we wait, we might as well go over your statement. The police probably won't interview you until tomorrow, but it's good for me to know what you're going to say before then."

"Okay, sure."

"Let's talk about what happened last night." She flips the page of her legal pad. "From beginning to end, nothing left out."

I fidget with the Tiffany ring on my finger. I flash back to Tucker seeing the "T" design and asking if it stood for his name. It almost makes me smile, thinking about that, even now. I remember what he said in the pool house earlier.

"Okay, sure," I say to Sheila. "Nothing left out. . . ." I go through the night but skip over any details having to do with Tucker. So basically, nothing after one a.m. Sheila takes notes the whole time, her small, neat handwriting running across her legal pad, putting quotation marks around words like "hella" and "stan."

". . . So then I just did my skin care routine and went to bed," I lie. But she doesn't seem to notice the difference. When she's done writing, I set my empty glass on the table and say, "Can I ask a question?"

"Of course, Gwen."

"Why haven't the police said that whole 'right to remain silent' thing to me?"

"Well, that's because you're not in custody," Sheila says. "Right now, you're not even a suspect, technically."

"I'm not?"

"You're a person of interest, Gwen."

"Well, yeah." I laugh and throw my hair over my shoulder. "I know that. I have like eighty million followers."

A look of confusion passes over her face. "Oh, no, that's not what—"

Just then, the door opens and Officer Moore walks in with my phone.

"I can have it back?" My eyes light up.

"Yup." He places the phone in my hand. "We got what we needed."

It's absolutely lighting up with alerts. I unlock it instantly. I scan for one person in particular, but I don't see her name. . . . Weird.

"Gwen?" Sheila says.

"Huh?" I glance up.

"Before we wrap up for today, there's just one more thing I wanted to bring up. My accounting office called to say your retainer check bounced."

I wrote the check this morning, signed with my pink pen and everything: $250,000.

"Oh my gosh, I'm so sorry," I say. "My mom is always moving money from account to account—you know, buying stocks, making money moves—and I must have written the check from the wrong one. I'll get it sorted out straightaway." My mother left an hour ago to take a Vicodin and a nap, so knowing her "naps," this will have to wait until tomorrow morning.

"Great," Sheila says. "We just need it by the end of the week so there's no gap in our representation. Firm policy."

"No worries, I'll have it to you tomorrow," I say. "You know I'm good for it." I hold up my custom ZHC Louis bag and wink.

"Of course," she says, but I'm already back to my phone.

I scroll through my contacts and head on up the marble stairs. I click the cell number of my manager, Carmen.

As it rings, I walk through my room and out onto my balcony.

"Hey, Gwen, I was just about to call you." There's a lot of air between Carmen's voice and the phone, and I can hear the click of a turn signal, so she must be driving.

"Yeah, I wanted to talk to you about the Domizio sponcon," I say. "I was supposed to post today, but we should prob hold it for a few weeks, until things blow over."

"Actually, it looks like they are going to pull the ad, unfortunately," she says.

"What? Like not do it at all?"

"Yes, with everything going on, it's a bit of a liability for them. But the good news is, you can keep the thousand-dollar deposit. But they will be canceling payment of the forty-five K."

"What? Can they do that?" My mind flashes to the Jeep in the driveway, which this was meant to pay for.

"There's a morality clause in the contract, and even if you didn't do anything, just the perception of impropriety is enough for them to invoke it."

It takes me a second to understand what she's saying. "'*Even if*'? Carmen, I didn't do this."

"Right, yes, of course, Gwen." Over the phone, I hear her honk at another car. "But all the same, they're not going to pay you. And they want the shoes back."

"The ones I wore in the video? But those were a gift," I say. "That's what the card said, 'A gift for our friend Gwen.'"

"Technically they were part of your payment package," she says.

I scoff. "I can't believe they even care. They're only worth like eighty dollars to begin with, and I've worn them."

Carmen is quiet for a second, and all I can hear is the white noise of her car. "Gwen, they don't want you to keep them because they don't want you photographed wearing their logo."

These are not words I've ever heard before. In fact, it's usually the exact opposite. *Gwen, hold this purse while I take a picture, drink this sparkling water on your livestream, TikTok with my client, Instagram Story from my restaurant, my spin class, my boutique, my hotel.*

People have always wanted to be associated with me. Just proximity to me could do more for their brand than a major television ad. My ability to sell products just by holding them—it was the most valuable thing about me.

"There's one more thing," Carmen says, and pauses. "I think we should talk about our arrangement, you know, and whether or not this is what's best for the both of us moving forward."

I look out at the ocean as she rambles on, and my heart sinks into my stomach. I recognize the feeling of rejection from my personal life, but I've never experienced it in my professional life before.

"Everything that's going on now, it doesn't really fit with the brand you've built, you know, of a carefree California teen," Carmen says. "This whole thing, it's a different image for you, and I'm just not sure I'm the one to guide you through it."

"You're dropping me?" It feels like the wind has been knocked out of me. "But I'm the most followed person on TikTok."

"Actually . . . you might want to check that."

"What?"

I put Carmen on speaker and pull up the app. And sure enough, my follower count has dropped by ten million in the past few hours. That means freaking Madison Reed from Clout 9 has already taken my spot at the top. As I stare at the screen, I continue to bleed followers. The number next to my name flips from 68M to 66M . . . 65M . . . 62M. At the same time, my comment section is blowing up with people leaving strings of emojis: skulls, blood drops, and knives.

The world starts to spin. I can't believe this is happening.

"People are kind of boycotting your page," I hear Carmen say. "Not wanting to follow a potential murderer and all."

I don't understand. One of my friends died. Shouldn't people feel sorry for me? Shouldn't Carmen—who's always talking about how she's on my team, she's like *family*—be helping me through this? Not abandoning me in my time of need, not betraying me?

I feel like crying, but I don't want to give her the satisfaction of hearing that. I already have sounded pathetic enough on this call.

"Ugh, whatever, Carmen," I say. "But when I'm on top again, don't come crawling back. If we're done, then we're done forever." I sound convincing, like I really believe that I'll be TikTok's darling again sometime in the future. But in truth, I'm not so sure.

I guess it worked, though, because Carmen starts to defend herself, say she hopes our paths do intersect again sometime in the future and we should still grab lunch sometime and yada yada yada, but I hang up before she finishes.

I fight the urge to throw my phone off the balcony. Instead, I grip it tightly and go back into my room, slamming the glass door closed behind me.

I toss my phone onto the duvet. I'm not sure what to do with myself. Not sure where to put this anger.

In the corner of my messy room, there is a stack of boxes, piled neatly by the cleaning lady last time she was here. Untouched, never-opened packages. Gifts to me. Not payments. These came from brands who only just hoped to work with me, ones I hadn't signed any sort of agreement or morality clause with yet. These were *actually* gifts. Dozens of them.

I float over to the pile and pick up a medium-sized box from near the top. There's a ribbon tied around it, with the name of the handbag company, a French one, written again and again in swirly writing.

I sit cross-legged on the carpet, the box placed in front of me. I feel that rush, the same one I have when I look out at my view of the ocean or drive a new car off the lot: That I am successful. That I am important. That I have what everyone wants. That I have what I wanted when I was sharing a room with my mom and only saw these brands on reality TV. I'd say I was drunk on the feeling, but this is *way* better than any alcohol I've tried. This feeling of having fancy things: it makes me feel alive.

I carefully pull the end of the ribbon so it unfurls gently. My heart rate picks up. I lift the top off the box, to reveal the expertly folded tissue paper, bound with a sticker that also features the designer's name, lest you forget in the time between untying the ribbon and now.

I run my fingers over the tissue paper gently. I inhale deeply, and the box smells like the brand's famous fragrance: vanilla and rose. The scent conjures images of Paris streets with sidewalk cafés, champagne flutes clinking, dancers in fluffy tutus.

I try to remove the sticker carefully at first, but when the thin paper tears, I just rip into it. Next there is a little fabric dust bag— another reminder that this is something of value: this leather bag comes with another bag to protect it. I untie the top of the cloth bag and turn it over so the purse falls into my lap.

It's a small shoulder bag, a sleek, minimalist design made of black patent leather.

I hold the purse up, turning it so the surface catches the light. So shiny and black, it reminds me of calligraphy ink or, like, the paint on an Escalade.

I toss the purse back into its box. I know that once I've used it a few times, the glamour will fade. I'll recycle the box, and the purse will just be another bag in my wardrobe. Which will eventually end up in the back of my closet, forgotten about, full of old gum wrappers and loose tampons.

But no sense in thinking about that now.

I grab another box off the pile. Another set of beautiful wrappings to unfold. Another magical item to discover. I shake it. *This one feels like it will be shoes!*

I continue like this for over an hour. Apparently, people used to send me a lot of gifts. At first, I savor opening each box: smelling the leather, running my fingers over the satin or the velvet. Savoring each beautiful design like I'm the mouse from *Ratatouille* with some cheese.

But the farther I get into the pile, the more furiously I un-wrap, until I'm manically tearing open boxes. Adrenaline rushing through my veins. I get a paper cut from one of the boxes, and I start to bleed a bit, but I can't even feel the pain.

I think of the phrase "money can't solve your problems." And I know Ariana Grande and Blair Waldorf say that people who say that just don't know where to shop. And usually I agree with both those people on almost everything. But here I find myself disagreeing with my ponytail and headband queens.

Because it doesn't *solve* your problems but, holy crap, does it distract you from them. Shiny things do not chase away the clouds of stress and grief and pain. Money does not bring you lasting peace or deep satisfaction. But it can buy five minutes of absolutely giddy happiness. Special, designer objects make me feel like I'm a special, important person. It's freaking intoxicating.

I end up lying on the floor among upended boxes, a rainbow of tissue paper, and thousands of dollars' worth of designer mer-chandise. I stare up at the ceiling, my heart still beating in my ears. And I smile.

12

13 HOURS AFTER

KAT

I stand in front of my window and pull the curtain closed to block out the lights from the pool. I wish it would also block out the memories of the day, that this piece of fabric would allow me to forget that my friend's body was found just down there, but that's not so easy.

It's almost eleven, and the police just left like twenty minutes ago, having finally sifted through every room in the house for physical evidence. They asked us to all stay here, at least until they're done with the interviews. They say we're not under house arrest but just being strongly encouraged to stay in place. Sure.

I felt almost jealous watching them load into their cars and drive off. Leaving us here, in this place that no longer feels like home.

Alone in my room, I sit on my bed, keenly aware of the eerie silence that's enveloped the house. I always knew the house was big, but despite that, it always felt so full—of people, of jokes, of parties. Tonight it feels big in a bad way: drafty, lonely.

The whole day was so loud. It started with Cami's scream, and then the noise just didn't stop. Between the police, the lawyers, everyone's parents, the press surrounding the property, the TV, and my phone notifications, the sounds were constant and deafening. And now it's so quiet, my ears are ringing.

Now it's like I finally have time to think about it. To really *feel* it. The fact that someone in this house killed Sydney. Someone in this house is capable of killing another human being. And in all likelihood, someone in this house is capable of killing me, too. The thought makes it sort of hard to breathe.

I look around the room, my eyes darting between the shadows. The hairs on the back of my neck prickle. I don't have an overhead light. Usually I prefer the softer ambiance of lamps. But right now, I wish I could have floodlights. For the first time since I was ten years old, I am afraid of the dark.

My heart racing, I stand up and walk from lamp to lamp, clicking on each one: my fairy string lights, my modern standing lamp. I get to my Himalayan salt lamp and I struggle with the wheel switch before realizing it's because my hands are shaking. *Pull it together,* I tell myself. But even with all the lights on, I can't get rid of the creeping feeling that something is very, very wrong.

Bang! My door flies open and slams against the opposite wall.

I scream and jump up. I scramble to grab something, anything, to defend myself. I whip around to see . . .

. . . Beau, standing in my doorway, also screaming and looking very confused. "What?!" He looks around frantically.

I breathe again. "Jesus, you scared me half to death. Who opens a door like that? What, were you trying to kick it down?"

"Well, I mean, my hands were full." He looks down, where two ceramic mugs have crashed on the floor, spilling liquid all over the wood.

"Well, I thought—" I can't bring myself to finish the sentence.

I thought you were the murderer, here to attack me. "I thought it might be someone else. I—I was scared."

Beau looks at the salt lamp in my hands, the cord, which I pulled straight out of the wall, dangling from it. My fingers are wrapped around the base of the lamp with a death grip. I lower it timidly.

"Oh, sorry," he says. He squats down to pick up the broken pieces of mug.

I help him, spotting a tea bag among the wreckage. "Chamomile?" I pick it up.

"Yeah." He smiles shyly.

"That's very sweet," I say. Beau hates chamomile but knows it's my favorite. He always remembers things like that. "Sorry I made you spill."

"It's okay," he says. "Sorry I scared you."

"I was already scared before." I turn a broken piece of ceramic over in my hand. This mug had little blue flowers on it. The edge of the piece is sharp. "Knowing I'm in the same house as a . . . murderer, I just . . ." I shudder.

"I know," Beau says. "But I've been thinking, I don't know, what if it wasn't someone in the house? I mean, maybe the police will dig further and realize it was someone else. I overheard them today talking about how Syd's parents had a million-dollar life insurance policy on her. That's a bit strange, right?" His voice is energized with hope. I wish I could match his optimism.

"That's definitely weird," I say. "But, Beau, I feel like there's a lot of space between being stage-parenty and murdering your child. And even if they were that greedy and . . . violent, I mean, she just got that Parker deal, right, so wouldn't she be worth more to them alive?"

"Yeah, I guess . . ." Beau mops up the tea with a bath towel.

"Plus, what about the post to the house account? There were only six people who could sign into that account, five now. How could anyone outside the house have done that?"

"Yeah, yeah, you're right," he says. "I just, I don't know, I just can't wrap my head around the idea that one of our friends did this."

"That's because you're you and you always see the good in people. It's one of the many things I like about you," I say. "But in this case, we can't ignore the evidence in front of us. It could be dangerous to trust the other people in the house."

I plug the salt lamp back in, and it flickers a few times and then lights up. It illuminates the shadow of a broad-shouldered man in my doorway. I flinch. "Tucker?"

"I heard screaming," he says flatly. He's wearing basketball shorts and no shirt.

"Yeah, that was just, we dropped some cups."

"Well, other people are trying to sleep," he says.

"We won't do it again," I say.

He turns around and leaves without saying anything else.

Beau and I share a look. "Now, that guy I could maybe see killing someone," he quips.

I know he's joking, so I smile. But below the humor, I can't help but think that if I was a betting girl, my money might be on Tucker.

I stand and close my door. I really wish I had a lock. "Hey, Beau, would you maybe wanna sleep here?" I ask. "I don't want to be alone tonight."

"Sure," he says. "Happy to."

A weight lifts off my shoulders. Suddenly I feel relaxed enough that I think I may actually get to sleep tonight. I take the throw pillows off the bed carefully and pull back the blankets.

I turn around to see Beau setting up a makeshift bed on my rug. He's fluffing one of the throw pillows and has got my bathrobe over his legs like a blanket. It's very small compared to him, and his feet stick out the end. I smile at the sight. "Whatcha doing?"

"Oh, is it okay if I use this?" He holds up the pillow.

"Yeah, but, um"—I turn to my double bed—"don't you wanna sleep in the bed?"

"Well, I didn't want to assume . . . I mean, just because you want me to stay here to protect you from a potential psycho killer in the house doesn't mean you necessarily want me in your bed, and I didn't want you to feel pressured to do anything or—"

"Beau."

"Yeah?"

I look him in the eyes. "I want you in my bed."

He raises his eyebrows. "Yeah?"

I nod. I giggle as, in one swift movement, he rises to his feet, sweeps me up, and pulls me into him. He kisses me and we fall back onto the bed, tangled together. I weave my fingers through his hair. His hand traces the curve of my neck.

I pull back just slightly and clarify: "I mean, I'm not ready to have sex tonight, but I would like to hook up for a bit. If that's okay?"

"Of course." He smiles, his eyes warm. "Whatever you want."

We kiss and kiss and kiss. His lips, his touch, his smell—all of it is intoxicating. I feel like here, in this little bubble, everything is good and beautiful, even with all the danger and fear outside this little room. I feel like as long as I am here, kissing him, holding him, everything will be okay. I will be safe. I will be happy, even.

A little while later, before we drift off to sleep, I reach over and click off the lamp. My room is now pitch-black. But wrapped in Beau's arms, I sleep easily.

13

20 HOURS AFTER

TUCKER

The sun starts to stream through the cracks in the curtains. I roll over and check the time on my phone: 5:53 a.m.

I haven't been able to slip into sleep for longer than fifteen minutes. My mind certainly feels tired enough. I'm so fried it's as if my thoughts are a video that keeps buffering and won't load right. But still my body won't let me sleep. My heart rate refuses to slow, and my muscles won't relax. I seem to have an endless amount of jittery energy propelling me forward. Toward what? I don't know.

The blue light of my phone shining on my face, I scroll through Twitter. Not laughing at anything, not really even seeing anything. Just stressed. I bite at the cuticle of my thumb until it starts to bleed.

The photo of Gwen and me outside the pool house still hasn't surfaced on social media or any of the gossip sites. Which is strange, because in the past it's seemed like the paparazzi sell photos as soon as they take them. Knowing that photo is out there and not knowing when it will surface is fucking with my head. It's like there's this big weight hanging over me, held up by a fraying rope.

I switch from Twitter to TikTok. The first video on my For You page is from Gwen's account, which I guess makes sense, since she's the most followed person on the app.

It's a photo montage of Gwen and Sydney over the years, smiling and laughing, set to the song "Angel" by Sarah McLachlan. Which is a little weird, if you ask me, because it's the same song they use in that commercial about homeless puppies.

But I guess this is Gwen trying, which is nice. My lawyer told me that it'd be helpful to express my sadness publicly, so the police think of me as a grieving boyfriend and not a suspect. I just haven't been able to find the words. I guess Gwen did. I glance down at the caption, which reads *Rip in peace Syd <3.*

This makes me smile, for the first time in a while. Oh, Gwen. Sweet, simple Gwen.

I roll out of bed. It's time to give up on sleep and see what food I can scavenge from the kitchen before everyone else wakes up, and before all the parents and lawyers descend again.

I pad down the stairs and toward the kitchen, rubbing my eyes. And I almost walk smack into a girl.

"Oh, Tucker, hey," says a flustered Brooklyn Reynolds. She's wearing a crop top and yoga pants. She looks pretty hot.

"What are you doing here?" I blurt out. And then, realizing that's kind of a dick thing to say, add, "I mean, how did you, uh, get inside?"

"My parents have a key," she says. "I would've knocked, but I didn't want to wake anyone. I didn't know you got up so early."

"I don't." I stretch, my back cracking in the process. "I actually haven't been to sleep yet."

"Oh, I'm sorry to hear that." Her eyes seem to hold genuine pity. "I can't sleep either. . . . I actually came here to get this stuffed animal that Sydney loved since we were little. I know it sounds dumb, but I thought, you know, if I held it, I might be able to fall asleep. Actually, maybe you've seen it? It's a white and blue teddy bear."

"Mr. Fuzzle Butt, sure," I say.

Brooklyn gives an inquisitive look, her mouth turning up into the faintest smile. "You know his name?"

"Well, yeah," I say. "You're right, Squid was obsessed with that thing. She talked about it a lot."

"I didn't think guys listened when girls talked about that kind of thing."

I shrug. I didn't care about the freaking thing. But with Sydney I found it was better to listen passively than ignore her and get yelled at later. "I know where he is. I can grab him for you."

It's not until I'm pushing open the door to Sydney's room that I realize this is the first time I've been in here since we found her. I didn't think about what it would be like. To see her bed, stripped of her sheets by the police; all the papers on her desk and the hairbrush on her dresser gone, taken into evidence. And then other things, like framed photographs and piles of books she loved, still the same, as if they're just waiting for her to return.

I realize I've been holding my breath. As if my dumb brain thinks that if I don't inhale, I won't take in any of the memories, any of the sadness or loss. I spot Mr. Fuzzle Butt on the shelf, grab him, and leave. I slam the door behind me.

Downstairs I hand the bear to Brooklyn—"Here you go." I try to act cool. Casual.

"Thank you." Her eyes glossy, she studies the stuffed animal. Its fur is matted and discolored from the wear and tear of the last decade. "Does this make me totally lame?" Brooklyn asks. "That

I drove across town before sunrise to get a children's toy? Am I a total baby?"

"Nah," I say. "Fuzzle Butt's not for kids. Look at this." I tug on the toy's right ear, which was half torn off years ago by the Reynoldses' dog. "This bear is one tough motherfucker. I think he got this in a street fight."

Brooklyn laughs, a real, genuine laugh. "Oh." She brings her fingers to her lips to cover her smile. "Wow. That's the first time I've laughed since . . ." She trails off. The sadness returns to her eyes.

And I realize that this is the first somewhat normal conversation I've had since this happened. That I haven't felt this much like myself since Sydney died. Even with Gwen I'm tense, worried about how much worse it will be if people find out about our relationship. The stakes are no longer just a dumb teenage cheating scandal. Now it's a possible motive. Kind of takes the fun out of it.

"Hey, do you wanna hang out for a bit?" I ask. "I was going to make some coffee."

She hesitates, biting her lip, considering my question. I shouldn't have asked. Of course she wouldn't want to be around me. I'm a "person of interest" in her sister's murder. She must hate me.

"Yeah," she says finally, setting the bear on the counter and sliding into a chair. "That would be nice."

Brooklyn sits patiently as I clang around the kitchen for a while, trying to figure out how to make coffee. I didn't really drink caffeine before, except for the odd Red Bull before a party. But I guess if I'm going to become an insomniac, I should get used to it.

Keeping up with dishes wasn't exactly our strong suit even before our lives were turned upside down, but I manage to find one clean mug at the back of the cabinet that says TOAST MALONE on it. I pour coffee into that for Brooklyn and into a glass measuring cup for myself. "And I'm not sure if we have any sugar . . ." I open a few drawers but don't have any luck.

"Oh, it's here." Brooklyn opens a cabinet, stretches on her tiptoes to reach the top shelf, and pulls down two packets of Splenda.

"Ha, you don't even live here and you know the place better than me," I say as I take one. "Shows you how much I cook."

"Yeah." She smiles politely at my joke, but there is a strange look in her eyes. Like she's distracted or upset. I worry that I've broached a sore subject.

I take a long sip of my coffee, then set it on the table with a clatter. "Listen, the thing that happened earlier this week, with the meeting, I'm sorry things went down that way."

She shrugs. "Don't even apologize. Losing Syd, it kind of puts that drama into perspective. How could I still be upset about something like that?" But still her voice is strained. I'm not sure if I believe her.

She changes the subject: "Hey you know what we should do? We could talk about our favorite memories of Syd. We did it when my grandma died, and I don't know, it kind of helped."

My mind races. I'm not good at sappy things. I never know the right thing to say. Brooklyn is watching me, waiting for me to answer.

Her face falls. "Or, I mean, if you don't want to, we don't have to. . . ."

"No, I do," I say. "It's a good idea. I'm just trying to think of a memory that's, you know, PG." I raise my eyebrows.

"Tucker!" She punches me in the arm playfully.

"Ow, easy there." I rub my bicep, feigning pain. "I'm sorry, okay, but your sister was hot. Can you blame me?"

She shakes her head. "That's weird to say. I look just like her." Her cheeks go rosy.

"Eh, I guess. I'm not sure if I really saw the resemblance," I joke.

"We're identical twins," she says flatly.

"See, that's what people kept telling me," I say. "But I'm not sure I believe it."

She snorts at this.

Eventually I get serious about her memory game and tell the story of when Syd and I drove up the coast and had a picnic on the beach. It's not necessarily my favorite memory of Sydney, but it's probably Syd's favorite memory of me, given how much she posted about it on all her social media accounts. It seems like the right thing to say.

"That's a really beautiful memory, Tucker," Brooklyn says, tears welling in her eyes.

I shrug. "Your turn."

"Okay . . . wow, my favorite Syd memory. Well, one time on a family vacation—"

She's interrupted by the sound of shouting from the other room.

Her eyes go wide. "What was that?"

14

21 HOURS AFTER

BEAU

I hold Kat's hand as we rush down the stairs. "My mom said to turn on channel thirty-two."

"And she didn't say what it was?" Kat asks.

"No, just that it was important." When we woke up, I had a missed call from each of my parents and my lawyer. An all-caps text from my mom said to turn on the TV.

Kat and I search the TV room for the remote. It used to be in that bowl on the coffee table until, well, until it was shattered during the fight on Thursday.

I find the remote under one of the couch cushions and punch the power button. Channel 32 is a cable news network, and right now a woman with short blond hair and intense features is talking at the camera. The logo lets me know it's the *Nora Caponi Show*. I've heard of it but never watched before. True crime isn't really my thing.

I turn up the volume: "There's been a confession in the case that has captivated the nation. That's right, in just a few moments Sydney Reynolds's murderer will be joining us in the studio."

Holy shit. A wave of relief washes over me. It's over. This hellish twenty-four hours is over. They found out who did this.

"Oh my gosh!" Kat exclaims.

"I know!" I pull her into my arms and spin her around. I can't believe it: it's over, we're safe. We're going to be fine.

"What's going on?" a female voice asks.

I look up to see Brooklyn Reynolds standing in the doorway, Tucker by her side.

"Tucker." Kat looks over her shoulder. "You're here . . . ?"

"Where else would I be?" he asks. He looks at the TV, where a headline now blares across the screen: TIKTOK MURDERER CONFESSES.

Brooklyn gasps. "I—I need to call my parents." She pulls out her phone. I think back to the life insurance. Part of me wonders if her parents will be in Nora Caponi's greenroom when they get the call.

"Mom," Brooklyn says into the phone, "are you home? Okay, wake up Dad, turn on the TV."

Or not . . .

"Let me see that," Tucker says, then rips the remote from my hand and turns up the volume.

On the television Nora Caponi says, "We'll hear from the murderer very shortly, but for now we are joined by Ollie Glover, our resident criminology expert. Ollie, are you surprised to see a confession this early in this case?"

Ollie is a man with a mustache and serious eyebrows. "In a word, Nora: no," he says. "This might be unusual for a typical murder. But this case is anything but typical. It's a celebrity murder."

He pauses for effect but continues before Nora can jump in. "In my experience as an investigator, I've seen two general types of people confess to a crime as serious as murder. The first is someone who commits a crime of passion, kills someone in a split second of rage or fear. When these people calm down and process what they've done, when they realize that they've taken the life of another human being, they are riddled with guilt. They confess to the world like many of us confess sins in our houses of worship. They want to admit to what they've done and pay their debt to society.

"The other kind of confessor is a much darker being. These are psychopaths who relish what they did. They want to brag. They like to walk us through exactly how they did it, and how they'd eluded our grasp; to tell us how we'd never have caught them if they hadn't turned themselves in, since, after all, they're so brilliant. These confessors seem to feel nothing, no remorse for what they did, no fear of a lifetime in jail. And might I say, Nora, ever since I saw that TikTok post yesterday, boasting about this terrible killing, I knew that we were dealing with that second kind of confessor."

Over my shoulder I hear the squeaking sound of slippers walking toward us.

"What's going on?" a voice asks.

"Don't know," someone replies. I feel a tug at my sleeve and turn to see Gwen. "What's going on?" she asks.

"Someone's confessed," I say.

She turns to Cami and repeats, "Someone's confessed."

I turn back to the TV. Wait. Hold on a second. I turn back. And yes, both Gwen and Cami are here, in this room, in pajamas.

And so is Kat, and Tucker and of course, myself. "But then . . . who confessed?"

"I had thought Cami," Tucker says, confused.

"I thought you," Kat admits.

Tucker recoils. "What the—" Everyone starts to shout over each other, and I can't make out what anyone is saying.

"Everybody shut up!" Gwen yells. She furrows her brow and points to me and then Kat. Under her breath, she counts, "One, two, three—"

Tucker scoffs. "This is ridiculous."

"Ugh!" Gwen whips her head toward him. "You made me lose my concentration. Now I have to start over. Okay, one, two . . ."

But then a graphic swoops across the TV, and our question is answered for us. A girl joins Nora Caponi in the split screen. She looks like she's about our age. She has a round face framed with wavy black hair, green eyes, and a small birthmark by her upper lip. And I've never seen her before in my life.

"Who the hell is that?" says Cami.

My thoughts exactly.

"Joining us now, in her first television interview, is the so-called TikTok Killer, Lucy Reid."

"Thanks for having me, Nora. That's *R-e-i-d*," she says cheerfully "And my Insta and TikTok are both @lucyreid26."

A lower third pops up with her name and social media handles. "What is she, a *Bachelor* contestant or a murderer?" Cami asks.

"So tell us, Ms. Reid," Nora Caponi says, "how did you come to know the victim?"

"I mean, I didn't, at least not before I killed her." She laughs. "I mean, I wish I knew her. I was just a fan."

"I see." Nora Caponi narrows her eyes. "So why don't you tell us what happened that fateful night?"

"Right, okay." Lucy Reid sits up straighter. "So first, I hitch-hiked to Malibu. Hitchhiking, you know, is very Manson-vibes, so it was a bit of an homage. So I get them to drop me at the house, but there's this big like iron gate, so I was going to give up, but THEN I spotted this little path down to the beach, right near the house. It was, like, totally overgrown with leaves and shit and I almost tripped like ten times, but I made it down. And then once I got to the beach, I could go up to their pool. Just like that, I was at the Lit Lair. And then I saw her there by the pool: Sydney Reynolds. She was alone, looking so peaceful and so sad, you know, just sort of dangling her feet in the water. And so I raised my gun and—"

"Wait, sorry." Nora Caponi holds up a hand. "You were across the pool?"

"Uh, yeah," says Lucy. "So, as I was saying—"

"That's strange," Nora Caponi interrupts again, "because the preliminary police report said there was no blood spatter found on the deck, nor on any of the foliage surrounding the pool area, and if you shot her from that distance, there'd be significant spatter."

"Oh yeah. You're right, I must've just misremembered," Lucy says, her eyes darting to the side of the camera. "I just got confused. I mean, it all happened so fast, you know?"

Nora Caponi seems unconvinced. "What kind of gun did you use?" she asks.

Lucy's eyebrows go up. "Oh, um—"

"A forty-five? A twenty-two? Or maybe you don't know the

caliber, that's fine," Nora says. "Let's make it easy. Just tell me, was it a revolver or did you have a magazine?"

Lucy looks from side to side as if trying to figure out if this quiz show has a lifeline.

"Ms. Reid," Nora Caponi says, incredulous, "have you ever even held a gun?"

"What's wrong with you?" Lucy slams her hand on the table. "Why are you asking all these questions? I'm confessing, aren't I?"

"It's my job, Lucy." Nora Caponi gathers the papers on her desk. "I think we're done here. But a piece of advice before you go: the next time you're going on TV to confess to a murder you didn't commit, maybe at least read the public information first." Nora Caponi looks beyond the camera. "And whoever on my staff vetted this girl can go ahead and resign before I get off the air."

I can't tear my eyes from the screen even as the hope of a confession falls apart. I've never seen anything like this on live TV before.

"This can't be over! I confessed!" Lucy Reid struggles against the grasp of security guards trying to guide her out. "This is my shot! You gotta let me have it! What if this is my only chance to be famous?"

Cami cackles. "This is my new favorite show."

Security drags Lucy out of the shot, and the split screen goes back to one shot. Nora Caponi, ever the professional, pats her hair into place and looks directly into the camera. "Well, there you go, ladies and gentlemen," she says. "The state of the world today. Some people would risk twenty-five-to-life just for fifteen minutes of fame."

GWEN

"Are you sure we can't just sneak out to Luxxe for a quick cappuccino?" my mom asks. She's sitting at the kitchen island, wearing a knit crop-top-and-cardigan set and tiny sunnies that have kind of gone out of style. Not that I'd tell her that. I don't have a death wish.

"No, Mom, the police just got here, and Sheila said they could call any of us in at any time," I say. "Plus, I can make perfectly fine coffee here." I slide a pod into the Nespresso maker and close the lid. I try a few of the buttons before I guess correctly and brown liquid starts to flow out of the machine into the tiny cup. I must admit that, despite my assurances to Jennifer—my mom prefers for me to call her by her first name so people don't know she's old enough to have a teenage child—this is the first time I've made coffee at home since we moved in. What can I say? I like to keep baristas in business.

I set the cup in front of her, and she sighs and takes off her sunnies in a dramatic sweep. "It's not the coffee. Being here just kind of gives me the creeps."

Yeah, try sleeping here, I think. I'd hoped Tucker would sleep in my bed last night, but he left after we hooked up. He said it would be suspicious if anyone saw him leave my room in the morning. That it would increase scrutiny on both of us. I said that was fine, but it wasn't. I mean, I'm used to sleeping alone, given the circumstances of our relationship. But last night, the night after my friend died, was especially tricky. My melatonin gummies were no match for a haunted house.

"Just try not to think about it," I tell my mom as I make a coffee for myself. My phone vibrates with a text from Sheila.

Almost there. Traffic on 101.

Kk! I answer.

That reminds me. "Hey, Jen, Sheila said something about the check not clearing. Did you happen to move anything out of the Chase account?" I slide into the stool opposite her, setting down my cup and grapefruit half.

My mom studies the empty espresso cup in front of her. "Actually, there's something I've been meaning to tell you, um, about the finances. You see, the thing is, once you started making a certain amount of money, we both adjusted our lifestyle, you know, to fit the status we had built. Which, as you may remember, was part of the branding plan, you know, to make you very aspirational. So really, a lot of these things were, at the time, business expenses—"

"Mom, I'm confused. What are you saying?"

She pinches the spot between her eyes she's Botoxed smooth. "We typically only have about a month's cushion," she says. "Between your paychecks and the bills. Sheila's check didn't bounce because it was drawn from the wrong account. It bounced because the Domizio deal fell through, so there wasn't enough money."

"What?" I almost choke on a piece of grapefruit. "How is that even possible? I've made like—" I try to add it in my head, but math was never my strong suit, and I dropped out of school before I finished Algebra II. "I don't know but I make like thirty grand a sponcon post, so, I mean, how, *how*, could we be spending money that fast?"

"How do you think, Gwen? It pays your rent here, and mortgages on my house in the Hills and the vacation house in Palm Springs. Then there's the tennis club, Soho House, and the Jonathan Club. SoulCycle and Pure Barre are like forty dollars a day each, plus you have to keep the Equinox membership so you can train with Calvin a few times a month. Payments on my Tesla, your Ferrari before you crashed it, the Porsche you gifted your father for some inexplicable reason, and now this Jeep you bought. Four major plastic surgeries plus the minor enhancements every six months. All that's before you add the shopping that you do. Not to mention all those meals out."

"You're one to talk, Mom. I've seen you order Nobu for takeout. On a Tuesday."

"You know I have a bad heart." She splays her fingers across her chest. "I need the omega threes."

"So eat an avocado," I snap, "not thirty-dollar-apiece sashimi."

She looks hurt by this, and I regret my tone. I'm not trying to blame her for the situation. I know I probably spend as much as she does, that I'm equally responsible for draining the bank account. But at the same time I'm pissed at her. Isn't she supposed to be the grown-up? Isn't she supposed to know when we're spending too much?

I exhale through my nose and down the rest of my espresso quickly. "You didn't put anything in savings?" I ask.

"Well, I mean, I'd always planned to do that. But then things come up. You know, and I have to draw from the account. Incidental expenses. Like, sometimes you need a mechanic for the car, or you know, the yacht."

"Right, right."

"But don't worry about it," she says. "I mean, who gives a shit about Domizio? Honestly, I didn't like them for your brand anyway. Just call Carmen to get something new on the books. The lawyers can wait a few days for their check."

"I can't," I say. "Carmen dropped me."

"Oh." Her thin shoulders fold inward. She stares down at the espresso cup in her hands, her eyes glassy.

"Yeah." My stomach churns. I think I might throw up all over the kitchen floor. I become keenly aware that the only things in my stomach are coffee and a bit of grapefruit. I reach into the box of Krispy Kremes Beau ordered, hoping something breadlike will stop the feeling of acid churning in my stomach.

I've only just raised the confectionary dough to my lips when my mom scoffs.

"Don't stress-eat, honey." She glares at the doughnut like it's poison. "The last thing you need is to add a muffin top to your problems."

"Really, Mom?" I stare her down. "That's really what you're worried about right now? What, that I'll look chubby in my mug shot?"

"*Gwen!*" She swats my arm. "Don't even joke about that. I don't know what I would do if—if—" Tears fill her eyes again, and she starts to fan her face with her hands, like she's going to dry the tears. She's probably worried that crying will ruin her monstrous lash extensions.

I sigh. And it really sets in. That I'm the one who's going to have to figure this out. How to pay the lawyer. How to keep my mom's house—or, rather, *houses*—from being foreclosed on.

"It'll be okay," I say. I stand up and hug her. "I'll take care of it." I leave the doughnut but grab a Clif Bar. Even those have too much sugar, according to Jennifer—who usually skips breakfast herself in favor of a questionable diet pill. But she's smart enough not to criticize the power bar this time. I grab a bottle of VOSS to wash it down and tell my mom I'll be in my room if the cops come asking, or if Sheila still shows up despite the continued lack of retainer.

I find my laptop under a pile of sweaters and open my email for the first time in six months.

When I first started, like a lot of baby influencers, I put my email in my bio on Instagram and then TikTok, asking people to reach out to me directly for sponcons. That was before Carmen. Before the management company I worked with before her. Before I was a "brand" or my videos were "IP." Back when I was just a kid goofing around on the internet.

After a few guesses, I remember the right password and I'm in. The inbox is absolutely overflowing. I haven't had to look at it because Carmen handled everything, and she said yes to only the top 5 percent of offers that came in for me. To protect my image, she said, the value of what I was offering.

Well, it's time to see what's up with the other 95 percent.

Even though the email address hasn't been listed in my bio for months, it still gets passed around the internet without my permission. After thousands of hate comments on my TikTok, I guess it shouldn't be a shock that the first email in my inbox, sent from lmr0485@hotmail.com, has "WHY DID U KILL HER??" in the subject line. Although I don't know if something like that is ever not shocking.

I promptly delete the message and scroll through the rest of my inbox. It takes me a while to weed through hate messages, press requests, and conspiracy theories from the last twenty-four hours, but then I get to the collab request emails. There are tons of them, despite the fact that I haven't responded to anyone through this email in so long.

People offer me free meals at restaurants, workout classes, tables at clubs (do they not realize I'm seventeen?), and even an invitation for a free stay at a five-star hotel in Dubai. I skim past these, although the last one is quite tempting. But no. Right now, it's all about cash.

I respond to every company that looks at all legit.

"Hi, it's Gwen!" I write. "Sorry I missed your email! Is this campaign still going? Would love to help out, xoxo!"

I send out at least twenty emails. Four of the companies respond that they "must politely decline" before I'm even done writing all my reach-outs. Which is freaking ironic, because yesterday they were spamming my inbox. What fair-weather bullshit.

Okay, well, maybe someone else will bite. In the meantime . . . what else can I do? I look around my room, trying to figure out what skills I have that might bring in money and fast, besides promoting stuff on the internet. My eyes stop on the piles of gifts I tore into yesterday. And beyond that, my closet. The collection of beautiful items I've built over the last year. A closet to rival Kylie Jenner's. A closet to rival Hannah Montana's.

I walk in and pull down a few items, displaying them nicely on the chaise longue, and snap a few test shots. I pull up Depop and make an alias account, since Carmen always said it was bad for my brand to resell gifts. The stuff I unboxed yesterday alone should be enough to cover one of my mom's car payments—and my outstanding balance on the Jeep for this month.

This will be fine, I tell myself as I list the first few items. *Everything is going to be fine.*

I dig through my closet for more things to sell. I toss shoes and bags and hats and belts onto the carpet floor behind me. Buried in the back, I find a purse I haven't worn in years but could never get myself to donate or throw away. I even brought it when I moved in here. There are interlocking C's on the front, but it didn't come from the store on Rodeo Drive. It has the quilting and the chain strap, but if you look closely, you can see there is no iconic double flap, and if you look inside, the lining is wrong.

I remember walking into school my freshman year, the first day back from winter break. That year at our school backpacks were out. Carrying your books and bringing a purse to school was in. And Sydney, the coolest girl in the ninth grade, had the best bag collection.

That morning the girls in our friend group, and the girls who wished they were part of it, were all gathered around Sydney's locker, as usual. When I walked up with my new purse, everyone came over to look. "Christmas present from my mom," I said proudly. "Omg it looks totally vintage," Katy M. said. "Can I hold it?" Brooklyn asked.

Sydney slammed her locker closed.

That same day, during fifth-period biology, I got my period. I was in the stall, getting a tampon out of my new purse, when I heard the door open.

Then my so-called best friend's voice: "You guys know her bag is fake, right? So tacky. I mean, the only reason she can even go to this school is because her mom works for my dad and we let them live in our guesthouse."

I stared down at my purse and held my breath so I wouldn't cry and they wouldn't hear me.

I wish I could say that was the only time Sydney said something like that. But it wasn't. Sydney and I met because, for about three years, Jennifer was the Reynoldses' personal assistant, which meant she did everything from scheduling appointments for Sydney's parents to dropping off their dry cleaning, picking up their coffee, and sometimes manicuring her mom's toes—whatever they needed. I was never ashamed of what my mom did. It was her job. Just like it was the Reynoldses' job to run their business. It was her job to help keep their household running.

But sometimes Sydney would act like I should be ashamed. She'd imply that I was indebted to her family, and to her specifically, for the opportunities I ended up having.

"Gwen had like no friends when she came to this school, because she didn't grow up around here, but luckily I took her under my wing," she said to the high school yearbook reporter our sophomore year.

When we got famous and publications with much wider circulations would ask how we met, I would simply say we knew each other since the eighth grade, but she always specified, "Gwen's family used to work for mine." That's how she phrased it: my family worked for her family, like we were in *Downton Abbey* or something and I worked for her, too. "Oh, do you not want people to know that?" she said once, after she'd told the reporter from *US Weekly* about how my mom used to rub her mom's feet.

"No, it's fine," I said. "Kind of like how Kim K used to work for Paris Hilton." She spent the rest of the week pissed that I said this. In her understanding of the world, she was the Kim K of any situation she was in.

When my star shot past hers and the articles started to come out calling me the "Queen Bee of Teen TikTok," comments like this from Sydney became more and more common. When we were looking for houses to set up the Lit Lair, she'd always say her vote should count double because her parents were fronting the money. She'd veto my favorites and say I had "new money taste." The truth is, despite the external appearances of our closeness, in the weeks leading up to forming the house, we were fighting more often than we were getting along.

So when I look back to that fateful night in the pool, I know I'm lying to myself a bit about why I did it. I mean, it is true that I was crushing on Tucker and that it was rare to have someone like me back who really knew me beyond the headlines. But if I'm being honest with myself, that's not the only reason I got involved with him. Part of me liked that he was Sydney's boyfriend. Part of me wanted to get back at her for all the years of snarky comments and looking down her nose at me. Part of me wanted to hurt her.

15

1 DAY AFTER

KAT

I used to say nothing kills a joke like having to explain it. That was before I had to do so during a police interrogation.

"In this video from a few weeks ago, you're filming yourself walking into Ms. Reynolds's room, correct?" Detective Carney holds up an iPhone, which is playing one of my TikToks. He had to put on his reading glasses to pull it up.

"Yeah."

"And this little song playing in the background, over and over again. "Don't be suspicious"—that's what they're saying, right? What exactly were you doing that may have been perceived as suspicious?"

"Nothing," I say. "It's just a meme."

"Hmmm." He considers this, the wrinkles in his forehead deepening. I wonder if he knows what a meme is.

"Now, in this other video, this caption." He points at the screen with his index finger. "What exactly does that mean when you say you are going to 'k-word' Sydney? What's the k-word?"

Oh my God, I cannot believe this is happening. I look over to Mr. Lambert, my lawyer, wondering if he's going to do something.

He's been nice enough, but he's never worked on a murder case before, and I can't help but worry he won't be as good as some of the fancy teams of lawyers I've seen meeting with some of my housemates. But quick Googling revealed that lawyers like that have retainers of roughly $200,000, aka all the money I made on TikTok, which is supposed to be for college and my future. And that's before the hourly rate kicks in. So . . . Mr. Lambert, a family friend doing my mom a favor, seems like the best option.

"Ms. Powell?" The detective asks, looking at me over his glasses. "Can you answer the question, please?"

"What?" I say. "I mean, sorry, could you repeat the question?"

"I asked you what you meant when you said, in a video at three-forty-three p.m. on July thirteenth that you were going to 'k-word' Ms. Reynolds?"

My lawyer just looks at me, like he's curious about the answer, too.

"Well, I think the reason you may be asking is because you already know that in Stan Twitter, people say 'k-word' when they mean 'kill.'" They start to react, but I hold up my hands. "But it was just a joke. Really, you have to understand. We had a . . . dispute regarding *Animal Crossing*—you know, the video game? So that's why I made the joke." I'm hoping that using words like "dispute" and "regarding," which sound kind of official, will help him understand.

"You told the whole internet that you were going to kill your friend over a video game? Is that the kind of thing you think is funny?"

Yeah, that's why I made a joke about it, I think sassily. But I bite my tongue and instead just give a polite nod.

"Kind of an inappropriate thing to say. Don't you think?"

"Well, it's only inappropriate now because she died," I say. "I mean, I know that sounds bad, but, like, I had no idea that was going to happen."

"So this is just a coincidence?"

"Yeah, it's a coincidence!" I snap. "Do you really think I'd decide to kill Sydney over *Animal Crossing* and then tell the whole internet about it?" By now I'm raising my voice. "I mean, c'mon, you can't be serious!"

"I must echo my client," my lawyer says. "I believe this line of questioning has gone past the point of being productive."

Past the point? I think. *At what point was this productive?* But I don't complain. At least my lawyer is helping now.

"Fine," Carney says. "Let's change the subject, then. Why don't you tell me why a week before she died, Sydney Reynolds accused you of stealing twenty thousand dollars from her?"

And suddenly I wish we were talking about my *Animal Crossing* jokes again. I swallow hard.

He slides a file over to me. But I don't have to unfold it to guess what it probably is. Feeling like I might vomit all over the table, I open it.

It's a printed screenshot of texts from "Syd the Kid"—the name for Sydney in my phone.

Syd the Kid: you bitch!! You're ruining my life!!

Syd the Kid: Wait till I tell my mom you STOLE 20K from me!! Where will you live then?

My heart speeds up, but my body feels frozen. I don't know what to say, what to do. I just want to cry, but I doubt that will help matters.

I turn to my lawyer. He's staring at the paper and looking like he might faint. Which is not comforting. I clear my throat to get his attention.

"Can we, um, take a recess or something?" I ask him.

He blinks and looks up at me, as if he's just remembering that I'm here. "Oh, well, Kat, it's only called a recess if you're in court."

That's what he says. Like the biggest issue right now is terminology.

"Whatever. Can we take a break?" I say. "I, um, need to go to the bathroom." I stare at him, trying to communicate with my eyes what I hope he already knows: we need to come up with some sort of strategy before continuing.

"Uh, yes," my lawyer says. "That's a good idea." He stands up, and his chair makes an ugly scratching sound. "I need a few minutes to talk to my client, if that's all right with you?" he asks the cop.

"Sure," Detective Carney says. "Take your time." His words are nice but far from comforting.

As soon as we're alone, my lawyer asks, "So what the heck was that about?"

It started about a month ago. I was sitting on the back patio, sketching and listening to *Fine Line*. The sun was high in the cloudless sky, and I was midway through sketching motifs from various songs on the album. I'd just gotten to "Cherry."

And then I felt someone walk up behind me. Sydney.

I turned to her, pulling out one of my earphones.

"You're pretty good at that," she said. I tried not to be offended at the surprise in her voice. "I'd like to talk with you about a potential collab."

She pulled up a chair next to me and explained that she had a catchphrase she wanted to get trending. "'TikTok killed the Instagram star,'" she said, waving her hands in a big arch. "Get it? Like the song from the eighties. But, like, relevant for our generation."

I nodded as I shaded in one of the cherries. "That's clever. I like it."

She beamed in response. "Okay, so here's where you come in."

She explained that she wanted to make merch with the phrase to sell to her fans. Laptop stickers, T-shirts, water bottles, and so on. And so I came to understand that by "collab," she meant that I design the logo and coordinate getting the merch made, and she, I guess, supplied the phrase. She offered to pay me three hundred dollars for the drawing and split the profits of the merch. But for me it wasn't really about the money. I decided to do it because, well, we'd been in the house two months, and Beau was my only friend. I thought doing something with her might help me get to know her, beyond a shy hello in the hallway or holding the camera for her and her friends while they did their dances.

It took me a few tries to get the design right, but eventually I had one I was happy with. Funky bubble lettering with a multicolored outline. Kind of a psychedelic aesthetic.

Sydney actually squealed when I showed her the mockup on Procreate. "You're a genius, Kat," she said as she hugged me. I thought that was a bit over the top, but Sydney and Gwen always talked like that. Nothing was good; it was *amazing*. Nothing was bad; it was *the freaking worst*.

I made a few small tweaks based on her suggestions and then

sent off the design to this company we found online. They wanted the money up front, and Syd Venmoed it to me without a second thought. She just had twenty thousand dollars on hand to spend on stickers, no problem. I put in the order that same night.

And that's when the trouble began. For weeks we checked the mailbox, the doorstep, the end of the driveway. But there were no boxes. Not one T-shirt or laptop sticker, let alone thousands of them.

The fans who'd preordered merch started to get angry with Sydney, and she in turn got mad at me. Everything came to a head when people who'd ordered the stickers started to use the hashtag #scammersydney. It didn't trend or anything, just a few tweets and a few dozen likes, but still Sydney was worried it would cost her important brand partnerships if it picked up steam. And that's why, in her frustration, she accused me of "stealing" the money she'd Venmoed me for the order.

I was in my room when I got the texts. I spent almost twenty minutes pacing around, trying to figure out how to respond. And then I heard her laugh down in the kitchen. She sent me that text while we were both in the house. And what's more, she'd sent me an incredibly stressful text and then just went back to laughing at TikToks like nothing was amiss. So I threw my phone onto my bed and went downstairs to talk to her.

In person, Syd had a fraction of the edge she projected in texts. And after I explained that I'd sent a bunch of emails to the company and that I'd make sure this was sorted out, Sydney thanked me and apologized for being so aggro.

It was the kind of argument that blew up over text but then was settled once we could talk it out. But there was no record of that conversation when we made up, only texts that reflect the moment when she was most intensely, irrationally pissed at me. And it's the last text she sent me before . . . well, I guess it will forever be the last text she sent me.

"So you see, I didn't steal from her. It was just a misunderstanding about stickers," I tell my lawyer. "Sydney, she just got really angry and said things like that. It was kind of how she reacted to everything. So, like, lost merch becomes I 'stole' twenty thousand dollars from her."

When I'm done, Mr. Lambert says, "Okay, Katherine, everything is going to be fine. We'll just go in there and you tell them that. Just like you told me."

His eyes are really kind. For the first time I'm kind of glad I have a family friend as my lawyer. Someone who knows my mom and has gotten our Christmas cards for years. Maybe this will be okay. He's not an expensive or infamous courtroom shark, but he seems to really care about me.

"Okay." I nod.

He places a hand on my shoulder. "Don't worry, Kat. Just be honest. The truth is always the best defense."

16

1 DAY AFTER

TUCKER

"I already told you everything I know," I say as soon as I walk into the dining room. The detectives have really set up camp today, bringing in boxes of files and even a computer monitor. "This is a waste of time," I say. But still, I take the seat across from Carney and Johnson, because my lawyer said cooperation will keep them from suspecting me.

"Just a few more questions," Johnson says cheerfully. "My team is just beginning to filter through the thousands of text messages sent between members of this house in the last three months. But a few of yours already stand out."

She picks up a remote and turns to the monitor.

What's going on?

"Do these look familiar?" Johnson asks. She clicks through a series of screenshots from iMessage: *"I want your body." "Waiting for you in the bathtub." "Goodnight baby <3."* The contact is cropped out. But I know who I sent them to. Syd hated me calling her any traditional pet names like baby or sweetie—we had our own ironic nicknames for each other—Squid (her, because it sounds like

Syd) and Sparky (me, who knows why). So anyway, if I was calling someone "baby," it wasn't her. I feel like the floor has dropped out beneath me.

"What's interesting about these texts," Detective Johnson says, her voice deceptively casual and light, "is that they weren't sent to your girlfriend, were they?"

She's not really asking for me to answer, so I keep my mouth shut.

"No"—the detective clicks a button and an uncropped image pops up, with Gwen's contact appearing at the top of the screen—"they were sent to your dead girlfriend's best friend, whom you seem to have been dating as well."

My lawyer gasps, then coughs to cover it. I guess this is the kinda thing he wanted me to warn him about yesterday. Too late now.

The detective punches the clicker, and I stare at the texts on the screen, filled with eggplant emojis and winking faces.

A sour taste floods my mouth. I want to spit, but I can't exactly do that inside, in front of the cops.

"You didn't really think you could just delete these, did you?" Detective Johnson asks. "Do you know how long it took us to get a warrant for your cell phone provider? Three hours."

I swallow. My throat feels like sandpaper.

"You may be used to getting away with all sorts of bullshit, Mr. Campbell. But I'm not Mr. Rooney, and this isn't high school high jinks. I'm a detective at the LAPD, and you're a murder suspect. You're out of your depth."

My lawyer tries to hand me another note, but I keep my eyes on Detective Johnson. I set my teeth and lift my chin higher. I don't want her to see me flinch. I remember what my dad taught me: speak with confidence, and people will believe anything you say.

"I didn't delete those texts because of you guys," I say. "After that weird post went up on our TikTok, I had to assume someone might be hacking us. Do you realize what would happen if *TMZ* had these? *That's* what I was worried about." I'm actually pretty impressed with myself that I was able to pull that out of my ass.

"*TMZ,* that's what you were concerned about in the hours after your girlfriend was found dead?" Johnson stares me down.

"Yeah," I say. "I mean, of course that's not the only thing I was thinking about; I was quite upset. But still, I'm a professional, and I have to think about my brand. My persona is bro-y, guys' guy with a heart of gold. Sure, I make douchey jokes that appeal to males fifteen to twenty-nine. But I also dutifully filmed Sydney's videos and surprised her with gifts she posted all over her Insta story. I mean, that's catnip to females fifteen to thirty-four." I leave out the small detail that these gifts were actually picked out by my manager and were usually advertisements for sponsors. "My relationship with Syd was part of my brand," I continue. "If the public found out I was cheating on her, I'd no longer be rough around the edges but sweet deep down. I'd just be an asshole. And no one wants that guy to hawk their products, ya know?"

Detective Johnson blinks. I don't think this is where she imagined this conversation going.

"In fact, are you guys gonna tell the press about these texts, because, like, I want to help you out in this investigation any way I can, but if you put me on blast like that, well, that would be less than chill. Would kinda make it hard for me to work with you."

"What the heck did you just say?" Detective Carney scratches his bald spot.

"My client wants to know, are you going to tell the press about the correspondence between him and Ms. Riley?" my lawyer says.

"We don't release details about ongoing investigations," Johnson says to my lawyer, then turns back to me. "But really, that should be the least of your concerns."

I keep my poker face. "How so?"

"Well, here's how I see it." She flips open a file. "Tucker, you have . . . let's see, twenty million TikTok followers?"

"Twenty-one mil," I say. "Leveled up last week."

"How impressive," she says. But her voice doesn't sound sincere. "I guess I'm just trying to figure out . . . how?"

"Whatcha mean?"

"Well, you aren't a comedian, or a singer. You dance a bit . . . but nothing that would get you past round one of *Dancing with the Stars*."

Dancing with the Stars, *that's what this lady thinks is cool?*

"But mostly in your videos you just kind of mouth along to other people's words. So I guess I don't understand, what's your talent? What's so special about you? What's the reason that you're famous?"

"Uh, not to sound like a dick, but most people in this house don't exactly have a 'reason' "—I make air quotes—"that they're famous. And my 'talent' is being Tucker Campbell," I say, which, honestly, if they weren't like, old, I wouldn't even have to explain. *What's so special about me?* I stand up and lift my T-shirt with one hand to show off my eight-pack. "I mean, *this* is why I have twenty mil followers. I don't know what else to tell you."

Detective Johnson is avoiding looking at me, but I'm pretty sure I see a hint of rosiness on her cheeks. I can't tell if she's angry or blushing. She turns to my lawyer: "Can you ask your client to please take this seriously?"

My lawyer grabs me by my collar and shoves me back down into my chair. "Keep your clothes on, Tucker," he grumbles.

"They asked." I shrug innocently. But I do wonder if maybe I overshot the line between confident and cocky for a second there.

Johnson glares at me. "Well, as *interesting* as that justification for your celebrity is, I'd like to present another theory. I think that when it comes down to it, you weren't so much famous as you were dating someone famous. I mean, you had only just started your account when you moved into the house, hadn't you? That's a bit unusual, to be picked for a house like this when you had, what, a few hundred followers and less than a dozen posted videos?"

She keeps glancing down to the folder in front of her. I lean forward to see what's in it, and sure enough, it looks like she has a printout of the *New York Times* article from a few weeks ago. I recognize the headline and the picture, even upside down. Of course, that's how she knows my follower count—from an old article. I bet this lady's never been on TikTok in her life. *Good luck with this case.*

"And then earlier this summer, Sydney starts to post videos with you for her millions of followers, and your own follower count skyrockets. Isn't that right?"

I always hated the way that article made me sound. Every other interview I'd done before with blogs and stuff, they just kind of posted whatever I told them, or what my publicist emailed. But the *Times* did a whole bunch of other things, including graphing my follower count over time. And just like this lady is saying, revealed how my account fluctuated based on how much Sydney posted about me.

I was so hyped for the article before it came out. My dad might not really get what TikTok is, but the *New York Times*, he knows that shit. Maggie Haberman is, like, his Addison Rae; David Brooks is his Gwen Riley. But then when the article came out, I didn't even wanna send it to him. It made me look like a gold-digging beta dude.

But of course, I didn't have to send the link for my family to see it. It was everywhere. Someone even sent the article in the group chat for my brother Ian's frat at USC. I don't exactly like them knowing me as "the dude who dates that famous TikTok girl."

"You said that your relationship was 'part' of your brand?" Johnson says. "I think it was all of it. From these numbers, I'd say your relationship with Sydney was the only reason you were famous at all."

I shrug indifferently. Inside I'm starting to think my whole *TMZ* excuse for deleting the texts may have done more harm than good.

"Maybe that's why, instead of breaking up with her for Gwen, you cheated on her. You wanted to be with Gwen, but you felt trapped by Sydney. How could you break up with her? You'd lose everything. She was the famous one, the princess, the reason your followers kept growing by the millions. She was the one with the trustee father who was going to get you into USC."

The other detective, Carney, joins in. "No way you'd get in on your own—straight Cs, a far cry from your valedictorian brother, Ian."

How do they know my brother's name? And how'd they get my high school transcript?

Detective Johnson shakes her head pityingly. "And for being so aesthetically fit, you certainly aren't the lacrosse star your brother Jeremy is. I mean, you didn't even make the team last year, so you weren't getting into college that way."

I clench my fist under the table. They want a reaction out of me. I struggle not to give them one.

"No, before TikTok, you were well on your way to becoming a nobody. A disappointment. But then you weren't. Because of this house, all of a sudden you were a star. Because of this house, you were making more at seventeen than Ian will with that business major. Because of this house, the kids on that dumb lacrosse team that cut you, they were jealous of you. Because of this house, you became *somebody*."

I blow hot air through my nostrils. "What's your point?"

"Here's what I think." Detective Johnson leans forward conspiratorially. I can see down her shirt a little bit. "I think Sydney did find out. I think she found out that you were cheating on her with her best friend, and she couldn't bear to look at you. So she ran off to her parents' house. And after a few days of licking her wounds, she stopped being sad. No, now she's angry. And she thought, *Hey, my parents pay for this house, why am I the one who had to leave?* So she comes back to confront you, to kick you out of your home, to kick you out of the whole lifestyle you built here, which you've grown quite accustomed to. You're drunk from celebrating your favorite singer visiting you, and you've been enjoying life in this house, enjoying the life Sydney gave you, without the inconvenience of dealing with Sydney herself. And now all of a sudden she's back—screaming and crying and being a total bitch. Maybe she's even the one who gets physical first. She's punching you and scratching you. Making your blood boil. So you reach for the gun, and in a single angry, drunken second, you pull the trigger, and you solve your problem.

"You get rid of Sydney, and now you can sleep with whoever you want whenever you want, and more important, you get to keep your spot in the Lit Lair."

I just stare at them for a second, trying to figure out if they're for real with this. "You think I killed Syd so that I didn't lose my place in the house?" I can't help but laugh at this. I mean, I know we all sometimes take TikTok drama a bit too far, but come *on*, murder over a spot in the Lit Lair? That's ludicrous.

But the detective doesn't laugh with me. Her mouth stays pressed in a thin, hard line. Then she says, "I think you didn't want to be with her. But you also didn't want to give up your place here. So you found a solution."

"There are just . . . so many things wrong with that incredibly fucked-up theory." I tug at fistfuls of my hair. "But let's start with the simple fact that Syd didn't have the power to kick me out. She didn't control who could or could not live in the house."

The detectives share a look. For the first time since I walked into the room, it seems like I know more than they do.

"Oh? You didn't know that?" I mock. "You had no problem reading all my texts but didn't manage to look at basic paperwork?"

"We've seen the mortgage agreement," Johnson says. "It's Sydney's parents who signed it."

I fold my arms over my chest and lean back in my chair. "I'm not talking about the mortgage agreement."

* * *

"I know it's in here somewhere," Gwen says as she roots around her room. The place is an absolute mess, just an explosion of designer labels and tissue paper.

She opens and closes the drawers of her "desk," which I doubt she's ever used for anything but doing her makeup in the giant mirror she's hung above it.

She sits down on the carpet and starts to remove things from the bottom drawer: a pencil sharpener made by Tiffany and Co., although there is not a pencil in sight; a single Gucci flip-flop; a book about the pets of the Kardashian family; a Ziploc bag full of loose AirPods, mostly lefts; a key chain made to look like a flask; a flask made to look like a bracelet; three different sizes of jade rollers; and a $2,000 designer fabric pouch sewn to look like a brown paper bag.

"Ah!" Gwen pulls a piece of notebook paper from the bottom. "Ta-da!" She waves the paper in triumph. "Here it is."

Detective Carney grabs the paper impatiently. It says "LIT LAIR CONTRACT" in large letters across the top.

"We made this at our first house meeting, after Sydney threatened to kick Cami out over that whole Parker fiasco," Gwen explains.

Carney examines the document with a furrowed brow, turning it over. "Is this signed in glitter?"

"Glitter gel pen," Gwen explains. "Pink, of course." She smiles. "But it's all very official and legally binding. We even had it notarized."

"I can see that." Carney scratches his mustache.

"Right, anyway," I say. "As you can see, it's right there in black

160

and white, or, uh, pink and *glitter*, I guess. Sydney didn't have the power to kick anyone out. It's majority rule for anyone to move out or in. Her parents may own the house, but she didn't have any sort of power over us. We were all equals."

Carney hands the contract to a cop waiting in the doorway, who shoves it into a plastic bag labeled EVIDENCE. "That's all we need from you for now, Mr. Campbell."

They file out of the room, giving no indication as to whether this eased their suspicion of me. But my interview is over now, at least, so that's something.

Head ducked down, I walk toward the door.

"Hey, Tuck, where you going?" Gwen calls after me.

But there's no way I'm hanging out in her room. Not during the day. Not with cops crawling around, waiting for me to incriminate myself further.

17

2 DAYS AFTER

BEAU

"Ms. Riley told us she heard a female scream, and then saw you and Ms. Powell coming in the window?" Carney reads from his notes.

"Yeah," I say. "We were coming down from the roof." I turn to my lawyer—he said to tell the police everything I know—but still, I worry about getting others in trouble. But I owe it to Sydney to tell the truth about what I witnessed that night. "We saw Gwen leaving Sydney's room."

I think back to that night. Trying to remember anything else. Gwen did seem kind of skittish. Was it possible she'd been fighting with Sydney right before we saw her? By then, was Sydney already back? Was Sydney already dead?

But Carney doesn't ask more about Gwen. Instead he says, "What exactly were you doing on the roof?"

"I don't know." I shrug. "Just hanging out."

"'Just hanging out'?" Johnson repeats. She clicks her tongue. "On the roof. You have this whole mansion to kick back in"—she gestures to a miniature model of the house and grounds they've

162

brought with them, which sits on the table—"and you decide to chill on the roof. Why?"

"I don't know," I say again. The truth is, we started hanging out on the roof so we could smoke without setting off the smoke alarm. And then going up there became a habit, even on nights we weren't smoking. But I'm not about to tell the police that. Marijuana is still illegal if you're under twenty-one. And we're, like, role models to little kids. I wouldn't want that getting out.

"There seems to be a lot you don't know," Johnson says. "Let's see if you know anything about this." She picks up a remote and turns on the TV screen. "There are four security cameras that surround this house." She clicks a button, and four windows open up on the screen. "Unfortunately for us, and conveniently for whoever killed Ms. Reynolds, none have a visual in the pool. But there is a camera on every door of the house, showing every single person entering and exiting the building."

She clicks one of the windows, labeled *Front Gate Cam*. "My team has scanned the footage from the twenty-four hours before the body was found." She fast-forwards past morning deliveries and Drake and his team coming and going. "And then, close to three a.m. . . ." She hits Play.

I watch as an SUV pulls up to the gate. The footage is grainy, shot through the dark. But a girl is still quite visible through the windshield. She's wearing a blue baseball cap, but even with the shadow on her face and the rough footage, her high cheekbones are distinct. She gets out of the car and types in the gate code, shielding her face from the rain. As the iron gates swing open, she looks up, right at the camera.

They pause the footage. It's Sydney. Undeniably.

Johnson clicks over to *Garage Cam* and scrubs forward a few more seconds. We all watch as the SUV pulls into the four-car garage and the door closes safely behind.

"And then: nothing," Johnson says.

"What?" I ask. "There's a camera on the back door." If Sydney went into the house that night, she had to come out. And if the person who hurt her was a member of the house, they would've had to as well. That should be on tape.

"You're right, there is a camera on that back door," Johnson says, clicking over. "But after the five residents enter the house around midnight"—she fast-forwards, and the screen goes from dark to light—"there is nothing until Ms. de Ávila exits the house the next morning, shortly before she finds the body."

What? How?

"There is nothing on any of the tapes that shows Ms. Reynolds walking back outside," Carney says. "Which means either she teleported to the pool or—"

"Someone messed with these cameras," Johnson says. "Cameras that"—she turns back to the model of the house—"are located here, here, here, and here." She presses thumbtacks one by one into the roof of the house. *Oh, shit.* "So I'll ask you again, what exactly were you doing on the roof that night?"

"What, you think I had something to do with this?" I gesture toward the footage.

"Well, you're certainly capable of it," Carney says. He slides a paper across the table. It's my transcript from before I left high school.

"Computer Science 101, A-plus," he recites. "Computer Science 102, A-minus, but hey, we all have off days, and you certainly recovered, because junior year it's Advanced Placement

Computer Science, A-plus. And then that summer your job was making websites."

"Shall we go on?" Johnson asks.

"What, do you think because I know some Java and HTML that I was able to hack security cameras?" I laugh, but they don't. "Jeez, you guys don't understand CS, do you? What, do you think anyone who knows some code can 'hack into the mainframe'?"

Carney leans forward. "Wait, can you do that?"

"Yeah, sure. Just let me travel back in time to 1985, and I'll hack into an IBM computer the size of this house."

"So that's a no on the mainframe?" my lawyer says. He gestures with his pen toward the recording device on the table. "For the record, you want to avoid sarcasm. This will be transcribed, and your tone will be lost."

I fall back into my chair. I can't believe this is what we're talking about. I look from my lawyer to Johnson and Carney. Carney has written *"IBM?"* in the margin of my high school transcript. Jeez, this is a case in a TikTok house—is this really what these guys know about technology?

"Beau?" my lawyer prompts.

"Yeah, that's a no on the mainframe," I mumble.

I have very little faith these cops are going to solve this case.

18

2 DAYS AFTER

CAMI

I slam my bedroom door behind me. For the last three hours the police have been questioning me about the Parker deal. *What happened? Why didn't you get it? Why did they pick her?*

It's my latest failure, another disappointment to add to a long string of them, and I'd prefer to forget about it. Instead I had to dissect it during a freaking police interrogation.

I pace across my room, my mind still reeling. God, this house is warm, and this stupid, scratchy sweater feels like it's choking me. I tear it over my head and throw it to the floor.

Why didn't you get it? Detective Carney asked repeatedly.

I don't know! I wanted to scream. *I sent them videos of three original dances I'd choreographed to three original songs I'd written. She sent them three videos she'd already posted earlier in the summer, one of which was to a dance I* had *choreographed for her.*

But I didn't say that. I told them what my reps told me: They went in a different direction. I wasn't the right "look" for this campaign.

The right "look." I know what that means. It's one of my least favorite phrases. They had their cookie cutter in mind. And I simply did not fit.

Sometimes people ask why I want this all so badly, the record deals, the followers, the fame. I always say it's probably for the same reason as anyone who aspires to sing or act or dance or create in any medium: I want to be seen, to be known. I want to create work that will connect with people, to have another human being relate to the part of myself I put in my art. Really, all I want is to feel less alone.

But when I lose out on opportunities because the "me" I'm sharing doesn't fit with a preconceived image of how people want a woman to look or behave, it reminds me that the business of making stars is still very much a business. And that for all the talk about the world connecting through technology, fame, on social media or otherwise, is not some come-as-you-are, warts-and-all utopia. That what the star machine wants to do is to take another young woman and package her, brand her, commodify her, and *consume* her.

I catch my reflection in my full-length mirror and stop pacing. I look terrible. My skin is red and blotchy from stress. And my old ratty bra is pinching my skin. My hair is askew; my eyes are frantic. I stare at myself, my chest rising and falling with my labored breath.

I blink and I am in front of another mirror. Back in New York, at the ballet studio, standing at the barre.

This is too tight, my ballet teacher says, pointing to my leo. *It's digging into your skin.*

Already outgrown another? the assistant teacher scoffs.

And then another day, as I lace up my pointe shoes, my

teacher staring at where my stomach rolled from my bending over: *Cami, watch the pastries, will you?*

And then another, watching myself do pliés in the mirror, a head taller than the petite girls that lined the barre beside me.

Cami is too tall for Giselle, one teacher says.

Cami is too wide *for Giselle,* replies the other.

Now I look at the mirror and my younger self looks back, pain in her eyes. Then, with a loud crack, the mirror shatters.

I blink. And I see the heavy brass paperweight in my hand, which, last I remember, was still sitting on my desk. And I see the blood on my hand, from when it cut on impact. And I see my mirror, here in the Lit Lair house, which I have just smashed into hundreds of jagged shards.

I step back, dropping the paperweight. Blood drips from my hand onto the white carpet. I swallow and look at my fractured reflection, my features distorted and my expression bewildered.

And for not the first time, I look at what I've done, and I'm terrified of myself. Of what I am capable of doing.

19

3 DAYS AFTER

GWEN

It takes me a really long time to decide what to wear to the funeral. I've already sold half my closet on Depop, and besides that, I don't have any sad clothes. My closet is full of bright bikinis, tiny crop tops, and flippy miniskirts.

Black and drab is just *not* my style.

In the end I borrow a simple little black dress from my mom. I examine myself in the mirror. I look pale. Maybe in contrast to the dress. Or maybe because I haven't been down to my usual tanning chair by the pool since . . . well, since the pool deck became a place of nightmares.

My eyes dart away from the glass. At the moment I don't like my reflection. I grab the umbrella and sleek black purse I laid on my bed and rush out of the room.

Cami, always the first one ready, is waiting at the bottom of the stairs, tapping her black Louboutins. She's wearing a black midi dress that hugs her curves and red lipstick that matches the bottom of her shoes. But the best part of her outfit is her hat— a pillbox with one of those black mesh veils that covers half her face. Like an old movie star or Cruella de Vil would wear. *God, she looks incredible.*

"Gwen," she snaps, "what are you looking at?"

"Just, I don't know, I like your hat," I say. "Do you think this dress looks okay, because it's my mom's and . . ."

"You're fine. Kitty-Kat looks like she's going to a freaking picnic."

"Hey!" Kat complains, looking down at her black-and-white-floral sundress. "This is all I have in black."

I can't help but laugh. Cami isn't wrong. Kat looks like she's headed to the beach, not the cemetery.

But then Cami turns her criticism laser vision on me. "Why do you have an umbrella?"

"Oh, you know," I say. "You always see that in movies. People at funerals have black umbrellas."

Cami stares at me through her veil. "Gwen . . . we live in LA . . . where there's a drought . . . and there's not a cloud in the sky."

"Yeah, but you bring an umbrella to a funeral," I explain. "Even if it's not raining." I look around. "Right?"

But no one backs me up. Instead they laugh at me. Even sweet Kat. Ugh, I knew I shouldn't have laughed at her dress.

A horn honks as a black coach van pulls up the driveway. The police are letting us all have a few hours away from the house and the constant questions, for the funeral and the luncheon. As we load into the van, it feels a bit like a field trip or something. Or it would if the atmosphere wasn't so sad.

Despite Cami's repeated texts to the group chat to hurry up, the boys rush out of the house just before we have to leave. Tucker gets in last and takes the only seat left, next to me. He looks so handsome in his suit. And his hair is still a little wet from the shower, so I can really smell his shampoo. I like it. It smells like his pillows. It smells like *him*.

"Hi," I say quietly. I bump the side of my knee against his. A movement small enough I'm sure no one else will see.

"Hey," he replies. He doesn't look at me, keeping his eyes straight forward, but the edges of his lips turn up into a slight smile.

His hand finds mine by the crease where our seats meet. He squeezes my hand, and then holds it, keeping his arm positioned so that no one else can see. My heartbeat speeds up. Tucker is so sparing with public affection that any little gesture like this always sends me into a sort of tizzy. I try not to react too visibly.

The van slows to a crawl as we approach the wrought-iron gate to the cemetery, clogged with the cars of fellow mourners. I twist the T ring on my free hand and try to keep my tears from spilling over.

In the last few days I've tried to wrap my head around the fact that Sydney is gone. But it turns out nothing could've prepared me for this. Pulling up to a cemetery, seeing the bright white headstones dotting the hills of green grass, and knowing that one of my friends is about to be placed in the ground, I shiver, even though it's stifling hot in this van.

Something slams against the window, and I startle. It's a photographer shoving his camera up at me. A flash goes off in my face. Tucker drops my hand like it's a limp fish.

More photographers swarm the car, pointing professional lenses at the tinted windows. Behind them even more people, including some kids who can't be more than twelve years old, film with their cell phones.

"What are they doing?" asks Beau.

"Being vultures," Cami says with disgust. "Just like they always are. But this time more literally."

"Should we have brought security?" I ask. We sometimes hire a guard or two, for events with big crowds where our fans might get into a frenzy. It didn't occur to me that a funeral might be one.

"There are police at the gate," says Cami.

And sure enough, when we finally are able to ease our way through the entrance to the cemetery, the sea of people is held back by the police. I watch over my shoulder as some of them argue with the officers at the gate. Others reposition themselves along the fence, leaning through the wrought-iron slats and switching to even longer lenses. My stomach churns. I really hope I don't throw up all over my shoes.

As soon as the driver puts the van in park, Tucker slides open the door and hops out without looking back. Everyone else gets out quickly, too. Except for me. I'm frozen in my seat.

Cami leans her head back into the car. "You coming?" she asks impatiently. She taps her nails on the car door. But she waits for me, even as everyone else walks off.

"Yeah," I say. I pick up my umbrella, take a deep breath, and join the guests at Sydney Reynolds's funeral. Praying that I appear to be the model best friend, even though I fell so short of that during her life.

Someone hands me a pamphlet with Sydney's photo on it. It's a headshot her mom had taken for her last year, during their family's Christmas card shoot. She's wearing this big, frilly blouse, and her "smile" is sort of forced and horizontal, nothing like her beaming natural smile. I can't help but be a little amused. There are literally thousands of photographs of Sydney on the internet, and her mother managed to choose one Syd would hate. I can just imagine Sydney's cackling laughter if she were here to see this. The thought makes it feel a little like she is.

There are dozens of people milling about near the plot of land that will be Sydney's final resting place. Most of them are dressed quite stylishly in black. Madison Reed from Clout 9 is wearing bright pink and telling anyone who asks, and many who don't, that she is just celebrating Sydney's life. As if she ever celebrated Sydney when she was alive. More likely, she'd rooted against Sydney at every turn, constantly jealous of our house's success.

I thought I knew most of the people Sydney knew. In fact, I didn't think there was anyone she was friends with that wasn't better friends with me. Yet there are so many faces I can't put a name to, or that I've never seen before in my life. I wonder if this is because dying makes you, well, more popular. Or because maybe Sydney had some secrets, too.

Tucker is loitering near the florist who is handing out long-stemmed red roses for people to lay on Sydney's grave. I avoid his eyes as I grab a whole bundle of flowers.

I turn to Cami. "Hey, can you get me?" I ask. I unlock my phone with my free hand and open TikTok.

"What?"

"You know, get me?" I hand her the phone. "As I set down the flowers. I think it would be great for my next post."

Cami stares down at the phone, not saying anything. But Tucker interrupts. "Don't you think it's in poor taste, Gwen? To film a TikTok at a funeral?"

"It's not like I'm doing the freaking Renegade, Tucker. This is a tasteful video. And if you think about it, this is what she would've wanted. Her mantra was 'If you don't post about it, it's like it didn't even happen.' If it's how she documented her life, don't you think we should document her memory that way too? My fans—*her* fans—can't be here today. But Syd touched their lives. They deserve some closure, too, and I think my video will help with that."

Cami looks at me, incredulous. "Do you really believe that, or are you just worried you've been content-light since Sydney died and you'll lose your sponsors?"

Well, that, too, I think. *In fact, I've already lost them and am trying to get them back, not that I'd ever admit that to you, oh-so-perfect Cami.*

Eventually Cami agrees to take a video of me laying a bundle of roses on Sydney's coffin. But when I think the angle is unflattering, she refuses to film another take, saying that people are staring. So I'm stuck just trying to edit it.

I'm still trying to pick a filter when Cami nudges my arm. "Incoming."

I look up to see Sydney's parents and Brooklyn walking toward us. They move slowly through the crowd, as a sort of unit, with Mrs. Reynolds leaning heavily on Mr. Reynolds's arm and Brooklyn following close behind, alone, missing her other half. As they pass, eyes look up from pamphlets and conversations fade to a hush. But they don't stop to talk to anyone, making a clear path toward us.

Shit. I try to get rid of my phone before they get here but panic as I realize I don't have pockets and I brought a dumb tiny purse that can't fit my phone. I end up stuffing it in my bra.

"Tucker!" Mrs. Reynolds says as they approach. She opens her arms and waves him into a big hug. "I'm so glad you're here. You were so special to her," she says into his shoulder.

I step forward a bit, ready to give the next hug. But Mrs. Reynolds avoids my eyes, her focus still on Tucker.

"You know, you were always like family to us." She makes a little squeaking sound. "And I really thought that one day you would be, officially." Tears well in her eyes.

"Oh, Mrs. Reynolds, here." I pull a package of tissues out of my little purse and hold them out to her.

She turns on me with such venom in her eyes, you'd think I was trying to hand her a snake or something. "The nerve of you lot, coming here." If looks could kill, they'd need to dig another grave for me.

Mr. Reynolds puts his body between us, perhaps to defuse the situation. He claps a hand on Tucker's shoulder. "Son, why don't you come stand up in the front with us?"

He doesn't make the same offer to me. He doesn't even really look at me.

So much for the three musketeers, I think. Before, I was "like family" too. But now it's Tucker standing up there with them and the nondenominational pastor. And I'm left out in the cold, treated like, well, like a *suspect.* I knew I was one to the police. But really, I never thought the Reynoldses would think I could possibly hurt Syd. I mean, they've known me since I was twelve years old. My family lived on their property for three years. Mrs. Reynolds gave me a tampon when I got my first period, during a sleepover. And when I was in eighth grade, Mr. Reynolds helped me flush my carnival goldfish, Goldie Hawn, after I accidentally shook her to death two hours after winning her. Okay, well, maybe that last one is a bad example for these purposes. But Goldie was a fish, not a person. And it was an accident. Can these people who helped raise me really think I'd be capable of hurting a person? Of hurting their daughter and my best friend?

The pastor steps on the little makeshift stage set up near the headstone. He reads some prayers and talks about Sydney in a way I barely recognize. He talks about a young woman who was a model citizen, a good Christian girl who volunteered with sick children and never got in trouble. A "sweet little angel."

Syd was a lot of things, but she wasn't an angel. She was fierce and messy and rebellious, and when she wanted to be, quite mean. But she also loved deeply and loyally. The real Syd did volunteer, but only because she had so many speeding tickets she had to do community service, and she complained every time she had to go. She was not well-behaved and partied a lot. But she was the type of friend who held back your hair for you while you were too drunk, even though she was probably almost as drunk as you were. And although she could be mean, she often reserved her cruelest statements for people who were her friends' enemies or bullies. Like once, back in school, she interrupted a bunch of guys picking on a freshman by saying, "I don't know how you can say those things to him when you guys are the ugly ones." She was far from picture perfect, but she had a good heart. I wish they would say that about her. That would be more honest. And I think it would honor her memory more.

The pastor wraps up his speech by saying Sydney will live forever in our hearts. Which is strange to me, because it kind of implies we will live forever. "And now," the pastor says, "Brooklyn Reynolds will read one of her sister's favorite poems."

All eyes turn to the family, where Tucker is standing holding hands with both Mrs. Reynolds and Brooklyn. Brooklyn hugs him, and then he takes a pink-cased iPhone out of his pocket and hands it to her. *Oh Tucker, what a gentleman, holding the phone of a girl without pockets.* I resist the urge to roll my eyes.

Brooklyn teeters across the platform in her black stilettos. Although she looks like her sister, she has none of Sydney's bravado or spunk. She looks like a baby bird with a broken wing.

She steps up to the mic. "Hi," she says weakly. She takes a shaky breath and begins to read off her phone, "Stop all the clocks . . ."

Just then her phone pings with an alert, ricocheting through the microphone speakers. Brooklyn startles at the sound.

Another ringtone goes off in the crowd, and then another. And then another, randomly and increasingly, like popcorn. *What the hell?* Who doesn't silence their phone these days? Especially at a funeral.

And then my own phone goes off, vibrating against my chest and *ringing.* Something weird must be going on; I haven't had my sound on since I bought this phone.

A slight murmur spreads through the crowd as everyone unzips bags or ruffles through pockets to find and silence their phones.

Up on the podium, Mrs. Reynolds leans over to look at her husband's phone. A look of shock crosses her face for just a second. Then she regains her composure, as if remembering she's on a stage. The movement is so subtle, I may be the only one who sees when she drops Tucker's hand like it's suddenly burned her.

Okay, screw it, I need to see what's going on. I dig my phone out of my bra, a motion I'm sure is unladylike. But as soon as I get my phone out, I forget about that. Because I have an alert that someone posted to the Lit Lair account. My chest tightens. With shaking hands, I unlock my own phone and click on TikTok.

I plunge down the sound button and glance up to the podium, where a shaken Brooklyn is struggling to resume her reading of the poem.

I tap the screen to play the video. It's a photograph of Tucker and Sydney hugging, all lovey-dovey. And then the photograph splits down the middle, and there is a picture of me, dressed as a slutty devil last Halloween.

The caption: *The best friend and the boyfriend? Poor Sydney, stabbed in the back even before she was shot in the head.*

My phone slips out of my hand, falling to the bright green cemetery grass.

20

3 DAYS AFTER

TUCKER

I have multiple missed calls from both my parents. The text from my father orders me to skip the luncheon and head straight to my parents' house in Beverly Hills where the lawyers will be waiting for an emergency strategy session.

This is fine by me. The last thing I want is to be in the same room as Sydney's family. And I couldn't eat ballroom chicken right now if my life depended on it. The way my stomach is churning, I doubt I'll be able to eat anything anytime soon.

I check my phone. The Uber is five minutes out from my family's house. I close my eyes and rest my head against the seat. Everything from the TikTok posting to getting in this car was a blur.

As soon as the final bars of "Amazing Grace" played, concluding the last item scheduled on the pamphlet, I bolted. More than a few people tried to talk to me, but I blew right past them. All my mind could process was: *Get the hell out*.

As I raced across the lawn, dodging around mourners and headstones, the sun was bright in my eyes, and I started to sweat bullets under my heavy suit. I tore off my tie before I was even out the cemetery gate.

Then there was the crush of photographers on the street, screaming questions. The flash of a camera in my face. I held my hand up to shield my face and searched for my Uber among the cars with funeral tags.

I saw Gwen as I was getting in the car. She was waving her umbrella, trying to get my attention, but there was no way in hell I was going to stand anywhere near her and let the paparazzi get another shot of us together. *TMZ* was already running the one from the pool house. I guess that's why they waited to post it before. They were waiting for something big. They were waiting for this.

The car jolts to a stop. I open my eyes to see my childhood home, stately on a large green lawn. My mother is standing at the door, her arms crossed. I was so worried about getting out of the press shit show, I forgot about the disdain I'd be facing here. I pop open the car door. Out of the frying pan and into the fire, as they say.

My mother doesn't say anything to me about the video. Instead she just shoos me inside and then looks down the block, checking for photographers. But I can see the disappointment in her eyes.

"Ayy, Tucker." Ian throws an arm around me as soon as I am through the door. "Gwen Riley, really?" He rustles my hair. "Didn't think you had it in you."

"Apparently, he had it in her." Jeremy punches me in the arm.

"Boys, please," says my dad. "Not in front of your mother."

I duck my head and try to fix my hair with my fingers as I

follow my dad into the den, where Tom Fleming and two other lawyers from his firm are waiting.

"Can we deny it?" my father asks.

Fleming shakes his head. "The press has the text messages. The police are saying the leak didn't come from them. But they've confirmed the authenticity."

The TV is on, playing the news. And apparently I am the story of the day. I sink into a leather armchair, the one my dad used to always read thick history books in when I was a kid.

Tom Fleming mutes the television but doesn't turn it off. Different photos of me keep floating past on the screen. God, do I really stick my tongue out in photos that much? Why do I do that? I look like a total douche.

And the worst thought hits me: maybe I look like a total douchebag because I've become one.

I clear my throat and look around at the group of people assembled to try to save me from twenty-five years in prison. "I'm sorry," I croak out.

My mother scoffs loudly from her spot in the doorway, and then turns and heads up the stairs. I hear her bedroom door slam.

"That's all right, Tucker," Tom Fleming says. He pats my knee. "What's past is past. You and I knew this could be a liability, and there was no changing that. Now is the time to move forward and deal with it." It's such a kind way to look at the situation. I wish my parents would say something like that. But I guess Mr. Fleming can see the situation through a rosy lens; after all, my problems mean more billable hours for him.

"The real issue now is perception," Mr. Fleming continues. "As you know, this case isn't just being fought in the court; it's being fought in the press. And if we do well in the court of public opinion, well, then we may be able to stay out of real court. There's a lot of pressure on the police to make an arrest, and we don't want the tides to push them toward arresting you."

I nod along.

"Now, before today your biggest advantage was the support of the family. We even had Mrs. Reynolds, the mother herself, saying she'd be a character witness for you. That goodwill, we have to assume, is gone. Which puts us in a precarious situation."

Shit. Right now I'd like the earth to swallow me where I sit. "What can we do?" I ask.

"Well, we can try to get you back on the good side of the press and of the family—"

"Do we really think that's possible at this point?" asks my dad.

"Well." Tom Fleming sighs. "Maybe not completely, but I think we can improve on our current position. But we need to act, and quickly. Do you understand, son?"

Both my father and my lawyer look at me.

"Just tell me what to do," I say.

3 DAYS AFTER

KAT

The luncheon is held in the ballroom of a fancy hotel in Beverly Hills. I sit at a table with my parents and Beau, near the back. I'm sure the food is good, but I can barely taste it. Sydney's extended family, aunts and cousins and other people I've never met before, give beautiful speeches. When I start to cry, my dad hands me a pack of tissues from his pocket. And I am so grateful that my parents are here.

Before we leave, we stop to sign the visitation book. There are so many names, so many lives that Sydney touched. It's so beautiful and so heartbreaking. I sign my name and set the pen back on the book.

"Are you sure you don't need a ride back to the house?" my mom asks.

I shake my head. "We have a car, plus Dad said you've barely slept. Go to the hotel and rest for a bit. I'll call you if the police ask to talk to me."

"Are you sure?"

"Yeah, Mom." I kiss her on the cheek. Then I give my dad a hug goodbye.

"Good to meet you, Mrs. Powell, Mr. Powell," Beau says, shaking each of their hands.

"Nice to meet you, too, Beau," my dad says.

"Thank you, sir."

As we walk through the lobby, I turn to Beau and say, "You're very proper today."

Beau's neck turns rosy. "I want them to like me."

I smile. My parents will like Beau because he's a kind soul and they will be able to tell that. Not because of formal things like remembering to say sir or ma'am. But still, it's cute he cares so much.

We approach the front doors of the hotel, and through the glass I see that a crowd has gathered. There are dozens of screaming teenagers, and even more grown men all in black, holding expensive cameras, blocking the way between the door and our waiting car. A bellhop tries to push back the crowd, but he's no match for them.

"So I think they know we're in here," Beau says.

"I'd say so." I peer through the windows, trying to see if there's a possible path.

"Move," I hear a girl shout. I turn to see Gwen pushing through the doors and opening her umbrella in the process. "Out of my way!"

Dozens of cameras pop off as she pushes through the crowd, but the umbrella shields her face and ruins any pictures, until she dives into the car. "Gwen may actually turn out to be a genius," I say.

Beau takes my hand. "Ready?"

I nod. We push open the doors and head into the fray.

"Kat!" one of the paparazzi yells. "Did you talk to the Reynolds family? What did they say to you?"

I turn in the general direction of the voice. "I'd just like to say it was a beautiful service and Sydney will be dearly missed. That's my only comment for today. Thanks, guys. Please give us some space to mourn."

But they don't listen.

"Did you know Gwen and Tucker were having an affair?" another paparazzo asks.

I just keep my eyes forward and don't acknowledge that I heard him. I know their tricks. They purposefully use provocative language to try to get us to react, so they can get a more lucrative picture or a more headline-grabbing quote. But I won't give them that.

"Did you kill her, Beau?" one yells.

"Kat, was it you?" another jumps in.

Beau squeezes my hand, and we keep moving forward to the car. I reach for the door.

And someone from the crowd grabs my arm. "I said, *Did you kill her?*"

I turn toward the voice, and a camera flashes in my face. I tear my arm out of his grip.

"Please don't touch me," I say, but my voice is barely audible above the shouting of the crowd. People push closer. I'm starting to feel claustrophobic. I'm starting to feel scared for our safety.

"Just answer the question, bitch," he says, his hand reaching toward me again.

But before he can make contact, Beau lunges toward him. He lands a punch square on the jaw of the photographer. I gasp as the man crumples to the sidewalk.

Beau shakes out his hand. "She said not to touch her."

Thirty other cameras go off all at once. The light is blinding.

21

3 DAYS AFTER

GWEN

"Hey, guys, it's Tucker. I just wanted to make this video to apologize to the Reynolds family as well as to my fans. A lot of you guys are young people who look up to me, and I feel terrible that I let you down. I am deeply sorry for all the pain I've caused. I loved my girlfriend, Sydney Reynolds, very much. This mistake I made is one that I will regret for the rest of my life. My brief flirtation with Gwen meant nothing to me. Sydney was the love of my life, and now we have all lost her, so abruptly and so young. And it really clarified things for me. The difference between a teenage mistake and what could've been a lifetime of love, if we weren't all robbed of such a beautiful soul. I know I can never make up for my indiscretion, but I hope to do whatever I can to be there for the Reynolds family as they go through this, and to help bring justice to whatever monster committed this horrible crime."

I watch the video only seconds after it posts.

When it went up, I was lying in bed, still in my black dress from the funeral plus an oversized sweatshirt, trying to fall asleep midafternoon just to escape this day. The luncheon had been a total nightmare: sitting with random relatives of Sydney's who apparently didn't have TikTok and weren't yet in the know, I picked at an overdressed, soggy salad while everyone else in the room gossiped about me. I just want this day to be over. Lying in bed, I heard my phone ding and reached for it with zombielike slowness. But five seconds into Tucker's little speech, I was sitting bolt upright in my bed, adrenaline running through my veins.

Unable to believe my eyes and ears, I watch it once more.

Suddenly I am very awake. Heart slamming against my chest, I hop off the bed and out my door.

"Tucker *fucking* Campbell!!" I yell as I tear down the hall. He made the video in his room, so I know he's fucking here. My stockinged feet slip on the polished wood of the hallway, and I almost fall on my butt.

Tucker doesn't yell anything back, but when I arrive at his room, he's standing in the doorway.

"What the hell was that?" I push past him into his room. I pace around the cluttered space, stepping over crumpled beer cans and dirty clothes. "A *brief flirtation*? An *indiscretion*? Are you kidding me? You said you loved me!"

"Well, actually"—he avoids my eyes, digging the toe of his sneaker into the carpet—"I only ever said I 'loved hanging out with you.' I was very careful about that."

"What?" The room is spinning. I press my palm against my forehead. "No, I . . . you definitely . . ." I struggle to remember.

But now that he says this, I realize I can't pinpoint an exact place or time when he said those words. I mean, he definitely has said it, right? Or is it possible I just assumed, after everything that happened between us, everything we did . . . "I thought you loved me," I say. "I did so many terrible things because I thought you loved me."

My mind flashes to all the times we kissed, all the times we snuck around, secret make-outs and hiding spots, sweet memories turning rotten as their true nature comes to light.

"What terrible things?" I hear him ask, but it sounds like he is far away.

"That's why you didn't want to go public with our relationship. To you it wasn't even a relationship. . . ." My face feels hot. Out of the corner of my eye, I see the Lakers sweatshirt I gave him hanging in the closet. I walk over and tug it down, throwing it onto the floor. This feels good, powerful, so I grab a whole row of hanging items and throw them down as well. I struggle to pull down the bar, too, but it's up there pretty good.

"What terrible things, Gwen?" he asks again.

I walk over to his tall stack of plastic drawers and push it over, knocking all sorts of crap out onto the floor—including a half-empty package of rolling papers and what appears to be Tucker's passport. My vision starts to blur with tears. I kick at the pile. Tucker stands by, watching me with wide eyes.

"I just hope you're happy," I say, "because after this, we're done. For good."

I barrel out of his room, tears running down my cheeks. I hear him call after me, his footsteps behind me. But I don't slow down.

I slam my bedroom door closed and turn the lock. I tear

through the room. "Alexa," I bark, "play *Music About Crappy Boys*. Volume ten."

The speaker plays Olivia Rodrigo's music, loud enough that it drowns out my tears. I fling open the balcony door. The wind whips back my hair, blond tendrils sticking to my wet cheeks. The cool air feels good on my skin. My body feels like it's running ten degrees too hot.

I struggle to yank the silver T ring off my swollen finger. Finally it budges. I hold it in my palm for a second, examining the tarnished silver. And then I wind up and, with all the strength I've built in two years of Pure Barre classes, I chuck it toward the ocean.

I don't see where it lands. I picture it splashing into the water, sinking to the bottom of the Pacific. Even though I know that all those reps with three-pound weights probably didn't make me strong enough to launch it past the rocks, I like the image. Either way, it's gone.

I fling myself onto my king-sized bed and cry. I cry in loud, dramatic sobs that seem to shudder through my whole body. I cry dark mascara tears that fall on fluffy white linens.

Through the music I can barely hear the aggressive knocking. "Gwen, open the door," Tucker commands.

"Never!" I fling a pillow in the general direction of the door. "Go away!!"

If Tucker Campbell ever wants to talk to me again, he can pay $250 for a meet-and-greet, just like everyone else.

22

3 DAYS AFTER

BEAU

"I can't believe you did that," Kat says. She digs through the freezer for an ice pack.

I fall into a seat at the kitchen counter. "That guy was being a total a-hole," I say.

"I know he was." She pushes the freezer closed with her hip. "But I could've handled it myself."

"Yeah, but you didn't have to," I say.

She holds up a bag of frozen Trader Joe's dumplings. "All we had." She examines my hand; it's a bit swollen, and a few of my knuckles have split. She sets the frozen bag on it gently. I wince. She brushes back the hair falling into my face and then rests her hand on my cheek. "Well, thank you," she says. "For doing that."

On the counter both of our phones vibrate like crazy. Kat picks hers up. She smiles. "My mom wants to know if we're okay; my dad texted *I knew there was something I liked about that Beau guy.*"

She rolls her eyes but doesn't stop smiling. But then she scrolls down farther and her face falls.

"What?" I ask.

"Oh, it's nothing. Just some articles. The picture is popping up on the internet."

I reach for my own phone, struggling to swipe up with my left hand. I click on Twitter, the page refreshes, and I see that the photo is not just popping up. It is blanketing my feed. We are everywhere. The image of me punching that asshole and of Kat looking shocked, snapped from every angle, and now published all over the internet. SYD IS DEAD BUT CHIVALRY ISN'T, one headline reads. TIK-TIK BOOM, reads another.

"Well, that one's pretty clever," I say, flipping the phone so she can see.

Her brow furrows. "This is serious, Beau. What if this hurts your case? I feel so bad—this is my fault."

"It's not," he says. "I made a choice. I saw a shitty man and I decided to punch him, okay? So this is on me. And not for nothing, I'd do it again, no hesitation."

"I know you would, but that doesn't change what it means for your case now. I mean, what if that guy presses charges?"

Yeah, that would suck, I think. But I don't say so. I want Kat to know that I don't regret this. Because I really, truly don't.

Kat opens TikTok and scrolls quickly through video after video. Half are about Tucker and Gwen and their leaked sexts, and half are about me throwing the punch. *What, is there nothing else people want to talk about today?* I think. *Or does Kat's FYP know she's a suspect?*

"Violent people do violent things," Nora Caponi's voice says from Kat's phone. Oh great, she's on TikTok, too. "If you are still doubting who may have killed Sydney Reynolds, I'd encourage you to watch this fight video—"

191

Kat scrolls past. "I think it's sweet that Beau defended Kat," a girl says.

"Hey, we have a supporter." I lean forward to see better. Her handle is @hannahbanana23. I've seen her before, I think, but I'm not sure where. The video only has about thirty likes, so I don't think it's that she's TikTok famous.

"Yeah, one supporter," Kat mumbles.

". . . you guys know I've shipped Bat from the beginning, and honestly this doesn't make me think Beau's a killer. This makes me think he is a good person who defends the people he loves. It makes me even more sure neither Kat nor Beau were involved in this murder, and I've been telling my mom—"

Kat scrolls past.

"Wait! Go back," I say. I think I know where I've seen this girl before. "Click on her profile."

She does and hands me the phone. Her bio says she goes to Santa Monica High School. I scroll down and sure enough, a few weeks back, there is a video of "Hannah Banana" in her house, and in the background you can clearly see her mother, Detective Elena Johnson.

"One supporter, but with the ear of someone very important," I say, handing the phone back to Kat.

23

4 DAYS AFTER

TUCKER

"Go away, Tucker," Brooklyn says. This is the second time a girl has said this to me in the last twenty-four hours. "You've done enough." She starts to close the front door of the Reynoldses' house.

"Wait." I shove my arm in the frame before she can shut the door. "I know you probably never want to talk to me again after what happened yesterday, and I understand. But before we never speak again, I just wanted to give you this." I hold out the book I brought. It's fancy and quite old, so I wrapped it in one of my T-shirts to protect it. It took me a while to find it among my things, especially after Gwen turned my room into even more of a disaster than it already was.

Brooklyn pauses, looking at the bundle and biting her lip, just like her sister used to do. Slowly she unfolds the T-shirt to reveal the cover. It's red leather, and there are these little gold flower designs all over it. The book looks nothing like the type of books I've read, with plastic bindings and pictures on the cover of the actors from the movie adaption. This book doesn't look like it belongs in this century. "Syd gave me this for my birthday last year—it's a rare book," I explain. "Poems by W. H. Auden. I guess she got the idea after we watched *Four Weddings and a Funeral*, and I said something about how it didn't suck as much as those other old rom-coms she made me watch."

My mind flashes back to Syd, giddy as I unwrapped the book. She was so excited to get it for me. But I was disappointed as soon as I felt the spine of the book through the paper.

I hate when my mom gets me books as a present. Why would I want one from my girlfriend? Shouldn't she get me an Xbox game or something I'd actually like?

"It's from your favorite movie!" she said as I flipped through the pages.

"*Die Hard*?" I replied, because that's my actual favorite movie. But also, just to be mean.

Now, standing at the doorway of her family home, I shake my head to dispel the memory. "I didn't appreciate the gift when she gave it to me," I tell Brooklyn. "Not like I should've. Anyway, I don't deserve it. So I thought, you know, you should have it. Especially after yesterday, when that poem got interrupted. It was from this book. The same one from the movie. I remembered it."

She examines the book. Her fingers find the page marked with a sticky note, flagging the poem. For a minute she's quiet, just reading the words on the page. Finally she looks up, brushing a tear from her cheek. "Oh, um, Tucker, you don't have to give this to me."

"No. I do," I say. "You and I, we were the ones closest to her. But I let her down. You didn't."

"Wait here," she says. She disappears into the house, book in hand.

I stand on the stoop waiting, praying Mr. or Mrs. Reynolds

doesn't walk by the front door. I'm not sure which of them I'm more scared of.

Brooklyn returns, holding Sydney's old teddy bear, Mr. Fuzzle Butt. "You know, ever since the other morning, I was thinking maybe you should have this. I think she'd have wanted you to keep it. You know, to remember her by."

I think of all the tabloid headlines, the TikTok and Instagram alerts crashing my phone, the lawyers and the police and the paparazzi stalking me. And I know that, teddy bear or not, there is no way in hell I'm going to forget the life—or death—of Sydney Reynolds anytime soon. But I don't say this to Brooklyn. Instead I take the bear, like it's my ticket to freedom. "I can't even tell you how much this means to me," I say.

She wraps her arms around my neck, and I hug her back. She cries softly against my chest and then sort of falls against me, surrendering the entire weight of her frail being to me. I hold her and make shushing sounds, like I would with an animal.

I inhale deeply, breathing her in. Her hair smells just like Syd's did. I guess that's more because they use the same shampoo than it is a twin thing. Still, it's nice to smell again. It's familiar, and I'm surprised how much I like it.

"I'm not saying what you did was okay," she says. "But I forgive you."

"Thank you," I whisper into her ear. A wave of relief washes over me. It worked.

As soon as I'm back to my car, I call my lawyer to tell him about the bear.

24

3 DAYS BEFORE

SYDNEY

"Always remember we're not just friends but family. The Lit Lair is not just another collab house but a collab home," I say to open the house meeting, like I do every time.

I look down at my agenda to see what's next. Today should be a piece of cake, but I want to make sure I go through all the procedures correctly today, so no one can complain later that I didn't do this by the book.

"Did everyone put their phone in the jar?" I look up from my paper to see that Gwen is texting away on her iPhone. I bring over the glass jar. "Come on, you know the rules."

Gwen drops her phone in reluctantly. I turn to set the jar on the table and see Tucker's phone screen light up inside. A new text from his dentist. He really needs to get that cavity filled; they text him appointment reminders, like, every day.

"Okay, so there are a few items on the docket today: we are switching from Spindrift to LaCroix housewide, because Gwen got a sponcon deal—no more other sparkling waters in the backgrounds of her videos, please.

"Clout 9 keeps tagging us in challenges—we're going to keep

ignoring them across the board. We don't want to give them the legitimacy of acknowledging them as rivals. Don't duet them. Don't reply.

"Also, whoever threw a ring light in the pool, please Venmo the slush fund to replace it. Those things aren't waterproof." I pause. "Everyone good with these? Any questions? Objections?"

There are various mumbles and hand gestures indicating approval.

I scratch these items off the list. "And now the last and most important item of the day. The proposal for my twin sister, Brooklyn Reynolds, to move into the house!" I squeal with excitement. "Now, this would mean that we'd convert the formal dining room to another bedroom and move the pool table and other games to the basement."

I flip the page of the house contract. This is the first time we've used this voting procedure since we wrote it.

Step 1: ALL CURRENT MEMBERS OF THE HOUSE MUST BE PRESENT.

Okay, check. Next. "All right, this is the part where we're supposed to have discussion and debate. But I think with this one the correct choice is clear." I smile.

"Is it, though?" asks Cami. She raises an eyebrow.

Ugh, I knew this might be an issue. As soon as I got the call from Parker today, I knew Cami would be trying to get back at me any way she could. But whatever. Brooklyn only needs a simple majority to get voted in. Cami can protest as much as she wants; it will still be five to one in favor.

"I'm not sure either," Gwen says. I look over at her, shocked. "I mean, her numbers are . . . not great. Like, what? Forty thousand followers. And her like ratio is weak even for that count. I'm worried it will bring down our house average. It could hurt our brand."

I huff. Gwen says this as if she hasn't been friends with Brooklyn and me for years. Long before she was famous. When she tagged along on family trips because her mom *worked* for my dad. Now she's Gwen Riley, TikTok Sweetheart, and what? She wants to leave Brooklyn in the dust.

"Yeah . . . I don't think she's right for TikTok fame," says Cami. "She doesn't have the right look, if you know what I mean."

"She looks just like me!" I protest.

"I rest my case." Cami scrunches her nose at me.

Beau raises his hand meekly. Oh, please, I can't imagine Mr. Hippie really cares about the sort of engagement stats Gwen just listed or Cami's clear revenge bullshit about Parker.

"Uh, yeah," Beau begins, "my worry is more about the homogeneity of the house. There are already more dancers than comedians, and this will just exacerbate that. And she's another person from LA, another white girl from a wealthy background. I think if we're going to add a member, we should think about, like, maybe someone from another state or from a different background."

"Yeah, like maybe a dude," Tucker jumps in. I glare at him. I can't *believe* my boyfriend is giving this conversation any sort of credence. "I'm just saying." He holds up his hands innocently. "This would make it five against two, like, that's a whack ratio."

I roll my eyes. "This is ridiculous," I say. "This isn't just anyone! It's Brooklyn, my *twin*. She should get to be part of the house my parents paid for."

"Hey, you're not supposed to lord that over us," Cami says, pointing to the house agreement in my hand. "If you do, then why are we even voting in the first place?"

"I thought this would be a formality! I didn't think there would be actual objections. I mean, she's my twin, for goodness sake. I thought it would be a no-brainer."

"I'm sorry to say it, Syd," says Gwen, "but I think it might be a brainer."

I struggle to contain a roar of frustration. These are the idiots who decide my sister's fate for the next year. Who decide whether or not to launch her to internet stardom. Who hold her dream career in their hands.

"All right, things have gotten a little heated," Kat says. "Everyone, let's calm down and keep it kind." She turns to me. "Perhaps it's best if we wrap up discussion time and move on to voting?"

I nod and she helps me hand out the pens and slips of paper.

I write *YES* in large letters across mine and toss it in the glass bowl. The first one in.

Despite their words of concern, I have to think I can at least count on my boyfriend and best friend to vote my way. Plus, sweet, wouldn't-hurt-a-fly, kind-of-a-pushover Kat won't cross me. And that gets me there, even without Cami, a hopeless case after Parker, and Beau, who, given his words just now, could go either way. It'll be fine. I just need a majority, and four to two works.

I watch as Beau puts his paper in the bowl, the last one in. But his face betrays nothing.

I dump the bowl onto the ottoman and unfurl the first one.

No

All right, that's fine, I knew there would be at least one. And it's girly handwriting, so probably Cami. I unfold the second one.

No

My heartbeat speeds up. But it's fine. It's *fine*. So it'll be four to two, no big deal. I unwrap the next one.

YES

Okay, yes, here we go, time for the good ones, I think. Although I can't help but notice that this one's in my handwriting.

I unwrap the next one.

No

Shit, what do we do if it's a tie? I look over to Kat, who's staring at the floor. What the hell? She acts like she's so nice and then does something she knows will hurt me. And she didn't even raise any concerns. She didn't even give me the chance to defend my sister. That's worse than what Beau did.

I reach for the next one.

No

My heart falls. What the fuck? It's written in glitter pen, so I know it's Gwen. Some best friend she is. Even though it's already over, I open the last one.

No

So that's it, then. Neither my best friend nor my boyfriend care about my sister. Or care about me, for that matter.

I. Cannot. Believe. Them. Rage surges through me. I feel so—so blindsided. For my best friends in the world to betray my twin, my own flesh and blood, like this. It's an unfathomable punch to the gut.

"Arhhh!" I sweep my arm across the ottoman, sending the glass bowl flying onto the floor. It shatters on impact.

Gwen startles. Kat's hand goes to her lips.

"Fuck you guys," I spit. "You all act like you're so nice, taking selfies with your fans, having your little giveaways, but to the people you know in real life, you don't show any of that kindness. In real life, you're just bullies."

I storm out of the room, my sandals crunching over the glass. "Oh, Sydney," says Kat. "Your feet, be careful."

But I don't slow my stride. I'm sick of Kat pretending to be a saint when she's just as self-centered and vain as the rest of them.

I pack quickly, throwing everything I see into my suitcase without using any of the special little pockets. I need to get out of here. To be with my real family. To be with Brooklyn. To get away from these fake friends.

I fly down the stairs, my suitcase banging behind me. Gwen stands at the bottom, a sort of bewildered look on her face. My best friend, the Kylie to my Kendall, the Serena to my Blair. Who has just stabbed me in the back.

"I can't believe you," I spit as I pass.

Gwen follows me outside. "Sydney, I'm sorry—"

"No. Don't even apologize." I throw my suitcase in the back of my SUV. "This is freaking classic, really, I should've expected it. You know, Tucker used to joke that you were going to kill me to wear my skin? That's how obvious it was to everyone: how jealous you were of me and Brooklyn." I slam the trunk closed. "It's so unfair of you to take that out on her now, your little issues that you weren't *actually* a part of my family."

"That's what you think this is about?"

"It's what everything is about with you, Gwen. You were a loser before you met me. You weren't even popular at your lame middle school! But being our friend wasn't enough, was it? It's like you always wanted to be me."

"Oh my God, do you hear yourself?" Gwen stands in front of the driver's-side door, blocking my way. "Talking about the freaking eighth grade. So you were the most popular girl in our high school? Big freaking whoop, Sydney. I'm the most popular girl *in.* *the.* *world.*" She laughs angrily. "Don't you see? I don't want to be you. I already am you. I'm you, but better."

I push around her, slamming the door behind me. I throw the car in reverse and speed out of the drive. I don't even stop to put on my seat belt. I just need to get out of here.

The way she said that, with such hatred behind her eyes: *I already am you.* How psycho is that?

I play it over and over in my head the whole drive to my parents' house. And I realize: I am genuinely afraid of my best friend.

25

5 DAYS AFTER

TUCKER

I wake to the sounds of voices outside my window. I reach over for my phone to check the time—8:13 a.m.—and see a TikTok alert for @LitLair_LA. I brace myself as I launch the app.

It's another unsigned post. A mashup of video clips of high-speed chases: footage of the O.J. chase, *The Blues Brothers*, and the end scene of *Bonnie and Clyde*. The caption: *Sometimes the getaway car doesn't have to go that far :) But the chase sure does get boring when the police just can't keep up :/ So here's a clue to even the odds: Want to know where the murder weapon is? Check the Lit Lair garage, duh!*

I head right to my window and look out to see the squad cars parked in the driveway. Phone still in hand, wearing only boxers, I pad down the stairs to the mudroom, where the door leading to the garage has been left half open.

I stand, barefoot on the tile, and watch silently as half a dozen police officers rifle through our cars. Police dogs sniff up and down the garage.

The police pull bags and boxes from the back seat of Gwen's Jeep, shaking out the brightly colored clothes and shoes onto the garage floor. They flip the seats of Cami's SUV and run their hands across the carpet of my Tesla.

I watch one of the dogs sniff the hood of the powder-blue VW Beetle with flaking paint and a Save the Turtles sticker. And then it moves on.

It gets to Gwen's Jeep and stops again. It goes up on its hind legs to sniff the tire cover that says UGH, AS IF! The dog starts to bark loudly. Another dog lunges toward the car, pulling on its leash. I watch as a gloved hand unzips the cover and reaches into the tire. I watch as it pulls out a black handgun.

The same kind I saw before, on the twins' birthday and in the photograph Detective Johnson showed me.

The memory comes back to me again, of Sydney unwrapping this gun. But this time the aperture of my mind's eye opens just a bit further. And I remember the girl sitting beside her. The girl who, of course, was sitting beside her, her best friend, leaning in to see what the present was, her blond hair shimmering in the light.

And just like that I remember who first told me the story about that day at the gun range. It was Gwen, who was in the back seat when Brooklyn wouldn't get out of the car. Gwen, who popped open her own door and said, *I'll go in with you, Syd.*

At least two of my girls know how to shoot now, Mr. Reynolds had joked. Gwen wouldn't shut up about his having said that. She always loved comments that made it seem like she fit into the Reynolds family.

I can't believe I'd forgotten: that while Brooklyn cried in the car, Sydney and *Gwen* went in to learn how to use the guns. Gwen knows how to shoot a gun. Gwen knows how to shoot *that* gun.

26

5 DAYS AFTER

GWEN

"So the good thing is, your fingerprints are not on the gun, okay?" Sheila says. "Which gives us a strong case for reasonable doubt. We could definitely argue that someone planted it there. Especially since the police had K-9s search the garage the first day and didn't find anything." I dab my eyes and press my phone to my ear as I pace around my room, still in my pajamas, my pink slippers squeaking against the floor. "But the bad news is, no one else's fingerprints are on the gun either."

"Is the bad news not that the gun was in my freakin' car?" I tumble into tears.

"Well, yes," Sheila says slowly. "That too. I'm sorry, I thought that was evident."

I struggle to catch up and breathe through my sobs. When I first woke up, my eyes were still puffy from crying over Tucker for the second night in a row, and now the murder weapon was found in my Jeep. . . . I feel like my life is in a freefall and I have nothing to grasp onto.

"Without another set of fingerprints," Sheila continues, "it would help if we had any idea as to who could have planted the gun. Who might have had access to the garage in the last few days?"

"I mean, like, everyone! All the kids in the house, all the lawyers and police and everyone who's been in and out all week."

"Right," she says. She clears her throat.

"Sheila," I say, "are they going to arrest me?"

She pauses and exhales. My heart sinks. Finally she says, "I don't think so . . . at least not yet. Because your fingerprints weren't on the gun. They only get one shot at trial, so they'll want their case as strong as possible before they make an arrest. But, Gwen, I do think, at this point, we may need to talk about what it might look like to plead down. To second- or third-degree. So if you did do this . . ."

"I didn't!" I can't believe she'd ask that. "You're my lawyer—I need you to believe that."

"Okay," she says, her voice neutral. "Got it. Then we'll stick with that."

I swallow and my throat feels like sandpaper. I don't like how she said *We'll stick with that,* as if there was another option.

"One more thing, Gwen. I don't work pro bono, especially not for celebrity clients. I'm going to need that retainer check by the end of the week."

"Right, yes, I'll call my accountant and figure out what the delay is," I lie.

"Please do," she says, "or else I can't keep working for you."

"I'll get it to you before the weekend, I promise. Just please keep me out of jail, okay? I do not look good in jumpsuits."

The line goes dead. I look down at my phone. I pull up Depop. I have a few more sales, bringing me to a total of $13,000—still just a fraction of what I need.

I check my email. But all the companies I wrote to about sponcon have either ghosted or straight-up rejected me.

Which is not to say I don't have messages. I have hundreds. Conspiracy theorists, TV bookers, podcasters, private investigators, and crime obsessives of all kinds want to know if I did it, how I did it, who I did it with, if I did it because I'm part of the Illuminati, if I did it because Sydney is part of the Illuminati . . .

People are as obsessed with me as ever—it just turns out being infamous is far less lucrative than being famous.

I hold down my phone's power button to silence the alerts and fall backward onto the soft cloud of my bed, letting the phone fall out of my hand.

27

8 HOURS BEFORE

SYDNEY

I wake up with a start, my eyes flying open in the darkness. I have this terrible, sinking feeling in my stomach. A sort of premonition that something very bad has happened.

I sit up in bed. I've sweat right through my T-shirt, and my head is ringing. I reach over for my phone to check the time: 1:43 a.m. I take a deep breath and remind myself that I'm not clairvoyant, and that this feeling in my stomach doesn't mean anything, except maybe I should stop eating my mom's questionable cooking.

Lightning flashes outside my window, illuminating my bedroom in gray light. Lighting up the various participation trophies from years of dance and gymnastics and the faded posters from when I still liked Shawn Mendes. The decorating is dated. It's nothing like my bedroom at the Malibu house, which is grown-up and sophisticated, with my puff-foam mirror and curated collection of crystals I bought off Goop.

I toss my hot-pink duvet aside and walk across the cold hardwood floor toward the Jack and Jill bathroom between my room and Brooklyn's. I'll splash some water on my face and feel a bit better.

As I'm patting my face dry with the hand towel, I notice the light coming through the crack below Brooklyn's door. Her lamp is on.

"Hey, Brook, do you feel sick, too?" I slide open the pocket door. "I think it's that horrendous seafood stew mom insisted—"

I stop short when I realize Brooklyn is not in her bed. In fact, her bed is perfectly made. Like she never went to sleep at all.

On top of the tightly tucked duvet, hot pink just like mine, there is a piece of thick stationery, folded in half.

I pick up the note and read it rapidly, my eyes flying across the page and picking up only key words. I get the message before I'm halfway done.

I shove the note in my pocket and fly out of the room. *No, no, no, no, no, no* is all I can think. I snatch my cell phone from the charger cord without slowing my stride, and the cord rips from the wall.

I click Brooklyn's contact, and the phone starts to ring in my ear as I race through the dark halls of our house. Looking, hoping, wishing that this note was written only seconds before I found it and that I'll find her just around the next corner, hidden in the shadows of our home. That she hasn't left yet.

I race down the stairs. Right as I get to the bottom, right outside my dad's office, lightning strikes again. And I can see in the flash of light that the safe is open. Thunder cracks and shakes the house. I rush over, but part of me already knows what I will see when I look inside. And I'm right: there is only one gun. The other is gone.

The phone in my ear goes to voicemail. Brooklyn's never set anything up, so it's just the generic robot voice. I hang up the call and click her location on Find My Friends. Her little photo is moving across the map. She's driving down the highway, headed toward Malibu. Toward the house.

But she's only halfway there. There's still time.

I grab my keys and get into my car. Adrenaline surges through my body as I wait impatiently for the garage door to slowly rise. *Come on, come on.*

As soon as I have an opening, I throw the car in reverse and barrel down the long driveway.

"*Call Brooklyn!*" I yell to the car voice command. It rings and rings and rings as I speed down the dark and deserted streets of our neighborhood, taking the cul-de-sac turns at full speed, sending waves of rainwater onto the perfectly manicured lawns of my neighbors. The suitcase I never bothered to get out of the back slides across the floor and hits the side of the car with a loud *thunk.*

Rain slams against my windshield in thick drops. The wipers fly back and forth, but even at their maximum, they do little to keep my field of vision clear in this storm.

The call goes to voicemail. That same automated "The voice mail for this caller has not yet been set up . . ." I slam the steering wheel in frustration.

"Hang up!" I yell. "Call Brooklyn!" I won't stop trying. I can't.

I look down at my phone. My little photo is gaining on her.

I press my foot on the accelerator as I race down the Pacific Coast Highway. The speed limit is fifty, but I push the needle past eighty. The streetlights fly by my window, a rapid blur of light. I can hear my pulse in my ears.

I flash back to the events of the last few days. The vote at the house. The smug faces of my housemates as the votes were counted. Five to one against my own sister joining our little "family." I can't believe I ever thought of it that way. It isn't a family; it never was. They are sharks, every last one of them. They may pretend it's a team sport, but all of them were out for themselves, whether it was Cami and her unapologetic cruelty or Kat pretending she was sorry but voting Brooklyn out nonetheless. They all put their own interests above all else.

I flash back to my sister's reaction when I told her. The way she sort of collapsed into herself when she heard the news, her shoulders falling.

My mother crying, wondering aloud if this meant she was a failure as a mother. My father sternly lecturing Brooklyn that not everyone could be a flower and that some people have to be gardeners. That some people were meant for show biz careers, like me, and others had to get real jobs. And that it was time that she found a career path that was a bit more realistic for her talents. That she better figure out what she was doing this year, since she'd turned down college and he sure as hell wasn't going to let her do nothing while she lived under his roof.

For the last two days, Brooklyn has just sort of stared blankly into space, her eyes glossy and vacant. She's barely eaten. She lay in bed all day. When I asked her if she was taking the antidepressants she's been on since sophomore year, she just shrugged noncommittally.

So she was already in a rough place. And then Cami posted a video as she was doing her makeup for the event tonight. She replied to questions fans left on her past videos. One of them:

What do you think of Brooklyn?

"Um, love the borough, love the borough. As for the person?" She smiled mischievously at the camera. "I honestly don't think anything about her at all."

The video has had three million views. Everyone on the internet loves it. They say it's so sassy and such a great clapback.

A clapback to what? I wanted to scream. Brooklyn didn't do anything to Cami. She didn't do anything to anyone. She was just trying to be friends with them. Trying to be seen and liked on the internet. Maybe her videos weren't that good or were even kind of "cringe," as some people said. But she was just trying.

But even worse than Cami's video is what it's inspired. Lit Lair fans have jumped on the bandwagon. They duet Brooklyn's old videos; they make fun of the times her dance moves looked awkward, outfits she wore that they think are ugly, trends she tried to start that flopped. They count how many times she says "like" in a single one-minute video (twenty). And someone we went to high school with even jumped in and made a video talking about the time Brooklyn failed geometry and had to retake it over the summer.

It's not just that Brooklyn didn't get into the house and didn't become an internet star. Now she's being cyberbullied for even trying, for doing her best to make videos the other members of the house might like. For trying to brand herself into someone the internet might love. For even thinking she might succeed at her dream.

Brooklyn said nothing at dinner tonight, just kept her eyes on her plate. Immediately after, she retreated to her room. I could hear through her door that she was watching the videos on loop. I was supposed to go to the house tonight for the Drake event, but

I knew the right thing was to stay home. I knocked on her door around eight p.m., asking if she wanted to watch a movie or something. She didn't respond. She didn't open the door.

I assumed she just wanted to go to bed early. I was wrong.

The rain starts to ease up and then stops, as if I've driven through the edge of the storm. The clouds part to reveal the full moon hanging over the ocean.

My heart rises. This is a sign. A sign that I will make it there in time. That I will get to Brooklyn and be able to stop her from doing something she can't undo.

I'm so close. I'm on our street now. I'm almost to the house. It's just down the road.

And then, through the misty air, I see it, peeled off by the side of the road. My sister's car.

I slam on my brakes and turn the wheel. My tires screech as I pull off onto the shoulder, right next to her car. I put my car in park, and through the window I spot a shadowy figure, about Brooklyn's build, down by the water. *What is she doing...?*

Without pausing to turn off the engine, I reach for the handle and pop open my car door.

And that's when I hear the gunshot.

The world tilts on its axis. My vision is blurry and spinning. I push forward through my confusion frantically, running down the rocky path toward the beach. Rushing toward the crumpled figure on the beach.

And then I fall to my knees in the sand. And all the air snaps out of my lungs. Because there is my sister. A gun in her hand. A bullet in her head.

I move closer to her. I frantically check her pulse, but seeing the state of her skull, I already know what I will find. She is gone. I pull her limp body into me. Cradling her head against my body. Rocking back and forth.

There's a loud sound like a wounded animal. It takes me a second to realize it's coming from my own lips. A sound I wasn't even conscious of making, that came from deep within me.

It's a loss I can't compute. My sister, my twin, my other half, gone. Gone from this moment, gone from any potential future moments. I can't even picture a life like that. Her not being there. Not being the person at the other end of the phone every time I get career news or Tucker says something annoying or even, like, there's a sale at Zara or a Starbucks Happy Hour. Not being there at my wedding to be my maid of honor, not being there for my kids to call aunt. Not having her own wedding. Her own kids. Not finding her own path, her own triumphs.

All the thousands of little dreams we dreamt of the future, when we played with Barbies or games of M.A.S.H, when we read horoscopes and took personality tests. None of them will happen now. *Poof!* They're gone. We came into this world together. I have no idea how to navigate my way through it without her. And I don't want to.

Through the blur of my tears, I look up, and I see it there, just a few yards down the beach: the house. This big, modern square sticking out unnaturally from the cliffs.

And I think of what Brooklyn wrote in her letter, in her . . . suicide note: that she wanted to come here to do it because it was their actions, *their* rejection, that broke her. She wanted them to feel bad.

The sadness I'm drowning in starts to recede, leaving anger

in its wake. *They* did this to her. They're callous and spoiled, and they don't realize what their thoughtless little lives do to people. How small actions they make can have a catastrophic impact on the lives of less famous, less "special" people. How a bit of kindness from them would've meant the world to her. And their coldness killed her.

My sister is dead. And what will happen to them because of this? They will feel a bit guilty, perhaps. For, like, five minutes. But then they will get to have futures, to have possibilities, all the things that she won't get. They don't deserve that.

My sister wanted them to feel guilty. But that's not justice. They don't deserve guilt. They deserve punishment. Just as much as if they'd walked out onto this beach and shot her themselves.

Just as much as if they had shot her themselves. An idea starts to form in my mind. Of a way to get them to pay. To trick the police into thinking that is what happened, so that those responsible will pay for her death. But it unravels almost as soon as I think of it. There are too many holes in the logic. The police would wonder why Brooklyn was even here in the first place. They would struggle with a motive, since the house members barely knew her.

"I'm sorry." I look down at Brooklyn's body. "I don't know what to do."

I stare down at the blood that has soaked into my T-shirt. Her blood. The same blood that runs through my veins. And not just in the way that families share. But in the unique way twins share. The exact same DNA. The same blood . . .

And this time, the plan snaps perfectly into place. The police may not be tricked into thinking Brooklyn was murdered. But if it was my body found here on the beach, or better yet, on the grounds of the house—the pool, even. Then no one would wonder why I was here. I lived here, after all. And the motives . . . they would invent themselves. There were so many lies and secrets and fights in this house, certainly the cops could find a reason why one of them, or better yet all of them, would want me dead. Especially if they are nudged in the right direction. Hope rises in my chest. Because I can do this.

The members of the house will pay for the death of a Reynolds sister. It will just have to be me.

28

7 HOURS BEFORE

SYDNEY

I brush the tears from my face and focus. If I'm going to pull this off, I need to concentrate.

Avoiding looking at my sister's face or the wound in the side of her head, I empty her pockets. I check for everything. Phone, keys, wallet—I flip it open and make sure her ID is there. It is.

Then I turn out my own pockets. I slip my iPhone, including the pocket on the back of the case with my photo ID, into her pocket.

I summon all my strength, squat down, and lift her. I know we weigh almost the same, and I've squatted my body weight before. But even so, it's much easier to carry her along the beach than I thought. Maybe because, with the fury racing through my veins, I'm pretty sure I could lift a car right now. Brooklyn slung limply over my shoulder, I make my way down the beach and up the rocky path to the pool.

I walk to the edge and set her down, easing her into the water gently, like they do when they send people out to burials at sea. She floats on her back, the water billowing up the fabric of her blouse like wings. She looks almost peaceful. Like she is just lounging, floating in the pool, like she often did in the pool at our family home. Like any moment, she'd flicker her eyes open and swim over to me and pull me into the pool. But of course, she never will.

No time for this, I remind myself. I can mourn her once those responsible have paid for what they've done.

I open the doors to the pool house and find the gloves I use for gardening. I slip them on and then grab an armful of pool cleaner bottles. I walk to the pool and uncap the bottle. I empty them out, one by one, the chemicals gurgling into the pool. This won't do much at all to hide the body. But it will look like someone tried. Which will lead the cops away from suicide. Toward murder. And by someone who wasn't too good at what they were doing. Someone like a teenager.

Trying to dissolve a body with a few bottles of commercially available pool cleaners. It's what Gwen would be dumb enough to try. It's what Tucker would be lazy enough to try.

When the last bottle is empty, I toss the bottles onto the floor of the pool house.

I jog back down the steps to the beach, across the dark sand, and back up to where our cars are waiting. I pop the trunk to my own car. I pull off my shirt, stained with blood, and shove it into the little hatch below the main trunk. I find my raincoat in the trunk where I keep it with my emergency kit. I zip it all the way up to hide that I'm wearing nothing but a bra underneath.

I close the trunk and get into the driver's seat. I open the front console and rifle through until I find a baseball cap. I pull it on over my wet hair and flip down the mirror from the ceiling to check my face. There's a bit of blood streaked across my cheek. I lick my thumb and rub roughly until it comes off.

I start the car, and the windshield wipers fly into action. I take off down the street. Ready to film what will likely be my most important video ever. The last time Sydney Reynolds will be seen alive.

Because in order for it to seem like someone in the house murdered me, the body in the pool can't just have materialized out of nowhere. The police need to see me coming home.

I pull up to the gate and get out of the car. I stare at the keypad as I type the code to keep it natural, but then, right as the gate opens, I turn and look right at the camera. Just for a second. But it'll be long enough.

I get back in the car, pull up the drive and into the garage. I grab my suitcase from the back and head into the house and up the main stairs. The house is dim and practically silent, save for the hum of ceiling fans turning. All the loud, big personalities asleep at 3:00 a.m. I push open the door to my room and lay my suitcase on the floor. I unzip and open it and pull out a few items, to make it look like I was getting ready to sleep.

I imagine how the police will interpret this tomorrow morning:

She came home but she never went to sleep, I can hear the police say; in my mind, they're played by the cast of *SVU. We have footage of her pulling in the driveway and her suitcase in her room, but she never went to sleep. The bed was still made.*

I walk into my private bathroom and pull tissues from the heavy decorative holder on the counter. I rub my face and crumple them up, leaving them scattered on the counter and in the otherwise empty little trash can by the toilet.

She was clearly upset about something that night—who in the house has she had fights with? the imaginary police say in my mind. It

219

won't take them long, talking with my dear housemates, to know that I was in a fight with each and every one of them.

Before I leave my room, I set my baseball cap and car keys on top of the dresser. Then I open the top drawer and pull out my Zippo lighter. I pocket it and head back down the stairs.

I can't exactly be seen leaving on any of the cameras, so I head to the wine cellar. I scan the labels of the bottles: Pinot Noir, Cabernet Sauvignon, Merlot, etc., etc.

And then there it is: a 1965 Bordeaux from Dixon Vineyards. Except there is no such thing as Dixon Vineyards. Robert Dixon was the name of the eccentric billionaire who originally built this house, before he lost all his money in the dot-com bubble. I pull the neck of the bottle up like a lever.

To my right, a piece of the stone wall shifts, and a wall lined with bottles of wine hinges forward like a door, opening onto a dark tunnel.

Excellent. One of the very few benefits, it turns out, of my parents being the ones who bought the house is that I'm the only one who knows about this.

I slip into the secret passage and push the door back into place behind me. It's pitch-black in here, and it smells like earth. Damp and musty. I slide Brooklyn's phone out of my pocket. The lock screen lights up as I raise it. An image of Brooklyn and me at Santa Monica Pier, hugging tightly, fills the screen. It sends a pang to my heart.

At the top of the screen, the lock icon senses my face and switches to unlocked. Just a little bit of encouragement from the phone's technology that I will be able to pull this off. The phone believes I'm her. And hopefully everyone else will, too.

I click the flashlight, and a beam of light brightens the passage before me. I keep moving forward.

When I reach the other side, I climb up the ladder and push on the ceiling of the tunnel, opening a trap door into the pool house. I climb out and close the trap door after me. You can't see it, really, but I throw a few pool floats over the top for good measure. Then I go out the door to the pool house, down the path, to the beach.

The sky is just beginning to brighten. The sun will rise in the next hour or so.

Standing on the sand, I pull the letter I found in Brooklyn's room out of my pocket. I read it, slowly this time, not in the panicked way I did when I first found it. Then I read it again. Trying my best to commit the words to memory. After all, these are my sister's last words.

Then I take the lighter from my pocket and ignite the corner of the paper. I watch as the fire grows, moving up the page, turning it to small, charred pieces that blow away in the sea breeze.

Of course, I'd love to have kept it. Because things like this are all I have left of her. But I couldn't risk its ever being found.

Once it's burned, I head back up to Brooklyn's waiting car. My car now. I get in and map the way to the nearest electronics store. I wait in the parking lot until an employee in a bright polo shirt opens the store.

The store's automatic doors glide open as I approach. It smells like AC, and the lighting is bright and sharply fluorescent. The sort of peppy, inoffensive pop music they always have in chain stores plays softly over a loudspeaker.

The environment is so . . . normal. It's so jarringly different from the dark and twisty world inside of me.

I have the sudden urge to smash the shiny laptops on display. To knock over the expensive flat-screen TVs and watch them tumble like dominoes.

She's gone!!! I want to yell. *Don't you understand? She's dead!!!*

I do not understand how the world can go on like normal when I feel like this.

I'm reminded of a fact I learned in childhood, during one of the few times my mom would get on a kick and decide we should go to Sunday school. There was this thing in Old Testament times, I think, where when people were grieving, they would tear their clothing to show how upset they were. I feel like that now, except I want to tear a hole in the world.

I head over to the phones and try to make sense of the different models. Of what I may be able to use without being traced. Of which one can do what I need it to.

I spot a guy in a polo and name tag stocking phone cases and try to catch his eye. He looks right past me.

What the . . . ? But then I catch a bit of my reflection in the flatscreens, and I realize I look like shit. I flip my hair over and shake it out. I pinch my cheeks so I don't look so much like a ghost, and I lick my lips. Then I saunter over to Polo Guy.

"Hi," I say, my voice an octave higher than normal. "I was wondering if you could tell me if either of these can be used for apps?"

"Uh, sure." The guy runs his eyes up and down my body. "What kind of apps were you thinking?"

"Uh, I don't know . . . like TikTok?"

"Yeah, sure." He unlocks the case to take a phone out for me.

"And there's one more thing. . . . My parents are, like, really strict. But I want to be able to text boys, you know? I want to get a phone I can use that won't let them see what I'm doing. That no one can tell is mine. Kinda almost like those burner phones they have in action movies, that can't be tracked." I giggle. "Would this be like that?"

And that's how I get this guy to walk me through setting up a burner phone, which I've paid for in cash, without any questions asked or suspicions raised. God, men are easy to manipulate. Especially the creepy ones, when you know how to turn their bullshit back on them. He even gives me his number, so he can be the first "boy" I text (vom, he's definitely like thirty, which, considering I'm seventeen, is major *ew*). I smile as he types it in, then delete it from the phone's contacts as soon as I'm out of the store.

I drive back to Malibu, making excellent time, since most of the city is asleep. No one is on the side street leading to our house; even the dog walkers haven't started their day yet. I inch Brooklyn's car as close to the gate as I dare, not wanting to be seen by the security cameras.

I take out the burner phone and type in our password to connect to the house Wi-Fi, which reaches three rings, even out here. Then I open TikTok. I type in the password I know by heart, and when it reads for facial recognition, I, of course, have no problem. It takes me only a few minutes to put together the post; after all, there are thousands of pictures of me from around the internet to choose from. Also, it helps that I'm the type of person who's thought a bit about how I'd want people to commemorate me after I die. I've even thought of ideas for my own funeral.

I look at the clock. It's not even seven a.m. yet. On a Saturday in the summer. A terrible time to post, engagement-wise. Plus,

I'm not trying to get caught with the phone in my hand right outside the gate when it posts. I queue it for noon and turn it off.

I arrive back at my family's house and park the car in Brooklyn's usual spot. I grab my bloody shirt and head straight up to the laundry room. I throw it in the washer, then strip naked and throw the rest of my clothes in after it. I pour about half a bottle of detergent into the machine and slam the door closed. My mom has one of those extra fancy washing machines with a million settings and that can connect to the Wi-Fi for reasons I cannot fathom. The knob chirps as I turn it all the way to Extremely Soiled. If there was ever a time for that setting, it's now. I considered burning my clothes in the backyard firepit, but I think that would raise questions from my parents.

I shower in scalding-hot water, scrubbing my whole body raw with my exfoliator. I stay under the water until our double-barreled water tank runs out of hot water. Then I change into a pair of Brooklyn's pajamas and slide into her bed. It smells like her, which is both beautiful and painful to experience.

I pull the sheets up to my nose and close my eyes. I pretend to sleep and wait for my mother to come wake me with the news that I am dead.

29

6 DAYS AFTER

CAMI

I tap Play on my Bluetooth headphones and roll my neck from side to side. I start to count out the music in my head, just as I've been able to do since I started baby ballet at four years old. This quasi–house arrest and the paps scouring the city for any sight of us made it impossible to sneak out to the studio to dance. I spent the last hour clearing the furniture out of the formal living room and cleaning the hardwood floor.

I take a deep breath, extend my arms in front of my body, and prep my stance for pirouettes. I pick a place on the front wall, the little T where the two windows meet each other, that I can keep my gaze on, to spot myself.

And then I turn, my foot en pointe, my gossamer skirt fluttering up into a circle around me, my spine perfectly straight. I love this feeling, as if in this moment, I may actually be a stationary axis and it's the world that's spinning around me.

On each beat of the music, I see the spot on the wall, then the room in a blur, then the spot again, a blur, the spot, the blur . . . one, two, three, fou—

Movement breaks my concentration, and I stumble out of my

turn. I see a figure through the window, coming up toward the house.

My heartbeat racing from my turns and my vision still a bit wobbly, I rush over to the window. And there they are, two men coming up the driveway, cameras in their arms. Cameras with long, intrusive lenses.

I storm over to the front door and yank it open. "Hey!" I shout. "You're not allowed on the driveway. This is private property." For days, there have been paparazzi lining our street and the edge of the property. But none of them have broken the law and gone past the gate.

The cameramen don't listen to me; instead, they keep walking toward the house. Right toward me. "If you don't leave, I'll call the police."

"Oh no! It's fine; they're with me!" Gwen comes flapping down the stairs like a frenzied bird. She's in full hair and makeup and wearing the dress she wore for Drake's visit. Which is strange. I don't think I've ever seen Gwen wear the same outfit twice. But then again, the last time I walked by her room, her closet was looking rather bare. So maybe she's on some sort of Marie Kondo kick. "You can set up in the living room!" she tells the camera guys.

"What's going on?" I ask her.

"Oh, just an interview for Nora Caponi."

"Nora Caponi?" I ask, incredulous.

"She has a TV show and podcast series," she says, answering my question literally but not filling in the blanks about why she'd willingly talk to someone so infamous for picking apart her guests. If Nora Caponi decides you committed a crime, she will make it her show's singular mission to ensure you go to jail. My lawyer told me that almost any case she features ends up with a sequestered jury. Before I can ask why she's doing this, Gwen tugs my arm and leads me toward a *Real Housewives*–looking woman who's followed the crew into the house. "Cami, I want you to meet Stacy Lipton. She's my new manager."

Stacy is blowing a gum bubble as we approach. It pops into a stringy mess across her overly lined lips. "Aw, shanty," she says, in what I can only guess is an attempt at French. She holds her hand out to shake.

I just stare at her extended hand for a second, and then I turn to Gwen. "What happened to Carmen?"

Gwen's eyes go wide. *"Cami,"* she scolds under her breath.

Whatever. I know it's not the thing I'm supposed to say in front of the new manager. But there's no time for politeness when my best friend may have made a grave mistake. No one, I mean no one, fires Carmen Marrero. She's, like, the best influencer manager there is. I don't know what Gwen is thinking . . . unless—no. There's no way Carmen dropped Gwen, right? I mean, yes, the whole house is under investigation for murder. And, sure, she's lost followers. But she still has, like, fifty million. She's still *the* Gwen Riley. That sort of status doesn't just evaporate in a few days, right?

"Carmen and I parted ways," Gwen says diplomatically. "Stacy, can I get you anything? LaCroix, maybe? We have Pamplemousse."

"Nah," says Stacy. "But is there somewhere I can smoke?"

"I'll show you," I offer with a smile. If I can get her alone, I can get the dirt.

I lead her out to the back patio. It's getting dark; only the gray-blue twinge of dusk hangs in the sky. Stacy lights up seconds after we're through the door. Over her shoulder, I watch as the camera crew sets up lights in the living room. A familiar-looking woman in a skirt suit and holding a microphone flips through flash cards. Nora Caponi. It's weird to see someone I'm used to seeing as a talking head, speculating about us and fueling rumors about the murder, here in person, in our house. People used to use the house for media stuff all the time. But that was before. Now it just seems kind of strange.

"Want one?" Stacy asks, holding a cigarette between her teeth.

"No, I'm seventeen," I answer.

She just shrugs and shoves the pack back into her knockoff pleather handbag.

I flash back to visiting Carmen's office, the time Gwen brought me along before we all got lunch at La Scala. Everything was so classy: the valet parking and the koi pond in the lobby. The bottled Evian her assistant offered us, and the expensive couches in the waiting room.

"So where is it that you work again?" I ask Stacy.

"Robson and Lipton," she says, and then blows a stream of smoke toward the pool.

"Never heard of it."

"We rep Audrey Farmer."

"That cheerleader who killed her baby?"

"*Allegedly* killed her baby," Stacy corrects me.

All right, I've heard enough. I spin on my heels, pull open the door, and charge through the house. I find Gwen in the dining room, fixing her lipstick in the reflection of the large decorative mirror.

"Dude, I don't know where you found this lady, but I don't think you should do any interview she sets up for you. She's bad news. Like Flat Tummy Tea bad news. No, like Fyre Festival bad news."

Gwen avoids my eyes, keeping her gaze on the mirror as she caps her lipstick. Then she turns to leave.

"Gwen!" I grab her arm. "Did you hear what I said?"

"I'm a little busy here, Cami."

"But you can do better than this—"

"I can't really afford to be picky right now, okay?" She pulls her arm back to her side.

"What does that mean?"

"We're ready for you, Gwen!" Nora Caponi pokes her head into the room.

Gwen smiles and holds up one finger toward her. Then she turns to me and says, "Don't worry about it, Cam. I've got this."

I watch her walk into the room and get mic'd up. She clips on her lavalier mic with ease and makes small talk with Nora like a pro; after all, she's done hundreds of interviews. There are many things Gwen doesn't know about, but shining when on TV was always in her wheelhouse. Watching her now, looking so at ease and capable, I almost want to believe her. But as soon as Nora Caponi starts the livestream with her infamous smug smile, my heart sinks. Because my guess is, Gwen very much does not have this.

6 DAYS AFTER

GWEN

"Tell us, Gwen, what was it like to see your best friend—such a young, beautiful girl—*dead,* floating in a pool, water mixed with

229

her own blood?" Nora Caponi stares into my soul, her beady eyes hungry.

I twist my hands in my lap. "It was hard, of course." I swallow; it feels like there's something stuck in my throat. "When Sydney died, I felt quite terrible."

"Felt terrible about her death, or terrible that you'd betrayed her trust and slept with her boyfriend?" She asks this question in a cheerful, fake voice, even though the words feel like a slap in the face.

"About both, I guess," I mumble. I know the answer is lame. That it doesn't make good TV. But I suddenly feel so out of practice. I used to be able to do press in my sleep. Now, this interview feels far too much like an interrogation.

I squint. Why are these lights so bright? Surely this much wattage isn't necessary when I bet the ring light in my bedroom would light us just fine. These are too strong; it feels like my face is baking. I hope I don't look red and blotchy. I had to do my makeup myself, since I couldn't afford even a cheap makeup artist on my current budget.

Nora tilts her head to the side, studying me. Her face has harsh angles, maybe from overdieting or a makeup artist too heavy on the contouring. Either way, it makes her look a bit like a bird of prey.

I can see Stacy over her shoulder, moving her hand in a circular motion, indicating that I should say more. I think back to her instructions for this interview: *Give them what they want to hear!*

I think of the $300,000 appearance fee they're paying me for this. I think of my empty closet, my maxed-out credit cards, my Birkin listed on Depop, the bills on my mom's kitchen counter.

But most of all, I think about the gun they found in my car, and my lawyer, who is a day away from quitting if I don't pay her.

I catch a sliver of my reflection in a camera lens, and I realize I'm slouched over, kind of shyly folded in on myself. As if I'm trying to take up as little space as possible. I sit up straighter. And I remember who the heck I am. I'm Gwen freaking Riley, and I can dazzle and entertain any crowd, in person or on the internet. And that's all this is, after all, a bit of entertainment, no different from the hundreds of TikToks and YouTube videos and Insta Lives I've starred in over the years.

I drape a curtain of hair over my shoulder carefully, so the camera on my three-quarter profile can get a good shot of my face, and start again.

"This situation in the house," I say, "not just with me and Tucker and Sydney, but with all the drama that comes along with this lifestyle, the fame and fortune thrust upon us so young— it was like a powder keg. I guess it was only a matter of time before . . . you know . . . *boom.*" I spread out my fingers, miming an explosion.

"Really?" Nora asks. "Everything seemed so idyllic from the outside."

"Yeah, I bet it did. What with the nice clothes and cool cars and all the followers . . . But people don't realize what it's actually like. To live in this sort of fishbowl. With the whole world watching your every move. Scrutinizing everything you do. You don't know what it's like to live under that kind of pressure. Someone could really . . . crack."

I pause for dramatic effect. "I think . . . *if* one of us did it, if someone here did kill Syd, that would be why. Because of the cutthroat competition and pressure cooker of social media, and what it does to the young, *vulnerable* minds of our generation. The thirst for fame, Nora—it can be poisonous."

"Wow." Nora Caponi nods her head solemnly and folds her note cards in her lap. "Are you saying you killed her?"

"No," I say. "I had nothing to do with her death. I'm just saying that I could see how someone in the house may have been pushed to that point. That's how toxic the environment was."

"Then what do you make of the gun being found in your car?"

"Well, first of all," I say, "the *suspiciously wiped clean* gun was hidden in my spare tire. Not in my car. Let's be clear about that."

"So you think it was planted there."

"I know it, Nora," I say. "Planted by someone with keys to the garage." I pause for effect. "Someone who lives in this house with me."

Nora Caponi is on the edge of her seat. "Gwen, it has been so enlightening speaking with you today. Before we go, one last question. Many of your fans are so young, and with everything going on, their parents are understandably quite concerned. What would you say to them now?"

"To the parents?" I glance directly into the camera, just for a second. "I guess what I would say is, keep your kids off social media. If you want to keep them safe. If you want to keep them alive."

30

6 DAYS AFTER

GWEN

"Gwen, what were you thinking?" Beau confronts me as soon as Nora Caponi's crew is out of sight.

"What do you mean?" I feign ignorance. But the phone in his hand is open to the livestream. We both know exactly why he's mad.

"You crazy bitch!" Cami comes flying into the room. She charges toward me, and I recoil against the door, worried she's about to hit me. Beau grabs Cami's arm to hold her back, but she lunges toward me anyway.

"Whoa, whoa." Kat puts herself between Cami and me, an arm extended toward each of us. "Violence is not the answer."

"I can't believe you said that shit," Cami yells past her at me. "You pretty much said it was someone in the house who killed her. You've totally screwed us over." She looks at Kat. "She can't just get away with saying something like that. It puts us all in danger."

"Okay, okay." Kat turns her head back and forth between Cami and me. "What about a house meeting?"

Cami scoffs. "Really, about this? Isn't this a bit more serious than that?"

"Really." Kat straightens her shoulders. She seems surer of herself. "I think the seriousness of the matter is the exact reason we need a house meeting. Everyone, TV room, five minutes."

I head down the hallway. Cami follows and I watch her out of the corner of my eye, still a bit on edge.

"Boo!" She lunges toward me.

I yelp and jump away from her, only to realize she moved only slightly in my direction. She's still more than a foot away. She just wanted to make me jump.

Cami cackles and tosses her head back as she walks past. I wait in the hallway for her to get settled before I enter the TV room and take a spot on the other side of the room.

Everyone else ambles in one by one. Each one staring at me as they pass.

I avoid their eyes, focusing on my phone instead. I scroll through my texts. *You were brilliant!!* Stacy said.

And then there are two messages from my mom:

Jennifer (Mom): *Saw the vid! You did good but that dress looked a little tight? Remember to take it easy on the treats! Just bc you live with teenage boys doesn't mean you can eat like them!*

And:

Jennifer (Mom): *When do we get the money again?*

I click the lock button without responding. When Kat comes around with the phone jar, I plunk mine in. Happy for her to take it.

"Okay," Kat says, once she has every phone. "Who would like to speak first?"

"Me!" Cami raises her hand and stands. "What Gwen did

was dangerous and irresponsible. We all know that the cops are watching our social media and will definitely see this interview. And she pretty much told the world that it was someone in the house who killed Sydney. And assigned them a motive that the tabloids will be talking about for freaking weeks. Her callous actions will make the police scrutiny on all of us worse. Now there's no way the cops will think anybody but one of us killed her."

"Oh, please," I say. "They already have decided it's one of us, but now—"

"Now what?" Cami demands. "You're half a million dollars richer."

"Well, not that much, but yeah." I fold my arms over my chest. "What's wrong with that?"

"Jesus," Cami says. "Like you don't have enough already?"

My face grows warm. "You don't know my financial situation," I snap. "Not all of us have a trust fund, you know." Cami always talks about money like it's a game. Who earns more than who, who holds the record for a single sponsored post. And in a way, earning money like this can be a game for her. She comes from money. Her college fund and her parents' house payment, even her lawyers—that's all figured out by her mom and dad. Any money she earns from TikTok is just extra.

"*Please,*" Cami says. "Don't make it about that. Kat doesn't have a trust fund, but you don't see her pulling a stunt like this."

"Oh," Kat says, "there's no reason to really put me in the middle—"

"Well, I guess I'm not as perfect as *Saint Kat,* then." I wave my hands. "So sue me. But I won't apologize for doing what I had to do."

"All right, let's try to keep this constructive," Kat says.

"Maybe . . . what if we came up with a set of house rules for talking to the press?"

"I really don't get what the big deal is," I say. "We never had to run our appearances by each other before."

"We weren't murder suspects before," Tucker says gruffly.

"Yeah, and whose fault is that?" I glare at him.

"Um, I'm pretty freaking sure it's yours," he says. "You're the one who had the gun in your car."

"Yeah, and who put it there?"

"Is there something you'd like to say to me?" Tucker asks.

Kat's eyes go wide. She's lost control of whatever semblance of a house meeting was left.

"Yeah, there is," I reply. "I think that you are two-faced and can't be trusted." I turn to the rest of the group. "And I think it's crazy for us to sit here talking about my interview when we should be talking about the fact that someone in this room did something unthinkable. I know no one has wanted to say it or even think it. But, you guys, the police have narrowed it down to us five for a reason. The post came from *inside* the house. It's time we say it out loud: someone in this room killed our friend." I turn back to Tucker: "And not for nothing, but I think it might have been you."

"Based on what?" says Tucker.

"How about based on the fact that you're a two-faced asshole who acts like you care about people only to totally betray them."

"Oh, please, you didn't seem to mind it so much when you and I were *'betraying'* Sydney in the pool," he says, a little muscle in his jaw rippling as he spits out the words through gritted teeth. He turns to the rest of the group. "I didn't kill Sydney," he tells the room. "Gwen is just bitter because I broke up with her."

"Hey! I broke up with you!"

"Sure," he says without even looking at me.

Fury burns behind my eyes. It's all I can do not to slap him across the face.

"Either way, why are we so sure sex was the motive?" Tucker says. "Are we just going to forget that Sydney and Kat were fighting over twenty G's only days before she died?"

"Hey!" Kat objects.

"Dude, what the hell?" Beau jumps in.

"I'm just saying," Tucker says. "Maybe this wasn't about sex. Maybe it was about money."

"Well, if it was about money, do you really think it would be about laptop stickers and not a major contract with Parker?" Beau says, cutting his eyes at Cami.

"I did not kill her!" Cami objects.

"Well, neither did I!" yells Kat.

Everyone is shouting over each other, pointing fingers and making accusations, when the phones go off. And even though we're all in the middle of defending our innocence, five pairs of eyes go to the jar. After all, we're still influencers; a phone alert is like our Bat-Signal. And this was five going off at once.

"The last time all our phones went off at once . . ." Kat trails off. But I don't need reminding; those posts haunt my nightmares.

Beau approaches the jar. The glass is shaking from the vibrations of all the phones. He reaches in slowly, as if something might bite him, and pulls out his phone. His face pales as he reads the screen.

"Is it . . . ?" I ask.

He nods. "Another post to the account," he says. "Bragging about the murder, just like before."

237

Everyone scrambles to get their phone out of the jar, shoving each other to reach in first. I pull up TikTok on my own phone, and sure enough, there's another anonymous video.

The sound is a snippet of "Lifestyles of the Rich & Famous" by Good Charlotte. The caption:

"When normal people kill, they go to jail. When influencers murder, they go on TV! All publicity is good publicity, right?"

The video flashes screenshots of different headlines from the past week. The photos of Beau punching the photographer on the cover of the *National Inquirer;* an explainer article digging through Kat's Instagram from *True Crime Daily;* a still from a *Dateline* segment with Cami's photo hovering next to the host's head. All culminating in a screenshot of my interview from today.

"Was this you?" Cami turns on me. "Maybe you queued another TikTok to promote your little tell-all?"

"What? No!" I'm taken aback. How could Cami think that I've been the one making these posts. "Did anyone else notice that Tucker was the only one not in this little montage? He is *clearly* the one who queued this. I mean, it's so obvious, it's kind of embarrassing. He killed her and now he's trying to deflect blame with the videos so he doesn't get caught."

"You know, I'm not entirely sure you two didn't do this together," Cami says, dragging her pointer finger through the air between me and Tucker. "So you could continue your little messed-up relationship. Even you accusing him now, it feels like it's still part of your twisted little game."

"That's ridiculous," I say. At the same time, Tucker says, "I wouldn't call it a relationship."

This sets me off again. I fly toward him, arm raised to slap him. "You know what—"

But Beau interrupts us with a big wolf whistle. We all fall silent. I didn't even know someone as laid back as Beau was capable of making a sound that loud. "Everyone shut up for a second," he says. "I think . . . I just figured out something." He looks back to his phone. "I was just looking at the metadata for this post. I do it for all the anonymous posts to see, you know, if they slip up and, like, use their own IP address."

"Did they?" Kat asks hopefully.

"Well, no, but I noticed that with the other ones, you could see in the metadata that they'd been edited and queued, like, hours before they posted. But this one wasn't. It was posted immediately after it was made, meaning less than a minute ago." He looks up from his phone. "This video was made while we were all standing in this room, yelling at each other."

"While our phones were in the jar," I whisper.

Beau nods.

"What does that mean?" Cami asks.

"It means that whoever is posting these videos to our account, and whoever killed Syd, they aren't in this room right now." He looks around the room, his eyes finding the faces of each member of the house. "It means we're being framed."

31

6 DAYS AFTER

KAT

"What about Mr. Nelson?" Gwen asks. We've been gathered around the kitchen table for hours, trying to brainstorm who might've framed us.

"Who, the neighbor?" Cami reaches across the table to flip open a box of the pizza we ordered at hour two of trying to figure this out. "You think he did this?"

"I don't know, it's just a thought." Gwen shrugs. "He was always complaining about the noise."

The rest of us laugh at this.

"I'm just trying to think of people who *don't* like us." She throws blond hair over her shoulder. "After all, most people do."

"Sorry, Gwen," I say. "But I don't think Mr. Nelson framed us for murder because we played music too loud."

"Yeah, don't even dignify that by adding it to the list," Cami orders me as she slides a veggie slice onto her plate.

I take a sip of kombucha and look down at my notebook. I've been writing down any leads that seem half-promising.

The list is a hodgepodge of people, from members of Clout 9, various boys Gwen rejected, and even that one journalist we snubbed at the *Teen Choice Awards* when we got stuck in traffic and missed the red carpet.

Reading back over the list, it really doesn't seem like any of them would be likely to frame us for murder any more than sweet Mr. Nelson with the corgis would. Sure, some of the kids in Clout 9 hate us enough to, say, create a bot account to spam our videos with hate comments. But frame us for a felony? Kill Sydney in the process? I honestly can't imagine anyone doing this to someone, no matter what weird grudge they harbor about sponsorship deals or Shorty Awards.

Tucker stands up, and I think for a second he might be about to contribute to the conversation for the first time in over an hour, but instead he just slides the last slice of pepperoni onto his plate.

"Hey, what about Sydney's first manager?" I suggest. "The one she fired over DM?"

"No, I don't think so," Gwen says. "I mean, sure, he hated Syd. But why would he frame us? I don't think he has anything against the rest of us."

"Definitely not him." Cami shakes her head. "Something this elaborate with the phones and everything, it takes someone smart, and that guy wasn't very bright." She taps her nails on the table, thinking. "Plus, the videos are so passive-aggressive and everything about this is so vindictive and calculated . . . I think we have to be looking for a woman."

"You shouldn't say that." I wrinkle my nose.

"Oh, I'm sorry to gender-stereotype the person *framing us for murder*." She throws up her hands mockingly. "Jesus, get your priorities straight, Kat."

I take a deep breath so I don't sink to her level and snap back at her.

Gwen throws her plastic fork down in frustration. "God," she says. "I didn't think there was anything shittier than being a suspect for a murder. But knowing it's not a coincidence, but that someone out there is actively trying to make it look like we did it, that is . . . so much worse."

I reach out for her hand. She looks up, her eyes red and puffy. She looks younger than usual, somehow. "I know it's difficult," I say. "But think of it this way, Gwen: this means we're all on the same team now. I mean, yes, things are quite difficult still. But now we know that no one in the house killed Sydney. We know that we can trust our housemates, our friends. It's us together against whoever is framing us." I look around the table. "We have each other again."

"Not to mention, now we have a common enemy," Cami says. "Someone we can blame for all this bullshit. Someone that one day, when we know who they are, we can hunt down and exact our revenge on." Her eyes twinkle at the thought.

I pause. That's not *exactly* where I was going with my train of thought, but I appreciate Cami's contribution to my efforts to cheer Gwen up, even if unconventional. "That, too," I offer.

Tucker takes a long gulp from his cup and then lets out a very long, very loud belch.

"Ew!" Gwen exclaims.

He just shrugs and says, "Is there any soda left?"

"Yeah, in the downstairs fridge," Beau says, his eyes back on his laptop.

Tucker heads to the basement.

"I can't *believe* he did that," says Gwen.

"I can," says Cami. "It's Tucker."

6 DAYS AFTER

BEAU

I try to tune out the commotion surrounding Tucker's burp and focus back in on Sydney's Instagram. I've already looked through all her TikTok videos and all her photos here, which is really saying something, considering how much she posted. But I'm convinced there has to be something I'm missing. It seems like nothing happens in the real world anymore without being somehow reflected in the online world. If someone's life was connected to Sydney enough that they murdered her and then framed us for it, there had to be traces of them on social media, right?

Like, maybe it's one of these high school friends in her "Homecoming" Stories Highlight that she seems to have dropped from her circle once she became famous, or one of these creepy men who comment eggplant emojis on half her posts.

I scroll to the next photo, a shot of Brooklyn and Sydney, dressed up last Halloween in matching black dresses, posed like the two-dancing-girls emoji. I've already looked at the comments on this photo. But it gives me an idea. While Sydney's social media has been mostly a bust, maybe there's something to be found on her sister's account?

Before Brooklyn Reynolds was a wannabe TikTok star, she

was a wannabe Instagram influencer. @BK_Reynolds is full of the expertly posed, perfectly filtered images of a professional. Always Brooklyn fake-laughing as she cheersed a lemonade toward the camera, Brooklyn in a bikini in front of a waterfall, Brooklyn riding an old-fashioned bike on the Santa Monica Pier with all the tourists Photoshopped out—you get the idea. I doubt this overly polished, antiseptic content will produce any leads.

But luckily, this is not the only place Brooklyn lives on Instagram. I toggle over and type in @abitch_notabridge. If there's anywhere online where something might peek through the cracks of the perfect-Reynolds-sister veneer, it may very well be here, a locked account followed by only fifty people. I've followed the account for a while, since Brooklyn was quite friendly to me around the time we moved into the house. But then I got the feeling that she was maybe a bit too friendly, and since I liked Kat, I took a step back. I muted both her accounts from my feed, so I didn't absentmindedly like too many of her pictures and give her the wrong idea. But I didn't unfollow, because that seemed rude.

I scroll through her finsta. She hasn't posted anything since her sister's death, which makes sense; after all, she must be quite sad. I click on the most recent posts. A poorly lit selfie with a towel bar hanging behind her head, clearly her sitting on a toilet, the caption complaining about food poisoning (yep, no glossy curation on this account). Next, there's a close-up of her rolling her eyes, and a caption complaining about being pissed at her sister for dominating the conversation while at dinner with their parents.

And then, about two weeks ago, a shirtless pic, where she has covered up her nipples with peach emojis, showing off a rib cage tattoo of a scraggly drawn turtle.

The caption: *Shhhh! Do not tell my parents but I got crossed as shit last night and let Jake give me a stick-and-poke. FML does anyone know if Dr. Malibu does tattoo removal? Or do I say screw it and keep this lil guy?* 🐢

I stare at the tattoo as I flash back to two days ago, when that Lucy girl "confessed" and Brooklyn was at the house. She was wearing a crop top, I remember, because it was quite chilly that early in the morning and I recall wondering if she was cold. Her bottom ribs were fully exposed, but I swear I didn't see this janky turtle. I mean, she couldn't have gotten a tattoo removed that quickly, right? Doesn't that take like months . . .

Oh, holy shit. *Holy shit.*

"It's her!" I exclaim. The rest of the table turns to look at me, confusion on their faces. "I know who's framing us."

Cami looks at me like I'm crazy. "Who?"

"Sydney."

"But she's dead." Gwen blinks. Then she gasps, covering her mouth with her hands. "Oh my God, is it her ghost?"

"No." I sidestep that one. "Actually, I don't think she's dead." I pull up the photo on my phone. "I think Brooklyn is dead. And Sydney is walking around pretending to be her sister and framing all of us. But the thing is, she didn't know that her sister had a finsta, which makes sense, you know, since Brooklyn used it to vent about her. But *because* Sydney didn't follow this account, and because Brooklyn hid it from her family, Sydney didn't know that two weeks before Brooklyn died, she got a tattoo. Look, look at this." I shove my phone toward them all. I'm so hyped up by this realization, so frantic, that I worry I'm not communicating well. But as crazy as this must sound, I know I'm right. I just know. "I saw, I saw her rib cage when she was here with Tucker the other

245

day. There was no tattoo, so that can't be her. The twin who's alive—it's not Brooklyn; it's Sydney. And I think she's the one who's framing us."

"Oh my God," Kat whispers, staring down at the phone. Relief washes over her face. And that's when I truly know that I'm right, because she believes it, too.

"That would explain how she can get through the facial recognition to make the posts," Gwen says.

Cami's eyes light up. "And actually, it would explain something I noticed: that 'Brooklyn' "—she makes air quotes—"was wearing Sydney's bracelet the day after the body was found. Even though you need a special tool to get those bracelets off."

My heart rate picks up. Another piece of potential evidence. I can feel this case coming together.

"What the hell are you talking about?" a voice says. I turn to see Tucker hovering in the doorway to the kitchen.

"Oh, um, I think I figured out who framed us. . . ."

"No, I heard what you said, I heard the whole thing. I'm just wondering where the hell you get off, blaming my dead girlfriend for her own murder."

"Hold up." I raise my hands. "That's not really what I'm saying. Let me explain. You know, when Brooklyn was here the other day, did you see a tattoo on her chest?"

"I don't know. I wasn't looking at her chest at all, because I wasn't being a perv."

"No, that's not what I . . . I would never objectify her like that. I wasn't looking on purpose or anything. I just know that if she'd had a tattoo, especially one that was sort of misshapen, I would've noticed it." I turn to Kat. "I wasn't—"

"I know." She puts her hand on my arm to calm me. "Tucker,

you have to agree that this makes more sense than some dude who used to be Sydney's manager or some Shorty Award sore loser framing us. There is only one person who has enough reason to be *this* angry at each person in this room: Sydney herself. It's totally clear."

"The only thing that's clear to me is that you guys have fully lost it," Tucker scoffs. "A finsta post and a bracelet? That's your proof that the person framing us is the one we all saw buried? Good fucking luck going to the police with that." Tucker goes over to the kitchen to get more ice for his soda.

The mood in the room deflates.

"Don't listen to him, Beau. Your theory is really smart," Gwen says.

"Thanks," I say politely, but it's not the best consolation coming from her, no offense. I run a hand through my hair. "But he's kind of right about the police. I mean, we're the suspects, I don't know if they will believe anything we say."

"And especially not if what we're saying involves some sort of psychotic *Parent Trap* switcheroo," Cami says. "Plus, it took Johnson days to stop calling it Tick-Tack; do you really think she'll be convinced by finsta evidence?"

Kat shakes her head. "Johnson wouldn't believe us short of, like, Sydney confessing."

"Well, what if we got her to?" Gwen asks. "Confess, I mean." Her wide eyes don't give any indication that she's joking.

Kat and I share a look.

"I don't think that would be so easy, Gwen," Kat says delicately.

"Actually . . ." Cami tilts her head, thinking. "Gwen may have a point."

"You don't have to act so surprised," says Gwen.

"We *should* confront her," Cami continues. "See if she'll spill the whole thing."

"What, do you really think she'd just admit it?" I ask, incredulous.

"Well, not to you or me, but..." Cami looks over her shoulder to Tucker, who's making a ruckus in the kitchen. She clears her throat.

"What?" He looks up from what he's doing to see everyone in the room staring at him. "No. No way."

"I'm just saying, you and 'Brooklyn' "—Cami makes air quotes again—"have been awfully . . . cozy lately."

"Yeah, well, me and *Brooklyn* are both grieving *Sydney.*"

"All you have to do is ask her a simple question: Who is she?" Cami says. "See what she says."

"It's not a simple question," Tucker says. "It's a ludicrously insulting question you want me to ask someone whose sister has been murdered. Brooklyn has been through enough. There's no freaking way I'm going to add to her pain by harassing her with your insane conspiracy theory."

"But—"

"But nothing." He throws up his hands. "The answer is no. I just—just won't do that to her." He huffs out of the room.

Cami makes an ugly face at his receding shadow. "That boy is completely useless," she says.

Gwen's shoulders fall in disappointment. She sniffles; tears well in her eyes. "Oh, don't cry," Cami says, patting her hand.

"It was a good idea, Gwen," Kat says. "Don't worry, we'll think of something else." But the look she gives me after she says this leaves me unsure whether she actually believes we will.

32

6 DAYS AFTER

CAMI

Later that night, I find Gwen on her balcony. "Hey." I step out into the cool night, closing the French doors behind me. "Sorry I called you a bitch earlier."

She gives me a funny look. "You've done it plenty of times before."

"Yeah, well this time I yelled it," I say. "And I kinda meant it."

She shrugs. "I'd gone on TV and implied that you might have committed a murder, so it's understandable."

"True." I tap my hands on the railing. I stare out to the dark horizon, toward the ocean. I can just barely see the waves breaking against the shore. "Can I ask . . . why'd you do that interview?"

"I needed the money," she says.

"For what?" I half-laugh. "To buy a Tesla for each day of the week?"

"No, to pay my lawyer." She sighs. "I'm kinda, like, broke."

I blink. "Like, you're money's not liquid or . . . ?"

"Like I don't have any money."

"What?" I think of all the times I've seen Gwen swipe a

platinum credit card, of all the lucrative deals she beat me out on. "How, Gwen? You've made like millions ..."

"And it turns out my mom's been spending it just as quickly." She holds her arms tightly against her body, goose bumps forming on her skin.

My eyes go wide. "Really?"

"Well, I mean, a bit of it was me," she admits. "But I got ahold of the credit card statements, and it turns out my shopping barely made a dent compared to what she did. You know they sell electromagnetic ghost detectors for fifty thousand dollars? She bought three."

"So it's all just ... gone?"

"Yep." She makes a popping sound with her lips.

"You're sure?" I still can't wrap my head around at least $10 million just, *poof,* gone.

"Yeah, I'm sure, Cami. I've been sure for days. Why do you think my closet is empty?"

"I don't know. I thought it was a Marie Kondo kind of thing."

"Cami, look at me." She waves her acrylic-nailed fingers. "Do you think I'm anything but a maximalist? I had to sell my clothes to make my mom's mortgage payment. I had to do that interview to pay my lawyer."

"Damn." I shake my head. "And I always thought my parents stressed *me* out. They put all this pressure on me, to get the best grades in school, the best role in ballet. *Be a winner, Cami.* But they still did all the parent things, you know? Like, it was my job to study hard and get As, but it was their job to pay the bills, so I never had to worry about those things. I can't imagine having a parent who expects you to be, like, the parent, too."

"I can." Gwen laughs hollowly. "This kind of thing happened

before I was famous, too. Like, she'd max out credit cards buying shoes, and then her card would get denied in the grocery line. Or she'd call me to pick her up at some bar before I had my license."

"Jeez."

"Yeah." She shrugs. "But it's life. What are you gonna do."

"Yeah, but it's *you*. I always thought your life was kind of perfect."

"Cami, please." She looks at me seriously. "If my life was actually perfect, do you think I'd spend this much time on the internet trying to convince strangers that it is?"

33

1 WEEK AFTER

SYDNEY

My plan didn't stop the night I "died," of course. It turns out, it takes a lot of hard work to ruin lives. Especially lives that are so privileged and gilded and picture-perfect. The good news is, if you push hard enough, they fall quite a long way down.

The work really snowballed as I schemed to keep up with the plan, but luckily, I'm smart. Smarter than the kids in the house, who keep pointing fingers at each other, and smarter than the cops, who follow every bread crumb I leave. Of course, it doesn't hurt that the people of the internet have quite skillfully turned my crumbs into three-course meals.

I don't know about you, but I'm, like, freaking obsessed with this Sydney Reynolds case. I roll over and turn up the volume of my floating Bluetooth speaker, bobbing along in the pool beside me and amplifying the sweet sounds of the world's most-listened-to true-crime podcast.

Oh my God, the cohost replies. *The Hashtag Homicide, as the kids are calling it, is about all I can think about. Was it Gwen? Was it Cami? Was it Kat? I'm glued to my phone, waiting to see if another post goes up.*

I slide my sunglasses off my forehead and down over my eyes.

I'm floating around my parents' pool on one of the lounge rafts, wearing a white bikini from Brooklyn's closet and chain-smoking cigarettes I filched from the cabinet under my mom's bathroom sink. I light up another with my Zippo and take a long drag.

I'm honestly not sure if I like smoking or not. It puts my head in a bit of a tizzy, a rush like drinking too much caffeine, but it also makes me feel a little nauseous. I never used to smoke. After all, I've seen the commercials; I had the talks at school. I know it kills you.

The Sydney Reynolds before last Friday would *never* have touched a cigarette. But as you've probably heard if you've been online anytime in the last week, that girl is dead.

We'll be bringing you updates on the Hashtag Homicide as soon as we get them, so be sure to subscribe. And use the code "WhoKilledSydney" for fifteen percent off your next mattress from our generous sponsors. But for now, on to today's main story. The podcast moves on to talk about JonBenét Ramsey for the umpteenth time.

Excuse me? Is my death not interesting enough for you? I scoff and switch back to music.

Over the last few weeks, I've been gobbling up the news coverage of my handiwork like it's SkinnyPop Sweet & Salty. The tabloids, cable news, murder podcasts, celebrity podcasts—even the proper news podcasts mention me at least once or twice a week.

There are as many theories as there are hobbyist investigators and social media sleuths. Some say Gwen's the culprit. Others are sure the gun was planted and that it was actually Tucker, or Cami, or Beau, or Beau *and* Kat together, or even, one said, Beau and Cami together (not sure I understand what that theory's based on, I have to admit, since I don't think those two have ever even had a one-on-one conversation, let alone planned to commit murder as a team). But no one, and I mean no one, has come close to figuring out what really happened. It turns out I'm quite good at this.

Not that it's been easy. I've had to dodge complications the whole way. There was the weirdness with Cami and the bracelet, though luckily the police shooed her away from poor, mourning "Brooklyn." And then, of course, there was that clout-chasing crazy girl who tried to confess and ruin everything I'd done. But thankfully, under the slightest pressure from Nora Caponi, she fell apart like a SHEIN dress the second time you wash it.

But then there was the difficulty of planting the gun. I wiped it down using the advice of an online video that was surprisingly easy to find. Once it was clean, I wanted to plant it as soon as possible, to really lock in the theory that someone in the house did it, and not for nothing, to get it out of my parents' house.

I had planned to hide it under the felt of the pool table, so it could point to anyone and everyone. I also loved the irony that it was literally right under Detective Johnson's nose the whole time. I knew that would frustrate the hell out of her—and put fire under her ass to get a conviction.

So the day after "the murder," I snuck back into the house through the tunnel at dawn, the only time I assumed everyone would be asleep. I came up from the basement, gun in my gloved hands, tiptoeing through the silent house. The rising sun had just begun to stream in through the entryway windows, lighting up little flecks of dust.

And then I heard a sound on the stairs. The staircase to the second floor was between me and the dining room, and whoever it was could see me over the railing if I tried to go back to the basement. I was trapped. I looked around frantically and pushed open the only door available to me—to the attached garage. I dove behind the nearest car, Cami's hulking SUV, and waited, my heart racing.

I was still holding the gun. I needed to ditch it, fast. There was no longer time for the poetic justice of hiding it in the table the investigators were using. I just needed to get rid of it.

I tried the door of Cami's SUV first, but it was locked. Same with Kat's Beetle. I made my way down the row: locked, locked, locked. *Wow, guys, keeping your cars locked, even in the garage.* I guess trust is hard to come by when your housemates are under investigation for murder.

And then I got to a car I didn't recognize: a white Jeep. I recounted the cars and realized Gwen's Ferrari was missing. Classic: she crashed another car. I looked more closely and noticed the tire cover: UGH, AS IF!

As soon as I saw that, I was sure the car was hers. That's from my favorite movie, and she was always stealing bits of my personality and claiming them as her own. *Clueless*, huh, Gwen? Well, here's a clue. I dropped the gun and rezipped the cover.

I peeled off my gloves and stuffed them into my gym shoes.

But I was still trapped. The tunnel was out of the question with someone awake and wandering around the house. And even though the garage door was right there, I couldn't exactly open it without the rumbling awakening Beau, whose room was directly above it. He could look out the window and see me fleeing. No, that wouldn't work. I needed to go out the back door and end up on the beach.

The only way out was to hide in plain sight. To be Brooklyn, here to get something of my sister's. I fixed my face into a look of vague sadness and walked casually down the hall toward the kitchen.

Looking back, I was lucky it was Tucker I first ran into that morning and not someone shrewder like Cami or even Kat or Beau. Tucker ate up my little story about that ratty stuffed bear. He didn't question me for a second. He even invited "Brooklyn" to hang out.

I told myself that I said yes so as not to raise suspicions. That hanging out with Tucker helped me to build out my lie and to gather information on him and the goings-on in the house. But if I'm honest with myself, I also stayed and had coffee with him because . . . well, Tucker still had a certain hold over me.

Oh, Tucker. Hot, dumb, infuriating Tucker. He's the only thing keeping me from executing this plan perfectly. The only thing that's distracted me from my singular goal of revenge. He's my Achilles' heel, that one. I'm honestly embarrassed by the basic nature of it all; after all, there's nothing like a fuckboi to be the undoing of an ambitious woman.

Like so many women who've been scorned by the one they've loved the most, I oscillate between hating him and still loving him, and make terrible decisions as a result.

The truth is, there weren't supposed to be this many posts to @LitLair_LA. The plan was meant to be simple. I was supposed to plant the gun and then make the post about where it was and then retire, sit back, and watch the police get revenge for me.

But then things got messy. The plan went off the rails just two days in. There I was, being Brooklyn, sitting in the police station at Detective Johnson's desk, waiting to fill out some paperwork for my statement about the last time I saw Sydney. She'd stepped outside to take a call. And I overheard the police officers a desk over. They were young men, the cops. Not as young as me, but not as old as Carney and Johnson. But they were truly acting like teenage boys. They were joking and shoving each other's shoulders as they looked at something on their computers.

"Can you believe these texts?" one of the cops said.

"I know." The other guy shook his head. "And have you seen that girl? God, that Tucker kid's lucky."

"You two disgust me," said another cop, a woman, peeking over the top of their monitor. "Isn't she a minor? And isn't she dead?"

"Nah, these aren't to the dead girl. These are to Gwen Riley. You know, the one who danced at the Super Bowl?"

That confused me. *What could Gwen and Tucker be texting about that would get such a reaction from these cops?*

"I don't care who she is; she's still a minor," the female cop scolded.

"Of course. We weren't looking at pictures or anything."

"Well, I'm glad not committing a felony is the bar. Those messages are evidence and should be treated as such, even if they're about sex."

Sex?

My head spun. All of a sudden, I felt like the fluorescent lights were too bright, that the TVs playing the news and the cops talking by the coffee maker were too loud. Like everything was just too much. My heart raced, but my brain felt like it was moving in slow motion.

And then I spotted it. The file on Detective Johnson's desk. Which was labeled *Tucker Campbell.*

I looked around, but no one was paying attention to me, and Detective Johnson was nowhere to be seen. I flipped open the file.

It was filled with police paperwork. And a flash drive labeled *cell phone.*

Without even thinking, I grabbed it, stuffing it into the pocket of my cardigan and flipping the file closed in a flash.

"Brooklyn?" My shoulders tensed. Detective Johnson was approaching the desk. *Did she see me?*

But she smiled kindly and said, "Sorry about that interruption. Let's finish this up so you can get home. I'm sure you'd like to be with your parents."

That night, in Brooklyn's room, I turned off the Wi-Fi on my old Dell computer from middle school (the police had taken my Mac into evidence, and I couldn't figure out the password to Brooklyn's) and plugged in the flash drive. I sat in the dark, the only light the bluish glow from my laptop, and read through the texts. Every last, heartbreaking one. All of it, right there in blue and white bubbles: the evidence of his betrayal. Of their betrayal.

I always knew Tucker was a bit of a fuckboi. I saw that he liked other girls' thirst traps. I knew he playfully flirted with girls at parties and joked around with other guys about what Instagram model had a great ass and who had the best boobs or whatever.

But I thought he was a sort of reformed fuckboi. That he had a soft spot for me. That for all this little stuff on the surface, the talk he talked and the photos he liked, the person he really was, deep down, was the boy I knew, who was so sweet to me, and who reached for me to cuddle in the dark as he slept.

So I let the little things slide. I thought I was being such a chill, cool girlfriend. For seeing the big picture, for trusting him. Never demanding to see his phone or telling him not to be friends with other girls.

And this is how he repaid me. By sleeping with my best friend.

Right under my nose, in the house we shared. In the house my family bought.

I slammed the laptop closed. And the wheels in my head began to turn, just as they did that night on the beach. And once again the only thing that kept me from spiraling into despair was the knowledge that I could make the people who caused this hurt just as miserable as I was.

So I shifted my plan a bit, decided that maybe instead of framing the whole house in equal measure, some people deserved to be singled out. I decided the gun post could wait, and that maybe Tucker deserved to feel a bit of singularly directed pain. I was already supposed to read the poem the next morning at the funeral. It was the perfect opportunity. The hardest part was being nice to him when I was pretending to be Brooklyn. But then I got to watch from a fabulous vantage point on the stage as the phones all went off and Tucker's life imploded. I even started to think about going back to the house and finding a way to move the gun to Tucker's room.

But then . . . things got a bit trickier. He made that video and he spoke so lovingly about our relationship, his regret about his mistake with Gwen, and the pain of losing me. He seemed to really feel bad about what he'd done. And he seemed like he really loved me, still. And then he came to the house and brought me the book, which I always thought he'd just left untouched in the bottom of his drawer and forgotten about. But he'd remembered. And I don't know, something shifted in me. All these memories came back from our relationship. All these feelings.

I started to think that maybe I'd made a mistake, leaking all the texts. Putting the focus on him. That maybe he'd made a mistake, too, and that he'd really loved me, despite everything. And while I wasn't ready to quite forgive him yet, I started to think that maybe I wanted someone else in the house to go down for this, not him. Since if I did end up forgiving him, it would be no fun to have a boyfriend stuck in jail for twenty-plus years. And after all, this was about Brooklyn, not about Tucker cheating on me. And that's what I needed to focus on.

So I decided it was time to be done with distractions. It was time to finish what I'd started. It was time to lead them to the gun.

I thought that if I served up evidence so digestibly to the police, they'd arrest Gwen immediately. But they didn't. Without fingerprints on the gun, they told the press, they needed to gather more evidence before they made an arrest. More evidence? Sheesh, I'd already given them so much.

And then Gwen gets on Nora Caponi's show and practically taunts me with the fact that she's still free to pull classic Gwen Riley publicity stunts instead of behind bars, where she belongs. I was so enraged watching it, I threw together another post and didn't even wait to queue it.

But it worked just fine. I got the conversation back to where I wanted it. Now the podcasts and YouTube channels and TikTok accounts have shifted away from suspecting Tucker and back to the others. They are talking about Gwen's longtime jealousy of me, Cami's all-consuming competitiveness, Kat and the $20,000, Beau and the cameras. They're talking about the toxicity of social media and the cutthroat environment of the house. If I'm lucky, the police will sense a conspiracy, and the hammer will fall on more than one of them. But if they only arrest Gwen . . . well, I still have the rest of "Brooklyn's" life to find new, creative ways to terrorize Beau, Kat, and Cami—and Tucker, too, if he crosses me again.

I finish my cigarette and toss it into the pristine turquoise pool water. What's my mom going to do? Yell at me? Concerns like that are just laughable now. The thing about a singular focus on revenge is that you're free of all other earthly worries. It's deeply clarifying.

I roll to the side, flipping off the float and into the water with a splash. I sink down a few feet into the pool.

My eyes sting under the water. I watch with a kind of detached interest as the bubbles escape my lips and float up to the surface. I stay under the water a long time, longer than is comfortable. Until my lungs ache and I see spots.

I've been doing things like this lately. Pushing my car past 100 while driving down the winding coastal road, touching the 500-degree curling iron. Taking the other gun out of the safe, loading and unloading it, just to hold it in my hand. It's like I'm reaching for the edge to see how far I can go. To feel something besides numbing, emptying loss.

When I finally come up for air, I'm gasping for breath. But I like the way it burns.

34

10 DAYS AFTER

KAT

I told Gwen we'd think of something. But so far, we have nothing.

For the last few days, we've been trying come up with any other plan, to dig up any sort of evidence that could help our case. We've combed through both twins' social media and scoured the house for clues, with no luck. Beau, Gwen, Cami, and I have been working tirelessly. Tucker has mostly stayed in his room, but so far, we haven't made any more progress than he has.

Tonight, Beau and I sit in the dining room, trying to figure out the security cameras. I search YouTube for explainers on how they work, but all the videos are about installing them, not hacking them.

Beau examines the surveillance cameras themselves. His hands move nimbly, his long fingers screwing and unscrewing the pieces of the camera he's disassembled and laid out across the table.

He shakes his head. "I just don't get it." He runs a hand through his floppy hair. "We've taken them apart and put them back together, but I can't find any sign of tampering, not the hardware or the software." He points to the screen on the security system modem. "It doesn't make any sense. A Reynolds sister enters the house and then, *poof,* there's a body in the pool. How?"

Before I can answer, we are interrupted by a crashing sound coming from the other room.

"What was that?" we say simultaneously.

We find the source of the sound in the kitchen, where Cami has slipped off a stepladder and brought down a shelf's worth of mugs with her. She seems to be uninjured and smiles when she sees us. "Oh, good, Beau, you're tall. We're trying to see if there are any more wineglasses back there."

I look around the kitchen at the half dozen used glasses and open wine bottles on the counter. "How many do you need?"

"We're doing a wine tasting," she says by way of explanation.

"Cami knows all about French wines," Gwen says, holding a glass in each hand. "Like the Pinot Noir, and Cabernet, and Coup d'état. So far, I can't tell the difference. But I'm willing to keep trying." She takes a large sip of each glass, then scrunches her nose in confusion.

"I'm sorry, what is going on?" Beau asks. "You guys know we're still under police investigation, right? And that the drinking age is twenty-one."

"Please, do you think I'm afraid of an underage-drinking citation with first-degree murder hanging over my head?" says Cami. "Don't you guys get it? We're no closer to proving she framed us than we were when we pieced it together. Just that much closer to twenty-five years in prison. And even if, even *if,* our lawyers could get us a not-guilty verdict, it's not like anyone will ever believe us again. How are we ever gonna get jobs, let alone be sponsored as influencers? I mean, our careers are over. So I say"—she holds up a bottle of wine—"screw it. If Sydney is going to try to ruin my life, I might as well spend the last few days I have—"

"Drinking your way through her family's wine collection?" Beau asks, unamused.

Cami smiles. "I was going to say 'living it up,' but that works, too."

Just then, a figure appears in the kitchen doorway: Tucker. The room goes quiet. We've barely seen him since the fight over confronting Sydney. He avoids eye contact with us as he walks through the room. He grabs his jacket off the back of one of the chairs and checks it for his wallet. He flips the keys in his hands and starts toward the back door.

"Where are you going?" Beau asks.

"Don't have to tell you, do I?" Tucker says gruffly. "I'm not part of your little team."

"Well, you're going to regret that when we order jackets," Cami mumbles, and then takes a swig of wine straight from the bottle. Tucker stops to stare at her. "Well, if you're gonna leave, leave," she says. "Buh-bye!"

He slips out the back door.

"Some people are just so unfriendly," Cami scoffs. "Now, where were we?" She clicks her phone to turn up the volume of the music. "Beau, Kitty, can I interest you in giving up?"

Cami hands me a red Solo cup. I'm not going to lie, it's a little bit appealing. Not the wine, really, but the idea of forgetting, at least for a moment, about everything that's happened in the last two weeks. But I can't stop thinking about it. About Sydney, out there scheming. And about Tucker and where he might be going. And if he might be going to meet *her*.

"Here." Cami brings a bottle over to me. "Oh, wait." She

shakes the bottle and laughs. "This one's empty. BRB, Gwen. You got Aux."

Gwen—who is bobbing along to the sounds of Lil Nas X and wearing Elton John–style sunglasses even though it's nighttime and inside—throws a thumbs-up. Cami scurries down to the basement.

Beau turns to me. "I can't believe these are the people we're in the fight of our lives with."

10 DAYS AFTER

CAMI

God, Beau is *such* a party pooper. Doesn't he see how nice it would be to just give up? I've spent each of my seventeen years of life dedicated, with an unceasing drive, toward goals: the best grades in school, the best dancer in my class, the most followers on the app. I felt like I couldn't split my focus or loosen my grip even for a second, or else I would lose everything.

But now it's all been torn away from me and I have no way to stop it. No control of my own future. And realizing that, I don't know, I just snapped. If it's all going to hell anyway, I might as well party. I feel like I finally understand the life trajectory of Lindsay Lohan, and also, possibly, the work of Friedrich Nietzsche, although I'm less sure about that, as I never read that book my mom gave me.

In the basement, it's dark and cold, thanks to the air-conditioning that's pumping. The motion sensor lights click on as I go, illuminating the gym, the game room, the movie theater. I get to the wine cellar and punch in the code—Sydney and Brooklyn's birthday. The lock chimes cheerfully, and I push open the door. It's dim in here, and even chillier. Goose bumps run up my arms.

I scan the bottles, looking for one I might recognize. They all have fancy lettering and line drawings of different animals or flowers or castles. For all my talk upstairs, mimicking words I've heard my dad say at business dinners or heard while watching prestige television, I don't actually know that much about wine. I just wanted Gwen to think I was sophisticated.

Gwen said she likes white because that's what they drink on *Real Housewives*, so I grab a Chardonnay. And I should probably get a red, too. Okay, let's see, Bordeaux? That sounds fancy; I'll grab that.

I lift up the bottle, but it doesn't slide out easily, like the white did. Instead, it turns like a switch. And something beside me shifts, the sound of stone scraping across stone, as the wall opens like a door.

Oh. My. God.

35

10 DAYS AFTER

TUCKER

Gravel crunches beneath the tires as Brooklyn pulls up to the overlook. She puts the car in park but leaves the engine running and her music playing softly over the sound system.

It was her idea to come here. I texted her that I needed to get out of the house and wanted to see her, and she suggested driving out to the overlook. It made sense, since the other house members were so hostile to her and being in public was out of the question when anyone with a cell phone could snap a photo of us. But still, I was surprised when she suggested we park here specifically. It has kind of a reputation.

During the day, this spot offers beautiful views of the ocean. But at night, it's usually only frequented by, well, high school kids hooking up in their cars. I'm sure Brooklyn must know this, since it was a running joke at our high school. But maybe not. She always seemed sort of innocent, especially compared to her sister. Maybe she didn't mean anything by suggesting we go here.

I look to her, trying to read her, but she's looking down at her phone, queuing songs.

I turn back, staring out the windshield. My eyes have adjusted a bit to the dark, but still, it's hard to see anything. This spot is far enough from the closest house that no light pollutes the sky. I know that just a few feet in front of us, the earth suddenly drops off in a cliff, plunging toward the ocean below. Where dark waves crash roughly against the cliff. But for now, all I can see is black. The ocean, the sky—it's all just a continuous, blank darkness.

When we were young, whenever we'd be near any sort of height, my older brothers would do this little trick where they shoved me and then caught me in one quick movement, shouting *Saved your life!* in my ear. It was meant to get a reaction out of me, so they could mock my fear. It was annoying, but par-for-the-course brother stuff. Except for one time, Ian pushed me a bit too hard and didn't catch me. I fell out of our tree house, at least ten feet down, onto the hard-packed earth. I broke my arm and had to wear a sling for weeks. But when I was on the ground scream-ing, he still laughed. So did Jeremy. Maybe that's why I'm so bad with heights now. I shudder and look away from the windshield.

"It's a bit creepy out here, isn't it?" Brooklyn says.

I just shrug. No way I'm telling a girl that I'm afraid of a cliff.

"I would've invited you to the house, but my parents . . ."

I nod. Even though she believes I'm innocent, I get that her parents might not be so sure. I bet I'm not one of their favorite people at the moment.

"I tried to tell them. That you never would've harmed Syd-ney. And about how kind you've been to me since it happened. I even showed them the video you made about the Gwen thing, but . . ." She shakes her head.

"I get it," I say. "Honestly, I'm not even sure my own parents believe me sometimes. I mean, they're paying for the lawyers and everything. But sometimes I think that's more because they don't want the shame of having a son who's a murder suspect. Because sometimes, the way my mom doesn't want to be in the same room as me . . . can barely look at me. It's like . . . she's scared of me." My voice cracks. I clear my throat. *Great, Campbell, you sound like a total sissy.* I stare down at the glove box.

Brooklyn places her hand on mine. "Oh, Tucker." I look up at her touch. Our eyes meet. Her gaze is so soft, her face so warm.

I lean forward across the console and kiss her, tentatively, unsure. Part of me thinks she'll pull back and slap me. After all, I was once her sister's boyfriend. But she doesn't. Instead, she kisses me back. Gently at first, but then with a sort of hunger, an urgency.

Brooklyn sheds her jacket, exposing one bare shoulder, then the other. She's wearing a thin black tank top and a red bra. I run my hands up her back, pushing the bottom hem of her tank top up and up and pawing at the clasp to the bra. I twist the lace, but I can't get it from this angle with the freaking steering wheel in the way and . . .

I lift her up slightly and pull her over to my seat, onto my lap. Brooklyn straddles me, kisses me deeply, her dark hair creating a sort of curtain around me, blocking out the already dim light.

She tugs at the edges of my shirt, and I lift my arms so she can pull it off. Brooklyn tosses my shirt to the side. Then she bites her lip and reaches down to pull her tank top over her head. Her hair rises up with it and then falls around her face like a wild black mane, tendrils pooling at her shoulders. I trace my fingers across her body slowly, my eyes taking in every inch, as I feel along the edge of her light-wash jeans, along the curve of her waist, across her ribs and . . .

I freeze, my fingers almost to the wire of her bra. The light is dim, but it is clear. There is no tattoo on her rib cage.

I pull my hand back like her skin has burned mine.

"What's wrong?" she asks.

"I'm—" I lift her off me, dumping her only somewhat gently into the other seat. "I'm sorry, I have to go. I'm not feeling well." I grab my shirt off the floor and shut the door behind me.

I take off toward the main road. I hear her window roll down.

"Wait, Tucker!" she yells after me. "What are you doing?"

But I don't stop. I tug my shirt over my head as I keep pushing forward as quickly as I can through the dark trees surrounding the overlook. I can't see anything, and I pray I don't trip and tumble down the hill, or worse, off the cliff.

I eventually get back to the road. It's dark and the wind off the sea is strong. It smells like rain, and the air is full of static, like lightning is about to strike. There's no sidewalk along the road—in fact, there's not much room for anything at all—so I have to run down the middle of the street. Watching for headlights coming up behind me or speeding around a blind corner. But I have no other choice. I keep moving forward, away from her. My lungs start to burn and my legs hurt, but I don't slow down. I just keep pushing on, my body moving forward but my mind stuck. Because the whole way back to the house, all I can think is: I've just done something I thought I'd never do again. I just kissed Sydney Reynolds.

36

10 DAYS AFTER

BEAU

"Wait, what are you saying?" Gwen asks, peeking into the tunnel. "She went through the tunnel to hijack the cameras?"

"No, she didn't need to mess with the cameras at all," Kat explains. "By going through here, she avoided them altogether."

"Guys—" Cami says.

"That's why Beau couldn't find anything wrong with them," Kat says. "Because there wasn't."

"Guys!" Cami says, louder this time. We all turn to look. "We're not alone." She points to the bottom of the stairs. Where Tucker has appeared, breathing heavily, with a crazed look in his eyes, wearing an inside-out T-shirt that he's sweat straight through.

"I'm in," he says. His Adam's apple bobbles.

Kat and I share a look. "What?" I ask.

"You're right," he chokes out, his words tumbling together in his flustered state. "It's Sydney. I saw—we were—well, it doesn't matter. But you're right. That's not Brooklyn. It's Sydney." He finally takes a breath and runs a hand through his hair, leaving

271

it sticking up wildly. "I'm in," he says again. And then, seeing we still don't understand, he adds, "I'll help you catch her."

"So how do we get her to confess on tape without her knowing I'm recording?" Tucker asks, stepping into the dining room, holding a red Solo cup. He's calmed down and taken a shower while I've mapped out a plan on the pool table, using various kitchen items as stand-ins for each of us and placing them on the model of the grounds the police left in our trash bin after a K-9 took a bite out of one of the walls.

"That's what we're working on," I say.

I grab the cup from his hand and place it next to the "pool" and the Toast Malone mug that represents Sydney. I write his name on the cup with a permanent marker.

"I saw that you guys had me as a coffee creamer," Gwen says, approaching the table with her arms behind her back. "But actually, I lead a dairy-free lifestyle, so I'd prefer to switch."

"Which do you want to be, Gwen?" Kat asks.

"Well, now that you ask." Her eyes light up as she presents what she was holding behind her back: the official Gwen Riley Doll™, complete with her own tiny cell phone and ring light. "I was thinking: who better to represent me than, well, me!"

"Ugh, not that thing. Its eyes are so creepy," Tucker complains.

Gwen ignores this and swaps out the coffee creamer for the doll.

"Be careful with that," Cami warns me. "It's a limited edition."

"Okay." I exhale, trying not to lose my patience. "Is everyone fine with their icon now?" I take the general grumbling as a yes.

"All right . . . now, here's the plan," I say. "Tucker." I hold up the cup. "You talk to Sydney out here, by the pool. You'll be wearing this microphone."

I hold up the little Bluetooth lapel microphone Gwen gave me from her video-making equipment. "I'm going to re-rig the security cameras down by the pool deck." I open the door to the cabinet that holds our tech equipment. The Wi-Fi router blinks. I turn on the little screen next to it. "The feed from the cameras goes to here." I hold up the auxiliary cord dangling from the security system. "Kat will be here with her phone, streaming the video."

Cami picks up one of the security cameras off the table and holds it up like she's taking a selfie, winking at the camera. Her image comes up on the screen on the wall.

Kat clicks the cord into her phone, and Cami appears on her screen, too. Kat gives a thumbs-up.

"Wait, no fair." Gwen leans into the shot of the camera, flipping her hair. "Let me in."

"Guys," I say.

"I'm just making sure it works," Gwen says innocently.

"It does," Kat says, showing Gwen her reflection.

I straighten Kat's saltshaker, in the little house. I had placed Cami's bear-shaped honey bottle and Gwen's doll in the house to help with whatever Kat may need, but now I'm worried they might end up distracting more than helping. "You two need to take this seriously," I tell them.

"And when it's people, not condiments, we will," says Cami. I'm not sure she has totally sobered up yet.

"Okay," I continue. "Now, once Sydney is headed toward the pool, I'll go out and let the air out of her tires, then circle back via the beach." I place my Tabasco on the beach part of the model.

"What about the tunnel?" Gwen drags a nail across the table, tracing the path from the pool to the house. "Couldn't she use that to get into the house?"

"I'm still figuring that out." I scratch my head. "But we can seal it off somehow."

"Hey, hey, wait a second." Tucker looks at the cluster of condiments in the "house." "This is bull. Why am I the only one outside with the crazy girl? What if something goes down?"

"I'll be outside," I say.

"Yeah, way over by her car. Not backing me up," he says. "There's no reason all three girls need to be inside the locked house to operate one phone." He shakes his head. "No way. I'm not doing this if I'm the only one out there."

I look to Cami and Gwen. Gwen is fixing her lip gloss in the view of the security footage, even though the other wall of the dining room has a large mirror.

"Cami," I say, picking up her honey bottle. "Would you be willing to be here in the trees between the pool and the beach? You could watch the stream and back up Tucker if anything goes wrong."

"What, why should I have to go out there?" she argues. "Why not your girlfriend?"

"Because Kat knows how to work the security system," I say. "She's been taking it apart with me while you guys drank through half of France."

"Hey, if we hadn't done that, we wouldn't have found the tunnel," she points out.

"And people say partying is a waste of time," Gwen says. She and Cami share a laugh.

Gwen reaches for her doll. "How about this?" She sets the doll next to Cami's bear. "That way Cami isn't out there alone. We both can be backup."

"Are you sure?" Cami asks Gwen.

"Of course. I wouldn't want you to be out there alone." Gwen shrugs. "And I want to help. I want to be part of the team."

"All right, it's settled, then," Kat says.

"Tucker." I pick his iPhone up off the table and place it in his hand. "Why don't you send 'Brooklyn' a text and invite her to the Lit Lair?"

37

11 DAYS AFTER

GWEN

I toss and turn, my duvet tangling up in my legs. I can't sleep.

Around eleven-thirty last night, Tucker sent the text inviting Sydney to the house today. By one a.m., when she still hadn't answered, we decided to turn in and regroup in the morning. Now it's close to two and I haven't gotten a wink of sleep. I'm so worried about whether she will take the bait, about what might happen if she doesn't, even about what might happen if she does. My head has never been full of so many thoughts. It's kind of giving me a headache.

I peel the blankets back on my bed and slip my feet into my slippers. I think I'll get a glass of water. Or pace the halls until I wear myself out.

I pause at the bottom of the stairs. A lamp is on in the living room.

Cami sits at the piano. Her eyes are closed, and she has big headphones over her ears. Her fingers move smoothly across the keys, and she sways slightly to the sound of music only she can hear. Her skin glows in the soft light. Her lips move slightly as she mouths the words. I'm entranced, watching her.

Her eyes flutter open, and she jolts backward, like she's seen a ghost. She pulls off her headphones. "Jesus, Gwen, you scared me."

My mouth feels like sandpaper. "Oh, um, sorry," I manage to say. I don't know why I feel so nervous all of a sudden. It's just Cami.

"Like, seriously, you were standing there staring at me like the girl from *The Ring*," Cami continues. "I mean, that'd be scary normally, but during a time when a psychopath is after us, like, maybe announce yourself when you enter a room."

"Right, yeah, sorry." I walk over and sit on the bench beside her.

"You wanna hear?" She holds up the headphones. "I just finished writing it."

I nod and she lifts the headphones. She places them over my ears carefully, and as soon as her skin brushes mine, my stomach flips. Cami doesn't seem to notice. She picks up the end of my braid and moves it carefully so it's out of the way of the headphones. She rests it on my shoulder and smiles. My eyes flicker away from hers. I look down at the piano, my heart racing.

Cami starts to play. Her fingers move deftly across the keys, her hands crossing over each other with grace. She moves her leg to push the pedal, and we're sitting so close that her bare knee brushes against mine. I suddenly feel very aware of every nerve in my body.

The way Cami plays is just like the way she dances: not the mechanical movement of plucking keys or hitting moves but a sort of organic self-expression, like there is a direct line between her heart and the music.

In a way, the song sounds familiar, but I'm sure that I've never heard it before. I know because this feeling I'm feeling right now, I've never felt before in my life.

I can't believe she wrote this. I can't believe any person wrote this. It's like now that I've heard it, I can't imagine there was a time before someone had played these notes in this succession. It seems like something this beautiful should have always been part of this world, like the sunset or the ocean.

I get it now, why Cami was so competitive and so angry so much of the time about record deals and sponsorships. She has a real gift. Of course she wants to share it.

When she's done, she pauses for a moment with her hands hovering above the keys, then turns to look at me.

I slide the headphones onto my shoulders. "Beautiful," I say, my voice barely a whisper.

"It's about you, you know," she says.

This takes my breath away. I don't know what to say. But I also don't want this conversation, this moment, to end. We are sitting so close together on the little bench. Her face is just inches from mine.

A bright light shines through the window behind her head. I gasp. We both duck down.

"What was that?" Cami asks.

"I don't know."

Staying low, we rush over to the window and peer through the glass. "Do you think it was the police or . . ." Cami trails off.

I swallow, the taste of adrenaline coating my mouth. ". . . was it her?" I ask.

"No." Cami stands back up. "I think it was just a car on the road. I don't see anything now."

But even though we're safe, my heart is still beating like crazy.

All of this, all of these different, confusing emotions, it's just too much.

"Well, I should go to bed," I say. I start to back away.

"Oh, yeah, well, thanks for listen—" Cami starts to say.

"Night!" I say as I scurry up the stairs and into my room without looking back.

38

11 DAYS AFTER

KAT

The door to the pool house is half open. I push it the rest of the way, flooding the dusty space with sunlight. Gwen and Cami are inside, looking through the trap door, each holding a partially inflated pool inner tube.

"Check it out," Cami says. "We put them in the tunnel half-deflated and then use this"—she holds up the air pump—"to fill them up."

"That way, no one can get through the tunnel," Gwen explains excitedly. "Once the tubes are full, you won't be able to pull them out."

"It was Gwen's idea," Cami says proudly.

I peek into the tunnel, which already contains an inflatable swan and a half-inflated doughnut Gwen is connecting to the pump. "That's brilliant," I say.

"Thanks!" Gwen smiles brightly. "Really proves Tucker wrong: when I bought them, he said, *No one needs a six-foot inflatable avocado.*" She does a cartoonishly deep voice for Tucker. "But *actually*, you never know when you might need one."

"Speaking of Tucker." Cami wipes her brow. "Any word?"

I shake my head. "I just saw him in the kitchen. She hadn't texted back yet."

Cami nods solemnly.

"Don't worry, guys," says Gwen. "She will. She's, like, obsessed with him."

I nod. I just hope she's more obsessed with him than she is with framing us.

"God, I wish she'd answer already," Cami says. "I'm anxious to get our revenge."

"She means justice, not revenge," Gwen says. Over Gwen's shoulder, Cami makes a face indicating that no, she meant revenge.

I'm still laughing about this as I leave the shed.

I spot Beau up by the pool. He's planting a camera in one of the trees overlooking the deck.

"You know it's funny," he says, climbing down. "I denied it no fewer than thirty times, but now I actually *am* tampering with the cameras."

"See, I always knew you were a hacker," I joke.

He smiles and greets me with a kiss on the cheek. He smells good. Like sweat and sun and soap and Beau.

Then the phone in my pocket goes off at the same time his lights up on the deck. I brace myself. Phone notifications have brought nothing but pain into my life for the last two weeks.

But it's a text from Tucker to the group chat, which Gwen has named "Scooby-Doo Squad." 🚐 🔍

She texted back. She'll be here at 8 pm

Beau and I share a look. Planning with Barbie dolls and

booby-trapping the tunnel almost made it feel like a game. But this text brings it back home. Makes it feel real. This is our chance to prove what she did. To prove that we are innocent.

"All right." Beau clears his throat. "Let's do this."

11 DAYS AFTER
GWEN

I crouch in the bushes. The house lights don't reach this far, and only a bit of moonlight filters down through the leaves above.

The hair on the back of my neck stands up even though it's 75 degrees. I sway back and forth, my legs already a bit sore from deep-yoga-squatting to stay hidden. Every time I accidentally brush up against a branch, my heart freezes. Because my mind doesn't picture a fern leaf but, instead, a hand reaching out from the darkness to grab me.

My phone lights up silently. A text from Beau to the Scooby-Doo Squad.

Target has pulled in front gate.

I guess there's no turning back. I click over to the stream from Kat's phone.

"Testing, testing," Tucker says under his breath. It comes through loud and clear on my AirPods.

On the screen, I watch the greenish-blue pool water move, air bubbles flowing from the filter. And I watch Tucker pace up and down the deck. No sign of Sydney on the video yet.

A branch snaps behind me. I whip my head around, my heart racing.

Cami steps out from the shadows.

"Jesus." I exhale. I pull out my right AirPod.

"She just got here," Cami says. "Beau's waiting to let the air out of her tires."

I nod. Cami looks me up and down. Before I took my position, I changed into my stakeout outfit. I'm wearing a tight, long-sleeve black shirt and black cargo pants I once bought at Target to be ironic. I dressed to blend into the background, really the opposite of how I usually put together my outfits. Cami's in all black, too, but it's Lululemon leggings and a tank. It's something she might wear in real life, and she looks hot. I tug at the end of my sleeve, suddenly nervous.

"Are you wearing eye black?" Cami asks.

My hand flutters to my cheek. "It's black lipstick," I admit. I had it left over from last Halloween, so I drew on thick lines below my eyes, like football players do. "Please don't laugh. I know it's silly. But, I don't know, it just made me feel less scared, you know? Like I was more prepared for this."

"I'm not going to make fun of you," Cami says. Although the twinkle in her eye tells me she does think it is a little funny. She steps closer and crouches down next to me, so her golden-brown eyes are level with mine. "I was actually going to say it looks cool. Do you have any more?"

"Yeah!" I pull the tube of lipstick out of one of my many cargo-pant pockets. "Here." I hold it out to her, but she gestures for me to put it on her. I uncap the tube, and Cami scooches closer to me. I can smell her perfume—vanilla. My hand starts to shake a little, but I manage to draw a smooth line across one of her cheeks. Wow, her skin is so smooth.

I swallow hard. "Other side?" I manage to say.

She turns her head slightly so I can do the other cheek. But this time, I mess up the line at the end.

"Hold on," I say. I set down the lipstick and raise my hand to her face. "It's a bit smudged." I trace my thumb along Cami's cheekbone slowly. When I reach the end, I don't want to pull my hand away. My heart pounds against my rib cage.

"Thanks," she says softly. Her eyes are locked on mine. My hand lingers.

She leans just a little bit closer to me, and I mirror her, moving just a little bit closer to her. And it's like we are both wondering the same thing, hoping the other will be brave enough to make the leap.

And then I do. I kiss her and she kisses me back and it's like a dam finally breaks and all of these feelings rush forward at once. We crash into each other.

My fingers weave through her soft, long hair. She wraps her arms around me, her hand brushing just under the seam of my shirt, her touch grazing the bare skin of my back.

We break apart just slightly. Her forehead against mine, both of us breathing heavily. I see her lips curl up into a smile before she leans forward and her lips meet mine again. Her lips are so soft, but she kisses me hard. There is an urgency behind it, like she is trying to make up for lost time. For all the moments we've been alone or our hands have brushed or glances have lingered and we haven't done this. *How have we not done this? How have we not been doing this the whole time?*

"Oh, shit, sorry," a voice behind us says.

We break away and turn to see a flustered Beau stumbling backward. He looks like he's about to tumble all the way down the hill.

"What's the matter with you?" Cami says. "You never seen two girls kiss before?"

"What? No," Beau sputters. "I mean, of course. All the time."

"All the time?" She raises an eyebrow. "That's a bit creepy, no?" She turns to me. "Can you believe this? We've only been a thing for, what, two minutes? And we're already being fetishized by a straight man."

"No, I would never." Even in the dim light, I can see Beau turning beet red. "I would never think of you like that. Like, gross, no, yuck."

"Excuse me?" Cami demands.

"Oh, no, no." His eyes go wide. "Not like that you guys are gross, or that there's anything gross about being gay or bi. I just mean like I love Kat and you guys are like sisters to me," he babbles. "It's just that to me, personally, it's weird to think of you in contexts that are not, you know, sisterly."

I place my hand on Cami's. "Will you please put the boy out of his misery?"

Cami cackles her iconic, Disney-villainesque cackle, falling backward against the branches.

"She's messing with you," I explain to Beau.

"Oh, thank God." He brings a hand to his forehead, relieved. "Also, please don't tell Kat I said I loved her, I . . . probably should've said that to her before I told you guys."

Then static crackles in my ear from the AirPod. And I hear a female voice say Tucker's name. My back straightens.

"Yo, guys, it's time," I say seriously.

The jovial mood evaporates. Beau quietly crouches down on the other side of me. I hand my other AirPod to Cami and hold out my phone so they can see. And we all brace for what's next.

$$\rightarrow$$

11 DAYS AFTER
TUCKER

I sit on the edge of one of the lounge chairs and stare down at the cracks in the concrete of the pool deck. Every muscle in my body is taut, but I try to look casual. I can't let Sydney catch on to the plan. I need her to think that this conversation is just between her and me. Part of me fears she'll know what I'm up to as soon as she sees me and turn the other way before I even have a chance to confront her.

But she doesn't. As she descends the stairs from the house, Sydney breaks into a big smile. She waves to me.

I raise my hand and manage to wave back, feeling like a robot who's not particularly good at acting human.

I stand as she approaches. She stretches onto her tiptoes to wrap her arms around my neck. I return her embrace.

She leans back, sliding one of her hands down my bicep and taking me in. I notice that her fingernails are painted a fresh, glossy crimson. "Tucker, I was so happy when you texted me. You had me so worried, running off like that yesterday. I thought something was wrong."

"You tell *me* if something's wrong, Squid."

Her face twitches for a millisecond, but then she recovers

her Instagram-influencer perfect smile. "Um, who?" she asks, her voice feigning innocence.

"You heard me, Sydney."

She starts to turn away, but I hook my thumb under her chin and lift her face so her eyes meet mine. "Look at me. I know who you are and what you did. I'm not mad," I say. A lie, but I need her to trust me, to open up. "I just want to know why."

A strange look passes over her face; it's like, even though we're still making eye contact, she's looking past me. Like I'm a ghost she can see right through. I can almost see the wheels turning in her head. Considering whether she can deny what I've accused her of. If she can weasel out of this and keep up the charade. And then something clicks and she sees me again. She decides. "Okay, yes. You're right. But, Tucker"—she reaches desperately for my hand—"you have to understand, everything I did, I did out of love."

I pull my hand away and stumble a step backward. "You loved me, so you framed me for murder?"

"No," she says quietly. "Out of love for *her*. Brooklyn. It was just something I had to do. To get justice for her. But, Tucker, I'm sorry, really I am, that you ever had to go through that, with the police and everything. Really, I only meant it to fall on the others. And yeah, when I found out what you did with . . . Gwen"—she says her name through gritted teeth—"for a second, I wanted you to catch the blame, too. But then, you know, I changed my mind. And then I tried to take the focus off you. That's why I kept making posts. The gun in the car, and then the post with everyone but you. I knew each one I made was a bit more risky, but I had to make sure they didn't end up arresting you."

She squeezes my bicep. "Tucker, you have to believe me:

except for that one moment of weakness, I didn't want you to be collateral damage. But this was something I had to do. And hey, look, I pulled it off—the police barely suspect you anymore. But Gwen will pay, and they think Beau and Kat may be accessories because of the camera thing. And Cami, please, with the whole Parker thing, I mean, a few more well-placed clues and I bet I can nail her, too. With all that for the police to focus on, they'll forget about you. And 'Brooklyn' can make sure it stays that way, you know, talk even more about how much you loved Sydney. She could even give an interview with Nora Caponi talking all about how great you are."

"I don't know, Syd . . ." My eyes glance down to the pool floor. I haven't been down here since Brooklyn died. All the traces of blood have been cleaned up, almost like nothing happened. Almost like all of this could easily be forgotten.

"Look at me, Tucker. I love you, okay? Even after that whole Gwen thing. I forgive you, all right? I forgive you for sleeping with my best friend. You just have to forgive me for this. And you and I, we can be together. You don't have to go down with the rest of them. You can join me. We can be together." She reaches out to place a hand tenderly on my chest, above my heart. I pull back, but I'm not fast enough.

She glances down at her hand pressed on my chest. For a second, confusion crosses her face, but then it quickly turns to rage. "What, what is this?" She reaches into my shirt and rips out the wire to the mini-microphone. "Tucker, what the hell?" She rips the wire in half in one swift movement. She throws the transmitter on the ground and crushes it under her boot. Then she reaches behind her back and pulls a black handgun out of her waistband. She raises it, aiming right at my chest.

Oh, fuck.

My pulse beating in my ears, I stare down at the gun. At her delicate finger poised over the trigger, her nail polish shining in the light.

It looks just like the one that killed Brooklyn. I flash back to the twins' sixteenth birthday. Two twins. Two identically wrapped boxes. Two guns.

My stomach drops. Of course Sydney would be carrying this now. How did I think confronting a psychopath would end any way other than with me dead? I feel like I'm going to vomit.

As strange as the gun may look in her delicate little hand, it's her gun, and she knows exactly how to use it.

I close my eyes and pray that when she crushed the transmitter, it didn't cut out video along with audio. That Cami and Gwen are seeing this happen right now. That Beau isn't still letting the air out of her tires. And most of all, I pray that I wasn't too much of a fuck-up, a cheating, lying, waste-of-space asshole, that if they are seeing this right now, they don't leave me for dead.

"Open your eyes," Sydney barks. "Hands on your head."

Gun trained on me, she closes the distance between us. She raises the gun to my temple. And I can't help but think—it's the same place the bullet entered Brooklyn's skull.

Sydney's hand shakes, and the metal edge of the gun rubs against my skin. "Where was that transmitting to?" she demands.

"Nowhere," I say. If I'm about to die, the least I can do is keep Syd from going after Kat next. "When you smashed that transmitter, you destroyed the only copy."

"You're lying." She presses the barrel of the gun harder against my head. "You're lying to me *again*, Tucker. Is that all you can do?! Lie?!" Hot tears well over the edge of her lower lashes

289

and stream down her face. But she doesn't seem sad. In her eyes there is pure rage. "All I ever did was love you, and you slept with my best friend, you voted against my sister, and just when I think you've found every earthly way to betray me, now you're trying to send me to jail." She's inches from my face, but she's screaming, sending spit flying at my face. Her usually perfect, clear skin is red and blotchy. A strand of her black hair sticks to the tears on her cheeks. She blows air out of the side of her mouth to clear her field of vision without moving her hand. "Don't you dare lie to me again. Where. Was. That. Transmitting?"

"Please." I look into her eyes and plead. "You don't really want to hurt me. This isn't you, Squid."

"No!" she says, her eyes wild. "You don't get to call me that. The girl you called that name—she's dead. She died along with her sister. And you—you killed her." Sydney makes a guttural sound that's somewhere between a sob and a scream. I hear a sound like thunder.

And then the world goes black.

39

11 DAYS AFTER

CAMI

". . . What, what is this?" Sydney says on the video stream. The picture jostles, and the audio blows out—sending a loud screeching noise into my ear. I yank the AirPod out.

"What just happened?" I ask. Gwen stares at her phone, which has gone totally black. She taps the screen frantically, but nothing comes back.

"He got made," Beau says seriously. "We have to go up there." He starts to stand, but I pull him back down by his arm.

"Wait! We don't know what happened. Maybe we just lost the signal or, you know, the mic fell out of his shirt."

"You heard Sydney's voice, Cami," says Beau. "She sounded pissed. What else could she be talking about?" He looks at me seriously. "If she's figured it out, she could hurt him."

I tighten my grip on his arm. "If she hasn't figured it out, we could give away the whole thing by running out there like the freaking Avengers."

He turns to Gwen. "What do you think? Would Sydney hurt Tucker?"

Just then a gunshot rings out.

All the air leaves my lungs at the sound.

Gwen bolts up, then takes off up the hill toward the pool deck at a dead sprint. I run after her, following the swoosh of blond hair she leaves in her wake.

I struggle to keep up. There is no clear path through the thick foliage. Branches and twigs cut the bare skin of my arms. My feet fall unevenly on rocks, my ankle twisting on impact. But I don't feel any of it—not really. I just feel adrenaline and panic. I just keep pushing forward in the dark.

And then, suddenly, I burst through the trees, and I'm on the pool deck. And there, just a few feet away, is Tucker, lying motionless on the ground, in a pool of blood.

Gwen makes a sound like a dying animal and falls against me. She sobs against my chest, crying tears onto my black tank. I manage to push through the fog of my mind enough to get an arm around her, but I can't tear my gaze away from Tucker . . . from Tucker's body.

Why did I hesitate? The video cut out, and not only did I not act, but I stopped Beau and Gwen from doing anything. We could have stopped this. We could've done something. They both thought we should. And I stopped them. *What have I done?*

Beau emerges from the trees behind us. "Excuse me," he whispers as he pushes past us. What is he doing?

He kneels and presses two fingers to Tucker's neck. Beau's face remains worried, lines drawn across his forehead. He doesn't react as if he feels a pulse. My heart sinks even lower, which I didn't know was possible. He leans down, his ear hovering just millimeters from Tucker's slightly parted lips, listening.

I lean forward. "Is he . . . ?" The words catch in my throat.

Before Beau can answer, Tucker's eyes flutter open just slightly.

Tuckers eyes flutter open! Holy shit, he's alive.

"Beau," Tucker grumbles hoarsely, "I'm going to need you to get your face much farther away from my face."

I let out a relieved laugh. I never thought I'd be so happy to hear that asshole's voice.

Beau sits back on his feet, a huge smile breaking across his face.

"Gwen, look." I peel her away from my body.

Her eyes go wide. "He's okay?" She starts to sob even harder, although I guess now it's out of relief.

"He's okay," Beau assures her.

"I mean, am I?" Tucker starts to sit up, looking around at the blood on the pavement. "Oh God." He pales, his skin turning a greenish tint. He looks like he's about to vomit.

"Don't look." Beau places a hand on Tucker's shoulder, easing him back toward the ground. Gwen rushes over to help, holding Tucker's head in her lap so it's not on the pavement.

Beau examines Tucker's leg. "Okay, so don't panic, but yeah, it looks like she shot you in the leg. That's probably why you fell and hit your head."

Tucker winces at Beau's touch. "Don't panic? I've been shot!"

"Yeah, but it's through-and-through." Beau tears back the fabric of Tucker's joggers to get a better look. "And she missed the femoral artery." And then, reacting to the confused looks on everyone's faces, he adds, "I got a ton of first-aid training when I was a lifeguard." He waves me over. "Cami, come here. Can you put your hands here?"

I will my body to move even though my head feels like it's full of cotton balls. Beau guides my hands to place them over Tucker's leg. Red blood stains my fingers almost immediately. His skin feels so slippery, like the time I got to pet a dolphin in the Bahamas. But this is a human, and it feels this way because of blood, not water. My mouth fills with saliva, a sour taste stinging my tongue. *No, Cami,* I will myself. *Don't throw up, not now.* I keep my hands still but look away from the blood, biting down on the inside of my cheek.

"Press down a little harder, Cami," Beau orders.

Tucker yelps in pain. A sheen of sweat beads across his forehead.

"I know it hurts, Tucker, but we have to stop the bleeding," Beau says. "Cami, keep your hands like this."

Beau leans back and, in one swift movement, pulls his T-shirt over his head. He starts to tear it into long strips. "Gwen," he says, "will you call nine-one-one?"

Gwen is still crying softly, still holding Tucker's head in her lap and tenderly running her delicate hands through his sweaty hair. I push back my jealousy at the sight of this intimate gesture. After all, he's been shot. This is a human-kindness thing, not a sign she's still in love with him, right?

"Gwen?" Beau demands.

"Oh, sorry." Gwen hiccups. She pulls her cell phone out of her bra with shaking hands. She struggles to type out her password. "Beau, I—I can't."

"I know you're upset, but you really need to—"

"No, I mean, my phone, it's not working. I have no service." She holds out her iPhone like it's a useless brick of metal.

"Huh?" Beau lets go of the T-shirt fabric he's been twisting around Tucker's leg and pulls his own phone out of his back pocket. His fingers smear Tucker's blood across the screen as he types out his password. *"Shit."* He looks up. "Mine, too. What the hell did she do? The Wi-Fi is totally down."

"What, none of our phones work?" I say.

"What about up at the house?" asks Beau. "There's got to be a phone on the wall somewhere, right? We had one of those, right?"

"A landline? What are you, old or something?" I snap. Then more gently, because it's not his fault we're in this position, I add softly, "No, we don't have one."

Panic swells in Gwen's eyes. "Without our phones, how can we—how can we do *anything?*" she says frantically. "Oh my God, we're all gonna die." She starts to sob again.

"Maybe not all of us," Tucker mumbles. His lips have lost half their color. "Just me."

Beau has returned to work on his tourniquet. I meet his eyes over Tucker's body. "What do we do?" I whisper.

His lips set in a straight line, he doesn't respond. Instead, he just nudges my hand slightly to the side so he can tie one of the makeshift bandages into a knot.

Behind us, the bushes rustle. Gwen yelps. Beau dives forward to cover Tucker's body with his own. I whip my head around, my eyes wide. My body frozen in fear, I watch as a beautiful red-tailed hawk bursts through the foliage, soaring above our heads and up toward the house.

We let out a collective sigh of relief. But the stressful thought of what—or rather who—else it could've been instead hangs in the air.

"Tucker, did you see which way she went?" I ask.

"No . . . I remember her yelling at me, and then it went black,"

295

he says. "Next thing I saw was Beau's ugly mug inches from my face."

"Do you think she'll come back?" Gwen squeaks.

"No, she won't," Beau reassures her, although he doesn't seem that sure himself. "She'll try to escape."

"Without air in her tires, she won't get very far," I say.

We fall silent. I wonder if they're thinking what I am: that the part of the plan meant to keep Sydney from leaving the property after Tucker confronted her has backfired. We thought we were so smart, taking away her escape route. We'd forgotten to think about how, when flight isn't an option, all that's left is fight. But we had no idea she'd bring a gun. I mean, framing us for murder is one thing, but I didn't think Sydney, our former friend, would've been capable of shooting one of us point-blank. But the lead in Tucker's leg says otherwise.

Beau swallows, his Adam's apple bobbing. "What if she goes into the house?"

Now it's my turn to reassure him. "Her keys won't work. We changed the locks, remember?"

Beau nods, but still, there's worry in his eyes.

The sharp sound of breaking glass erupts from the house.

"You don't need keys to do that," Tucker mumbles.

I think of the patio doors that make up most of the back of the house, designed to show off the ocean, not to keep out intruders. And the alarm system, which without Wi-Fi doesn't do shit.

My eyes fly toward the house up on the hill, dark and looming.

Kat.

She's alone up there. Someone needs to warn her. To help her.

I look around. To Gwen, who's crying so hard I bet she can barely see straight. Then to Beau, who's dropped one of the T-shirt strips he was holding. His eyes, full of pain, are turned up toward the house, toward Kat; but he hasn't moved from Tucker's side. Then I look to my own hands, pressed against Tucker's wound. They're covered in dried rust-colored blood, but fresh, bright red blood still seeps through the cracks between my fingers despite my best effort to hold the pressure. My hands aren't enough—Tucker needs this tourniquet, and Beau's the only one who knows first aid.

And suddenly I just know. That this time, I can't hesitate. That this time, it's up to me. To step up. To be the one who helps. To run toward danger.

"Gwen, come here," I say.

A hiccupping Gwen shuffles over on her knees. Her hands are shaking.

I look at her seriously. "I need you to be strong, okay?" I say. "I know you have it in you. You're one of the bravest people I know."

"But I'm not," she whines, her voice thick with tears. "I'm useless."

"No, you're not. You just feel a lot. But that's okay, that's good, actually. And it doesn't mean you can't do a lot, too. Okay, now can you place your hands right on top of mine?"

She takes the spot next to me and places her hands over mine. I slide my hands out smoothly, and hers fall right into place. "Okay," I say. "You can cry if you want to, but you just cannot move your hands. Not until Beau's done, got it?" Gwen nods seriously, her eyes still welling with tears.

"Focus on this, Beau." I place the end of the bandage back

in his hand. "I've got your girl, just"—my eyes dart to a tearful Gwen—"watch out for Gwen, will you?"

"What are you doing?" Confusion passes over his face, but I don't stop to explain. He'll understand soon enough. I rise to my feet and take off toward the stairs leading to the house.

"Cami!" I hear him yell after me. But I don't stop running.

Broken glass crunches under my feet as soon as I reach the top of the stairs. Little pieces coat the stones of the patio like hail. There's a gaping hole in one of the doors, and an outdoor chair is upended inside the kitchen.

I try to picture lithe, delicate Sydney chucking the chair through the window. I can barely imagine it; I've never seen her pick up a weight beyond the cute little three-pound ones she used with her Peloton. But I guess people can do a lot of things with adrenaline on their side. My heart in my throat, I keep walking forward.

I step through the hole in the door, careful to make sure my shin clears the half a foot of jagged glass around the bottom.

A glint off something on the ground catches my eye. It's a large piece of glass that landed on the carpet. It kind of looks like the blade of a knife. I carefully pick it up.

Holding the glass out in front of me, I walk forward.

I check the dining room, but it's empty. I notice sparks trickling down from a hole through the middle of the Wi-Fi router. This bitch *shot* the Wi-Fi. No wonder our phones were all duds. I flinch as a spark falls right next to my foot.

The security monitor is in equally terrible shape. I lift the cord Kat's phone had been plugged into. The end of it is frayed, and her phone is gone. The chair next to the monitor has been knocked over, I pray from Kat running away in a hurry and not because a fight took place here. I take solace in the fact that there's no blood on the white marble floor.

I ease into the dark hallway, the hairs on the back of my neck standing on end.

"Kat?" I whisper as loud as I dare. I want to find her, but I don't want Sydney to find me.

And then, above me, I hear footsteps running down the hall. I don't know which one of them it is, but there's no time to guess.

I race up the stairs, gripping my makeshift knife so hard that tiny cuts open along my hand. I don't loosen my grip.

The hall is dark, but my eyes can just make out Sydney, gun in hand, kicking open the hall door to the girls' bathroom. A scream rings out. *Kat.*

My heart racing, I stalk down the hall, trying my best to make out what the muffled voices are saying through the wall.

The bathroom door is a few inches ajar, a strip of golden light refracting onto the dark hall floor. I gently push open the door just a bit more, praying the hinges won't squeak. I peek through the crack.

A terrified Kat stands against the glass shower door, holding up her hands in surrender. Her phone is in her right hand, and both her hands are shaking. Tears stream down her face. I open the door a bit more, and Sydney's black ponytail comes into view. Even with her back to me, I can see that she has her gun pointed right at Kat's heart.

"Don't—don't shoot." Kat hiccups.

"Delete it! Delete it now," Sydney yells.

Kat slowly lowers her arms, pulls out her phone, and starts to type out her phone password with shaking hands.

Glass shard in hand, I push the door open and creep toward Sydney's ponytail. I step carefully so she doesn't hear me approaching. I pray Kat doesn't look up from her phone and react to me, at least not until I can raise the glass to Sydney's throat.

"Why isn't it unlocking?" Sydney demands.

"I'm sorry, my hands— I just typed the wrong—"

My foot slides on a stray towel on the floor, and my heart squeezes in panic. But I manage to catch myself before I fall. I take a deep, relieved breath and look up. Only to realize I'm looking right at my own face, my hair askew and eyes wild, staring back at me in the reflection of the glass wall opening out into the darkness of the night. I also see Sydney's face, almost in slow motion, as she sees me. The reflection in the window bounces back to the reflection in the bathroom mirror, refracting dozens of images of us both—my panicked eyes—and Sydney, turning, gun in hand, to face me.

A smile spreads across her face. "Cami, what's this? Bringing a piece of glass to a gunfight? You always were a bit B-team surrounded by A-players, weren't you? I guess this makes sense." Nothing like an ex–best friend to really know how to push your buttons. "Drop it," she orders.

"No," I say. I look around the bathroom, trying to figure out a plan. But without the element of surprise, she's right: in a head-to-head match, I'm toast. But it's not one-to-one. I'm part of a team. I step forward, putting my body between the gun and Kat. "I won't let you do this." My heart pounds against my ribs. And every nerve in my body screams for me to run, to save myself. But I dig in my heels. "If you want to hurt her, you'll—you'll have to go through me."

"Please, Cami, you?" Sydney scoffs. "You of all people are not going to take a bullet for someone else. And definitely not for a girl who, if I recall correctly, you called an 'overrated hipster.' There's no way you actually mean this. You're selfish. You always have been, and you always will be."

"Yeah, well, maybe I was before," I say. "With the Parker thing, and with your sister . . ." I tread carefully in bringing up Brooklyn. It may be the only way to get to whatever compassion, whatever softness, is still inside Sydney. Or it could set her off and make her pull the trigger. "Maybe we all were a bit shortsighted and immature, seeing Brooklyn as a statistic, as engagement numbers and a brand, instead of as a person, as your sister. Maybe we should've let her in, or at least been nicer. And yeah, we could be better people—I could be less selfish, and Gwen could be less shallow, and Tucker could be less of a douchebag—but Syd, we're all still seventeen. We're not even like fully formed people yet. We're still learning how to, like, not suck. How to be decent. Do you really think the rest of our lives should be determined by the mistakes we make as teenagers?"

Anger flares in her eyes. "My sister doesn't get a rest of her life because of what you did. She killed herself, you know. Because of what happened with the house, and then the whole freaking internet making fun of her."

This takes the air out of my lungs. I suspected that might have been what happened, once we knew Sydney was framing us for her sister's death. But to hear it in so many words breaks my heart, for Brooklyn, for her parents. And even, despite everything, for Sydney.

"I'm so, so sorry that you lost her. I really am." I look into Sydney's eyes. "But, Syd, you have to know, at least on some level, that she was sick. That she didn't die because she wasn't voted into the Lit Lair. That her illness killed her. And that her death, while such a tragedy, wasn't our fault. And that framing us for murder won't bring her back. That, you know, the best way to honor her would be to try and be better people. That's what Brooklyn would want. Not this."

"You're right. If it was Brooklyn here instead of me, she probably would forgive you, let you go. So I guess it's too bad you all killed her," Sydney says, her face hardening. "Because I'm not nearly as forgiving as my sister."

At those words, I realize any sort of negotiation is futile. And that I'm running out of time. So I lunge forward, aiming the glass toward her hand holding the gun.

Sydney tumbles backward, and the gun goes off. A burning sensation rips through my arm, and I fall back onto the hard tile. On impact, the glass slips out of my hand and spins across the tile floor.

I look at my arm, at the blood blossoming from the wound, and feel the room spin. So this is it, this is how I die. At seventeen, on a bathroom floor. And if my past is any indication, I will probably throw up all over myself because of the blood. I can see the *TMZ* headline now: B-LISTER CAMI DE ÁVILA FOUND DEAD IN BATHROOM, COVERED IN HER OWN VOMIT. No, wait: B-LISTER DOLORES "CAMI" DE ÁVILA FOUND DEAD IN BATHROOM, COVERED IN HER OWN VOMIT. Even worse.

"Cami!" Kat lunges for me.

"Move and I shoot you, too!" Sydney screams at her. The glass shard, dotted with a few drops of blood from where I nicked Sydney's hand, glistens on the tile between us. Just out of Kat's reach. The gun trained on Kat, Sydney steps forward and crushes our only weapon under her boot. It shatters into dozens of tiny, useless pieces.

"Give me your phone!" Sydney barks at Kat.

Kat hands it over, and Sydney slams it against the marble counter furiously, sending pieces of glass and metal flying. Destroying the phone and the recording of her confessing: our proof that she is Sydney and that she framed us.

"Okay." She lets the husk of the phone clatter to the floor. "Now don't try anything else," she says.

Gun still trained on us, she eases toward the exit. But just before her fingertips touch the handle, the door flies open. Three dudes with large guns in their hands and black body armor that says SWAT across the chest burst into the bathroom and start yelling all at once.

"Freeze!"

"Drop the gun!"

"On the ground!"

Sydney screams and falls to her knees. She sets the gun on the floor, and one of the cops kicks it away from her reach, sending it sliding. Another cop pulls out a pair of silver handcuffs.

"No, wait, you have the wrong idea!" Sydney wiggles her arms to avoid being handcuffed. "I was just defending myself! These girls attacked me, just like they did to my sister."

She glares at me and Kat, who's rushed to my side with a giant wad of tissues from the box on the counter. She presses them against my arm. *Like that'll fix a bullet wound.* I resist the urge to roll my eyes, because after all, she's helping me, and I've been shot.

At Sydney's words, the cops handcuffing her seem to notice us for the first time. They pause, studying our faces. And my heart sinks. It's our word against hers again, isn't it? And we all know how that went last time. Without the video she just destroyed, Sydney can keep ruining our lives with her lies.

"Listen," Sydney continues, "call Detective Johnson. She's like your boss, right? My name is Brooklyn Reynolds. Tell her it's me versus the same girls who killed my sister. She'll tell you who's the victim here and who are the ones who should be arrested."

"Oh, don't worry, we know *exactly* who you are." Detective Johnson steps through the doorway wearing a bulletproof vest. "Back from the dead are we, Sydney?"

"What?" Sydney laughs anxiously. "No, I'm *Brooklyn*, I don't know what you're talking—"

"Save your breath," says Detective Johnson. "I heard your whole confession."

"What, how?" Sydney whips her head toward the demolished phone, her dark hair flying. "How?!"

"Oh, Sydney, did we forget to tell you?" Kat says without looking up from patting tissues onto my arm. I've never heard her voice so caustic. I quite like this side of her. "We weren't just recording video. We were livestreaming it."

All the color drains from Sydney's face.

"I heard the whole thing as you said it." Detective Johnson waves an ancient-looking iPhone. "Along with about a million other people."

"It's like you always said, Syd," Kat says. "If you don't post about it, it's like it didn't even happen."

The cops pull Sydney to her feet. Detective Johnson glares at her as they lead her out the door. "Ms. *Sydney* Reynolds, you're under arrest."

40

11 DAYS AFTER

KAT

"I'm fine, don't touch me!" Cami lunges away from an EMT who's trying to help her. She's sitting on the back bumper of a parked ambulance. Our whole driveway is filled with various emergency vehicles, their lights swooping. "You said it was just a graze, right?" Cami says. "If I'm not dying, the only one who is going to put stitches in me is a plastic surgeon. I swear to God, skip the hospital, take me to Dr. Malibu straightaway."

"Ma'am, we're not Uber," says the frustrated EMT.

"Evidently," she says with a roll of her eyes. "Because if you were, you'd have, like, zero stars."

I stand a few feet away and wait for this to play out so I can thank her. Moments after the police hauled Sydney out of the bathroom, the EMTs rushed in to help Cami, making her lie back in a stretcher, even though she insisted she could "walk just fine."

After they took her, I ran down the stairs and out the door to find Beau, to make sure he was okay. I found him by another ambulance, watching as they loaded in Tucker, who had an oxygen mask over his face but was still conscious. As soon as I saw Beau there, alive, unharmed, and for some inexplicable reason shirtless, a weight lifted off my chest. I called out his name and ran and jumped into his arms. He lifted me up and kissed me firmly, desperately. Even when my sneakers returned to the ground, he didn't let me go. He squeezed me tight and kept whispering my name into my hair over and over again, his voice thick with tears of relief.

"If anything had happened to you . . . ," he started.

"I know," I said.

"I love you, Kat."

"I—" I was taken aback. We've only been dating for like a week and a half, even if we were best friends for longer. But to be honest, none of that mattered. "I love you, too," I said, and we kissed again.

Our bliss was interrupted when an EMT pulled me away to evaluate me for injuries. I told him I was fine, that the only wounds I'll have to deal with will be dealt with in therapy. But he insisted I get a physical workup. He finally cleared me and began evaluating Beau, so I went to find Cami, only to discover she was going ten rounds with her own EMT.

Eventually, she badgers the paramedic enough that he walks back to the front of the ambulance to call his boss. I take my chance to step forward.

"Hey, Cami." I approach slowly. "I just wanted to say . . . thank you. I can't believe you took a bullet for me."

"Okay, calm down," Cami says. "It was just a graze, all right? And this doesn't change anything, so don't get used to it. This doesn't mean I'm going to be like . . . a nice person all of a sudden."

"Oh, of course not." I nod seriously. "You did your one extremely nice thing and now you're free to be mean forever."

"Exactly."

I take the place beside her on the metal bumper of the car. I reach over and squeeze the hand of her uninjured arm. She doesn't pull away.

"Cami!" Gwen comes tearing through the crowd of emergency workers. Her face is streaked with tear-melted black lipstick, and there's a twig sticking out of her hair. She almost pushes over a confused crime scene investigator as she makes a beeline toward Cami, throwing her arms around her.

"Oh my God, *your arm!*" Gwen squeals. She starts to cry as she takes in Cami's injury. "Does it hurt?"

"Well, yeah, it *hurts*. Sydney shot me," says Cami. "But they said I'll be fine."

"She shot you! Oh my God!" She looks around. "Where is she? Did she get away? I swear, I'll kill that girl!"

"The police took her into custody," I say. "They got here just in time." I look across the yard to where Detective Johnson is lingering by the front door of the house, talking to a uniformed officer.

"Well, *just in time* would've probably been before she pulled the trigger," Cami says. "But yeah, they got her. Johnson saw the livestream. Heard her whole confession."

"Really?" Gwen raised her eyebrows. "I thought we'd have to send them the recording afterward."

"Yeah, it's kind of a miracle she was even on TikTok," Cami says. "I mean, this is the same woman who asked me if the Charli all the videos talked about was *Charlie Sheen*."

"Actually, it wasn't totally luck," I say, raising my hand. "I had an idea. Right when we went live, I sent the video to Hannah Johnson. The detective's daughter. She's one of our fans."

"Oh, brilliant, Kat!" Gwen says. "So smart to work back channels. This is just like the time I befriended Scott Disick's dog walker to get Met Gala tickets."

"Yeah, a bit like that."

Detective Johnson notices us watching her and walks over.

"Ladies." She nods at us. "I just wanted to apologize for any inconvenience our investigation may have caused you. This is perhaps the strangest case I've ever worked, and I don't mind saying I'm glad it's over. And while I would never condone vigilante means, I have to say thank you for your . . . unconventional help in this case." She clasps her hands together. "Well, I'll leave you be. Have a good night, and, Ms. de Ávila, I hope you have a quick recovery."

"I hope you get fired," Cami says back.

Detective Johnson just acts like she doesn't hear this and walks away.

"What?" Cami says at my and Gwen's shocked reactions. "Are you going to tell me I'm wrong? I'm sorry, but she botched the investigation. We basically had to do her job for her."

"Okay, but even if you think that, maybe don't say it to her face," Gwen says.

The EMT hangs up the phone and walks back around the side of the rig. "I'm sorry, ma'am, but we are going to have to take you to the hospital, just for a few stitches." He holds up his hand to stop her before she can argue. "Which you can have done by the hospital's resident plastic surgeon, who, before you ask, does not have his own TV show, but I'm told is still very good at his job."

"Ugh, fine," Cami says.

The EMT helps her into the back and reaches for the door.

"You guys family?" He turns to me and Gwen. "If you are, you can ride along."

Gwen looks at me, her eyebrows raised.

"Yeah," I say as I step into the back of the truck. "Yeah, we are."

41

11 DAYS AFTER

SYDNEY

At the county jail, they take all ten of my fingerprints. The black ink ruins my manicure.

"Ms. Reynolds, you're gonna be inmate number one-four-three-eight." The guard uncuffs me and hands me a little chalkboard with my name and the number on it.

He grabs my shoulder and walks me over to a tripod-mounted camera, pointed at a gray wall. "All right now," he says. "Time for your close-up."

42

1 MONTH AFTER

KAT

There's a moving van in the driveway, and boxes are piled all over the house. The weather has turned cool, or as cool as fall gets in Malibu. A canvas cover has been pulled over the pool, and a few sparse leaves have fallen over the top. The For Sale sign in the front yard has been updated with a diagonal red sash: SOLD.

I hold down the flaps of a cardboard box and pull packing tape across the crease with a satisfying unpeeling sound. There. My last box is done.

I've decided to go back and finish high school. My mom was offered a new job at a great school in LA, and the principal said that once I fill out some paperwork, I can join the senior class, picking up where I left off in Fresno. My mom is quite excited about my decision, of course. And honestly, I'm looking forward to it, too. To be a normal teenager again. Or as normal as I can be, given that I was a TikTok celebrity and previously accused of being responsible for one of the most high-profile deaths in the last decade.

It's not that I'm giving up on my dream. But, I guess, realizing that I'm not in such a rush.

If you spend enough time on social media, you'll start to think that fifteen to seventeen need to be the peak years of your life and career. That by twenty-five you'll basically be washed up.

But that's not true.

There is plenty of time to do everything. I can finish high school and go to college, where I can study environmental science and join an improv club. And then, who knows, maybe I'll try the professional-comedian thing again, maybe here in LA or maybe in New York or Chicago. Maybe I'll make TikToks, or maybe I'll focus on performing in person, in real life, at open mics and sketch shows. Or hey, maybe I'll make content on an app that hasn't been invented yet. Heck, by then social media might all be holograms that float out of your phone like in *Star Wars*. I have no idea what the future will look like. There are so many possibilities, so many paths my career could take. But none of it needs to happen before I turn twenty. For now, I think I'd actually like to write a paper about Emily Dickinson and go to prom with Beau and, I don't know, even AP Calculus sounds good to me at this point.

I take my last box and bring it out to the driveway, where Beau is lifting Cami's boxes into the U-Haul as she looks on, her arm in a sling. "Please be careful with that. My Shorty Award is in there."

Beau, ever patient, reassures her. "I got it, don't worry."

"I seriously think you should let me do it myself. Really, everyone acts like I'm on my deathbed. It was just, like, a scratch."

"Babe, you were shot," Gwen says, wrapping an arm around Cami's waist. "Let people help you."

Cami stretches her neck to see into the truck, where Beau is sliding around boxes to make more room. "I swear, even with this sling, I could do better than him. I'm pretty sure I can lift more than this Timothée Chalamet–bodied fool."

Beau laughs and runs a hand through his sweaty hair. "You're welcome for the help, Cami."

He greets me with a peck on the cheek and takes the box from me. "This the last one?"

I nod.

"One more photo before we go?" Gwen holds up her bedazzled phone.

"Yeah, because we don't have any of those," Cami deadpans. But she helps her girlfriend prop the phone against the truck and set up the self-timer.

We gather together. Gwen fluffs her hair. Beau throws his arm over my shoulder. Out of the corner of my eye, I spot Tucker coming out of the house, a duffel bag slung across his body and crutches under his arms.

"Tucker!" I shout. "Photo."

He crutches over, sliding into the shot just before the timer goes off, sticking his tongue out and waving a crutch.

Gwen picks her phone up and starts sliding filters over the image. "Don't worry, I'll tag everyone!" she says.

"Not me," I say.

"Oh, right!" Cami's eyes go wide. "You deleted your socials."

I nod.

"All of them?" Tucker asks.

"Mmm-hmm."

"Even Insta?" Gwen asks. "Even Snap?"

"Even the Facebook I never used."

"Whoa." Gwen blinks as this sinks in. "How do you—how do you feel?"

"I feel . . . good," I say. "More free, and also like, I find myself daydreaming again. Like, I hadn't realized when, but at some point I'd stopped really doing that, 'cause like every moment was filled up with sights and sounds from my phone. But now it's like, I get bored again but in a good way."

"Bored in a good way?" Cami shakes her head. "Could never be me."

We all laugh.

A little while later, after we've said our goodbyes (both girls hugged me and promised to hang out soon; Tucker gave me an awkward high five), I'm waiting for Beau to unlock his car, and I lean down to tie my shoes. A gust of wind blows down the street, tossing back my curls and rustling the palm trees above us. And my phone vibrates in my back pocket.

An alert blinks across the top of the screen. Since I got rid of all social media, I really only get calls and texts. But this is neither.

The alert is from the news app, and my heart rate picks up as soon as I see the headline.

Suspect in TikTok Fraud Case Makes Bail
Sydney Reynolds, who allegedly framed her famous housemates for the supposed murder of her sister in an elaborate scheme, was released on $1 million bond this morning.

43

1 MONTH AFTER

GWEN

"It was such a traumatic thing, what we all went through. Someone dying so tragically, someone trying to frame us for murder—it really puts things in perspective, you know. All those things I used to worry about—how many followers I had, how much money I made, whether I won a Shorty Award—none of that matters. These things, they aren't real life. You know, I was measuring myself by all these arbitrary numbers, but what I was really seeking, what I really needed, was true human connection.

"When something as intense happens as what happened to me and my housemates, it really shakes you up. Wakes you up, really, so you can see what's genuine and what's fake. It made me want to leave that world of plastic and smoke and mirrors behind and seek out things that are real, things that are true. And that's when I knew I needed to make a radical change in my life. To leave that old Gwen Riley, the one who was more brand than person, behind. And start anew. Which is why . . .

". . . I've decided to form the Real House, a revolutionary new content house of anti-influencer influencers. Our videos will be more raw and real and authentic than anything you've seen on

TikTok before. And this time, the house is twice as big!" I pan the selfie video I've been filming to show off the ah-mazing backyard and mansion my realtor secured for us, all paid for by one of my new sponsors.

I bring the camera back to my face. "Stay tuned for next week, when I will reveal the members of the new house!"

And there I end the video and head back inside to edit it. I type out the caption: "6 days and counting . . . 👀 👀"

Now that I'm no longer under investigation, everyone wants to work with me again. Even Carmen reached out, sending me a huge bouquet of hyacinths and a note asking if I'd want to partner with her. Yeah, right. Even I'm not that dumb.

I've got a new manager, one who sees me as a true partner in strategy and not just a pretty puppet with strings to pull. It's one of the ways that this time, I'm doing things totally differently.

I take a deep breath and prepare to post the video to my ninety-eight million followers. Yes, that's right, *ninety-eight* million. I'm back on top as the most followed person on TikTok. In fact, I've beaten my own record.

It turns out that as long as you come away looking like a scrappy vigilante who helped save her friends and not like, well, a killer, then any scandal can be spun. Even being accused of murder can be good for your brand.

ACKNOWLEDGMENTS

Much like a collab house, this book is the product of teamwork. There are a number of talented and generous people who helped make this story what it is. I feel so lucky I got to work with them.

I am so grateful to everyone at Underlined and the larger Delacorte Press and Random House teams who helped this book become a reality.

Thank you to my editors, Wendy Loggia and Alison Romig. Wendy, it's been a dream come true to work with you. For years I've been a fan of books you've edited and written, and working with you was even better than I imagined. Thank you for taking a chance on this project, and for all your notes that helped it become the book it is today. Thank you, Alison, for your spirited support of this project, and your invaluable insight. You truly "got" this project, and your notes and edits were very much appreciated.

Thank you so much to the copy editors who worked on this book. You make me look so good and saved me from so many embarrassing errors (like how I thought cul-de-sac was cold-de-sac). I cannot thank you enough for your hard work and attention to detail.

To the design team, and to Casey Moses specifically, thank

you for the awesome cover. You captured this story in a fantastic way, and I would be so lucky to have people judge this book by its cover.

To the sales, marketing, and publicity teams and everyone at Random House who helped connect this book with readers, thank you for all your hard work.

Thank you to my rock-star literary agent, Nicole Resciniti, and to everyone at the Seymour Agency. Nicole, you believed in me when the phrase "I'll finish up the draft after prom!" was one that made sense, and you've encouraged and guided me from that day to this one. Thank you for all the phone calls talking through anxieties and for your ever-helpful notes. You are my rock through the publishing process, and I am forever grateful to have you on my side. Thank you for all your work championing this book from premise to finished project.

Many thanks to Dana Spector at Creative Artists Agency, for believing in this story and in me. I'm so excited to see what other forms this story may take thanks to your shepherding.

Thank you to my friends and family for all their encouragement during this project. Thanks especially to my sister, Maggie, who is always my first reader and biggest cheerleader. Thank you for talking through plot points with me between classes and work that is much more important than mine. Thank you for reading my words and encouraging me, and for making sure to document my progress with photographs. Also, Mags, remember that time you tried to Amy March this book? Consider me bringing it up now my revenge.

Thank you to my parents, who have always encouraged my writing and believed in me even when I doubted myself. Thanks to my mom, who encouraged this idea when it was a "what if" during a late-night conversation. Thank you to my dad, who set me up a desk in his basement and let me plaster the wall with character vision boards and plot notecards. Sorry I forgot to use painter's tape.

Thank you to both my brothers for their encouragement of my writing, and particular thanks to my younger brother, Ryan, who taught me how TikTok works.

Many thanks to my friends, especially Maddie Bradshaw, Becca Rose, Nicolas Lozano, Kristin McIntire Kennedy, Ana Caro Mexia, Maddie Bouton, Sarah Manney, Maya Lorey, Ethan Flanagan, Julia "Jade" Fletcher, Carrie Monahan, and Tony Bruess. Thank you for taking calls in which I rambled in detail about the drama of people I made up in my own head. You're the best friends a girl could ask for.

Thank you to the teachers who encouraged my writing and taught me so much over the years, from St. Francis Xavier and Nazareth Academy to Stanford and Columbia Journalism School. Especially: Jessica Radogno, Amelia Garcia, Lori Wasielewski, Mary Kate O'Mara, Janine Zacharia, Phil Taubman, Steve Coll, and Adam Tobin.

Thank you also to those who have mentored me and helped to sharpen my writing outside the classroom, from my early days as a teen reporter at *The Mash* and *Huffington Post Teen* through my time writing at the *San Francisco Chronicle*, Reuters, and Bloomberg, including: Taylor Trudon, Liz Perle, Morgan Olsen, Michelle Lopez, Phil Thompson, Jessica Mullins, Molly Schuetz, Katherine Chiglinsky, Gerrit De Vynck, Sarah Frier, and Jillian Ward.

Thank you to real-life social media creators, big and small, who share pieces of themselves and their lives with the world.

Social media is far from perfect and at its worst can make us feel isolated and alone, but at its best, it really does have the potential to connect us across boundaries. Thank you to everyone who tries to make the internet and the world a kinder and more welcoming place. I hope you appreciate the elements of the book that satirize some of the more unusual elements of your job, and know I respect that what you do really is hard work.

And last but not least, thank you to my readers. The time since my first book was published has been surreal, and I cherish every Tweet, email, and Instagram DM I receive from you. I am so glad my words have connected with you and started a conversation, and I hope we can keep chatting for years to come.

EVERYTHING YOU WANT TO READ
THE WAY YOU WANT TO READ IT

Discover a new must-read paperback every month!

Underlined
Paperbacks

GetUnderlined.com • @GetUnderlined

1450

Art used under license from Shutterstock.com

Underlined

A Community of Book Nerds & Aspiring Writers!

READ

Get book recommendations,
reading lists, YA news

DISCOVER

Take quizzes, watch videos,
shop merch, win prizes

CREATE

Write your own stories,
enter contests, get inspired

SHARE

Connect with fellow
Book Nerds and authors!

GetUnderlined.com • @GetUnderlined

Want a chance to be featured? Use #GetUnderlined on social!

Art used under license from Shutterstock.com

31901067341208